Tribulation

Also by Thomas A. Lewis

The Shenandoah in Flames

The Guns of Cedar Creek

For King and Country

The Wildlife of North America

West from Shenandoah

Brace for Impact:
Surviving the Crash of the Industrial Age

Praise for the Work of Thomas A. Lewis

Tribulation

a novel of the near future

Thomas A. Lewis

ACKNOWLEDGMENTS

I want to express my thanks to the little band of nit pickers and nay sayers who helped me weed this manuscript of typos, infelicities, impossibilities and other flaws, including son Andrew (where's the dog?) Lewis, sister Marion (the the) Yourkowski, brother-out-law Richard (Situation Room) McCarthy and decades-long friend Russ (Willy or Billy?) Adams. Likewise to my personal, chapter-by-chapter cheerleader Kathleen, whose enthusiasm on my behalf makes those ladies who work for the Dallas Cowboys look drab and apathetic.

It should be clearly understood that any mistakes that survive in this work are entirely the fault of the above named people.

Cover photo: Katrina approaching New Orleans by bnpositive/Flickr
http://www.flickr.com/photos/bnpositive/45817296/

ISBN-13: 978-1494768454
ISBN-10: 1494768453

CONTENTS

1. THE GATHERING STORM
2021

Of course I remember how it happened. Every one of us who was alive back then remembers exactly how our world ended. We had for years expected every day to be just like the last one, and then one day, just like that, it was the last one.

Surprised? Not really. No more than a 100-year-old man is surprised when death comes, or a deer when the headlights finally arrive. We knew it was going to happen, and spent our whole lives acting as though it were not. Hoping that we would be dead before it came. Age-based optimists, we called ourselves. Gallows humor.

Every one of us who lived through it knew, instantly – the second we grasped the enormity of what was happening – that we were the ones who had done it. We had lived lives of depraved indifference, of luxury unimagined in eons of human existence, apparently believing (if we thought about it at all) that the bills would never come due.

We had allowed ourselves to become fatally distracted from reality.

And what about those of us who got a look at the bills coming due, who might have changed what happened? We who, had we thought of the right things to say, or do, might have saved millions, and our way of life? There is a special corner of hell prepared for us. And we live in it now.

Brian called early that morning, the day it all started to come apart. It was a beautiful mild day in late spring, about this time of year but not as hot as it is these days. We used to have slower springs, and gentler rains.

"Dad, we're on the way to the Farm. You should come, too."

"Really? You mean to stay?"

"Listen. They just released the latest computer models for the hurricane. And they all agree, it's coming ashore west of New Orleans and tracking straight up the Mississippi River."

"Damn." I stared out the window of my little retirement bungalow on the PGA golf course in New Market, in the Shenandoah Valley of Virginia, and thought about Brian heading west on I-66 from his place in Northern Virginia. "You're in the car?"

"Yep. Me and the kids."

"No Kathryn?"

"Of course not. I tried to tell her how this thing could take out the Old River Control Structure, break the Mississippi clean out of its bed. Tried to explain what that could mean. But when it comes to this stuff, she just will not listen."

"Well. No doubt she's thinking of the last time."

"Oh yeah, she brought that up. 'You're absolutely sure,' she says, 'like you were sure that when Iran closed the Strait Of Hormuz, it would crash the economy? You holed us up at the Farm for nearly a month that time. Took the kids out of school. Damn near lost me my job and yours too.' Yeah, that was embarrassing. Nobody thought they could reopen the channel that fast."

"So how'd you leave it?"

"We're going for the weekend, I'm under orders to have the kids back Sunday night."

"Are you going to?"

"We'll see."

"Holy crap, Brian, you could get in real trouble,"

"Dad, we are in real trouble. Everything is breaking down. Food, water, electricity. All the systems are right on the verge of crashing. If this hurricane does what it looks like it's going to do, we're toast."

"Pretty big *if*, Brian."

"Yeah. So I'm going to do what I gotta do, and I want you to turn on the Weather Channel and pay close attention to what they're saying about Hurricane Seven. Then I want you to Google the Old River Control Structure, and the flood of 1973. Okay? Will you do that?"

"I'll do that. But Brian..."

"Not now, Dad. I've got to get going. If I'm wrong...again...then fine, I'll eat the crow. If I'm right, I'll see you at the Farm. You'll have a few days, you're a lot closer to it than I am and you don't have to use an Interstate to get there. But don't leave it too late. Oh. And you know you have to come alone."

"Well, I don't know how I'll manage that."

"You'll think of something. This is going to be a challenge for us all. See you on the other side."

I turned on the TV as instructed. No point in looking at the regular channels, they were full of our military buildup along the Mexican border to hold the line against the starving millions who were now sometimes coming across the Rio Grande in human waves; the tense three-way naval confrontations with Russia and Canada over the oil drilling platforms everybody was trying to build in the ice-free Arctic Ocean; the turbulent refugee camps holding the tens of thousands of people displaced by the rising sea water of the Atlantic and the spreading deserts of the American West; the food riots in Europe, the climate refugees of North Africa, on and on. I put on the Weather Channel, and there was Hurricane Seven.

Years ago, the National Hurricane Center had given up on naming tropical storms. There were simply too many of them, and keeping track of the retired names, and avoiding the names of living notables, began to give even the computers headaches. Now they just number them and here we were in early June already up to Number Seven.

Seven was a huge, dark comma on the map almost filling the Gulf of Mexico, whirling slowly toward the northwest, looking just as ominous as Katrina had looked, back in the day, not that many people would remember her now. According to the animation and the excited announcers, Seven was two days from landfall near Morgan City. Huh. A real monster. There was a time when you never saw a North Atlantic or Gulf hurricane before July, but now the overheated waters of the equatorial oceans spawned them just about anytime except the dead of winter.

I remembered a little of what Brian had said about what could happen if a Gulf hurricane came up the Mississippi. It was hard to pick out from all his other rants – about peak oil, running out of food, desertification, sea-level rise, water shortages – but even when he was being hysterical about his conclusions, his facts were usually pretty straight. I remember when he started getting worked up about this stuff, I thought, why is he the only one who knows this stuff? How come the experts aren't worried, and he is? Boy, did I find out.

He told me that the strongest winds, heaviest rains and highest storm surge in a hurricane are to its right front. So if the eye of Hurricane Seven made landfall west of New Orleans and traveled along the river, as they were now forecasting, it would give the city and the river its worst. Unlike Katrina, which had come ashore east of the city and had nearly destroyed New Orleans with the back of its weak left hand.

What had pretty much finished the job of destroying the city had not been another hurricane, but sinking land and rising Gulf waters. Most of what had been flooded by Katrina was now under water again, permanently, and except for a levee'd-up area including the French Quarter, the Warehouse District and part of the Central Business District, the City of New Orleans by 2020 had been largely abandoned (along with huge chunks of the Gulf Coast, South Florida and of course the Florida Keys). The Port of New Orleans, and the miles of oil refineries and tank farms and commodity-handling port facilities along the river to Baton Rouge upstream was another story – still unharmed behind their ever-growing levee walls.

So Hurricane Seven looked like the worst-case scenario for what was left of New Orleans. But that wasn't the worst of it. That wasn't why we might all have to head for the Farm and pull up the drawbridge.

Why are you so interested in this? Why does it matter? You're making a record? You're setting it down so people will remember? Huh. I miss books. I miss the Internet.

Well. I thought that might be the case, and since it is, I should take a minute to explain about the Farm. For the readers of your book a century from now.

It was, of course, much more than a farm, but Brian insisted we call it that to avoid attracting the attention of strangers.

2. PREMONITIONS

2010

Let's go back a few years from the day Brian called about Hurricane Seven. Maybe ten, eleven years, back when the grand-kids were in grade school, Daniel maybe 8, Julie 6, something like that. I was visiting them in their suburban Virginia five-bedroom Victorian with the in-ground pool and the three-car garage. Life on the salaries of a *Washington Post* national reporter (him) and a Federal Trade Commission attorney (her) was well equipped.

But that weekend, life there was awful. The tension swirling through that house, touching everything, changing everything, was an almost visible fog.

It's hard to be around dying people and fighting spouses. For one thing, they are so preoccupied by their problems that they barely know you're there. And for another, you never know what to say. I always want to start by saying, "Well, Jeez, count your blessings." Almost always, I stifle myself.

Pre-teens are pretty self-absorbed, too, but on this weekend one glance at Kathryn was enough to muzzle the usually boisterous Daniel and Julie. Kathryn's glare looked like she was practicing to kill goats with psychic energy. Brian looked like a goat that was losing its will to live.

It was a gorgeous Indian Summer Day. (The use of that phrase, by people who obviously thought it referred to some Disney-movie notion about nature-loving Indians, always amused me. It referred to the season, during the years of the 18th-Century French and

Indian War, during which attacks on settlers' farms in the Shenandoah Valley had been most intense.) Dottie had a Saturday event for her breast-cancer-awareness organization, so when Brian had called Friday night to ask if we could talk, she had said, "Go, go!" while making shooing motions with her hands.

The drive in from Winchester had been peaceful, the sunlight spreading like melted butter over a landscape of extravagant colors – from the bright crimson of the sugar maples and sumac to the wild yellows of the oak. I passed long lines of cars headed for the Skyline Drive in the Shenandoah National Park, leaf-peepers headed out to gawk at the spectacular tapestry of fall colors. This was back when gasoline was still so cheap that such trips were taken without thought of their expense.

I got to Brian's house in the self-consciously rustic village of Clifton, Virginia, just after nine that morning, and sensed immediately that there was a crisis. Brian greeted me tersely at the door and escorted me to a seat at the breakfast bar at one end of their great room, behind which Kathryn was at work amid a great clashing of dishes and pots. She reminded me of a tornado; she looked dark and threatening, she was writhing with pent-up energy and looking for something to blow away.

Brian and I perched glumly and silently at the granite breakfast bar like two crows in the rain, nursing our coffees, waiting for better weather. The kids slouched at the breakfast-nook table with orange juice, their ear buds jammed in and their stares unfocused, everybody trying to think of a compelling reason to be somewhere else.

"So." Kathryn grated out finally, to my consternation picking me to address as she slammed a plate of bacon and eggs down in front of me. I had hoped to keep my head down until I could reasonably say that I had to get back home, and get the hell out of there. "Has he shared his big plans with you?"

"Kathryn, whatever is going on here, I am not in it. I do not know what you're talking about."

She scooped a sheaf of papers from the end of the counter and flung them down next to my eggs. "This is what I'm talking about. Brian's better idea for the money we were going to fritter away on our childrens' education and our retirement."

They were photographs printed on plain paper. I glanced at a few of them, saw scenes of a ramshackle old house, some overgrown fields, a barn.

"Kathryn," I said mildly, pushing my stool back and standing up, "You and Brian obviously have some things to work out. I'm not interested in being the stick you use to beat him with, and you guys are obviously not much interested in having company right now, so I think I'll just..."

"Oh, Dad, I'm sorry." Kathryn let both hands fall to her sides in a gesture of surrender. "I didn't mean to put you in the middle of anything. Please. Eat your breakfast. I'll be nice."

I was not much reassured, but I eased warily back onto my stool.

"Do you know what he's planning?" she asked again. "If you don't I'd like him to explain it to you, I'd like to hear your reaction. NOT...." she raised a hand to ward me off because my mouth had opened... "to take sides. I'd like to know what a kind-of-objective observer thinks about this."

Through all this Brian had sat staring at his breakfast, mute, unmoving, damn near inanimate. "Brian?" I said, just to see if he was still conscious. "Do you want me in this?"

He summoned his soul back from the regions of the bright light, heaved a sigh, and looked at me with the eyes of a caged hound dog. "I know what you're going to say."

"Well, good," I said brightly, rising from my stool again. "That relieves us of a lot of unnecessary chatter. I, on the other hand, do not know what I'm going to say, but I know what the rest of this day is going to be like, and I'd just as soon skip it. So, if you don't mind..."

"Dad," he said wearily, flapping his right hand up and down in surrender or something, "Please. Sit down. You could help us talk this through. I just meant that you and I have argued about a lot of this stuff before, and I know where you stand."

I looked at the sheaf of pictures, and then I looked at him. "What stuff?" But I knew what he was going to say.

Brian had been getting more and more pessimistic about –

well, about everything – for years by that time. It started, I guess, while he was a general assignment reporter for the *Post* where he soon developed an affinity for, and before long a specialty in, environmental reporting.

I've never seen anybody whip through the five stages of grief so fast, or so often. Whatever subject he got into – air pollution, water pollution, industrial agriculture, energy, food, climate change, whatever – he would spend the first day in denial, saying, "This can't be happening!" On the second, he'd get angry; "Those bastards!" Then came bargaining, "We've got to organize! Campaign! Do something!" By the fourth day, he would be in a blue funk and finally he would sum it all up with an explosive "Shit!" Acceptance, of a sort.

Take peak oil. That was one of the first things he got his hair on fire about, that we were going to run out of oil. Well, okay, to be fair, not run out, but run short. All the oil fields were playing out, he said, and demand was skyrocketing, especially from China and India and Asia, and pretty soon there wouldn't be enough to fill all the orders. Prices would head for the stratosphere, conflicts would flare, supplies would be interrupted and economies would crash. Thing is, you could watch a month of Sunday news programs and never hear a word about this. Just Brian.

As for me, back then I never got very far past Stage One: denial. Now, don't get me wrong, he's a smart guy (have I mentioned that?) and he'd come up with a lot of information about, oh, say, what they were doing wrong in cattle feedlots. The crowding, the pollution, the overuse of antibiotics, the weird feed they used, on and on. And I'd hear this stuff from him, or I'd get it second-hand from his mother – back then, he called Dottie almost every day – and you couldn't really argue with his facts.

Do you remember Dottie at all? A little? Yes, it's been a long time.

But, I mean, back then I always thought there had to be more to the story, more facts on the side of the people doing it. I mean, they were experts, there were thousands of them, and here comes

Brian to glance at what they're doing and say, well it stands to reason that this is a disaster. How could he be right and all of them wrong? Besides, I just couldn't believe that people could be as greedy and cruel and destructive as he described them, and I also couldn't see any other way to keep the burger joints open. I mean, there are 300 million of us, and on any given day half of us want beef and the other half wants chicken. I don't remember Brian suggesting another way to do it, either, back then. So Dottie and I would listen, and make sympathetic noises, and wait for him to come to his senses. "Do you think he's a Communist?" She asked me one day. "He seems so, oh, I don't know. Anti-American."

Okay, that was over the top. But he made a lot of enemies. Take that feedlot thing. Lobbyists for the food industry and the cattle industry and the grocery stores started calling up his editors and complaining that he was getting stuff wrong, that he was harassing them, had it in for them, all this before he ever wrote the story. So his editors would call him in, over and over, and make him double-prove and triple-source whatever he was getting ready to write. But, see, here's the thing. He was always able to do it.

But I told him, I said, "You're not going to get promoted this way. What you're doing, it's a constant pain in the ass for your superiors, and when it's time to hand out the raises and the promotions, that's what they're going to remember." Yeah. I did, I actually said that. I was trying to give him practical advice.

Sometime around 2005, with the country in the middle of one of its biggest and strongest booms, Brian did two things. He told me to get everything I had in the stock market out of it, and into cash, because we were about to see an enormous crash. The bankers, he said, the biggest financial firms in the country, had completely lost their minds over the quick money they were making with sub-prime mortgages, derivatives of sub-prime mortgages, tranches of derivatives of sub-prime mortgages, and simultaneous bets that the whole sub-prime-mortgage system they were operating was going to fail – bets called credit default swaps.

I told him he had to be wrong. That the best financial minds in the country could not be as stupid and criminal as he described. I mean, there it was again: the hedge funds had *theoretical mathematicians* on their staffs, for crying out loud, and statisticians and data crunchers, and here comes Brian, looks over the fence at what they're doing in their yard and says, Whoa, that's not going to work. And every night on TV there are guys in suits with resumes as long as your arm saying, yup, it's kind of counter intuitive, but real estate will never lose value and this boom will never run out of steam.

But I didn't sleep well for a couple months after we had that conversation. Finally, late in 2005, I cashed out my 401(k), my annuity, and my modest portfolio of favorite stocks. It hurt to do it, but it saved my ass. I had good friends, people just like me, who ended up homeless after the housing bubble burst. Early in 2006.

So like I said, he's a pretty smart kid. But the second thing he did at about that time was to start telling everybody that the whole system was going to come down, was already in the process of crashing. Not just the big financial firms, and not just America, either, but the whole western industrialized global economy. I told him he had to be wrong. That there were lots of smart and powerful people in government and business who would not let that happen.

Yeah, I actually said that, at a time when we were watching the best and the brightest of our government and business go on television every night talking and acting really stupid. I remember one night, I think it was in the fall of '07, when the Treasury Secretary and the Federal Reserve chairman went up to Capitol Hill and briefed the top people on what was going on. And the Members of Congress came out of that room afterward, and you could see the fear of God on their faces. And that night I thought, "Holy shit, Brian's right."

But the whole thing didn't crash, they pulled it out, and that made me right. Right?

Brian didn't think so. He kept researching, and writing, and --the way he put to me – "looking for a way I could be wrong." But he just got more and more worried, until that day in 2010 when he told us about the plan that changed all our lives forever.

3. THE DECISION

2010

"What we have to face," Brian said to me and Kathryn on that long-ago, peaceful Saturday morning in his fancy suburban house, "is the fact that this country is coming apart. I've reported on every industrial system that provides us with food, water, energy, you name it, and they are all deteriorating, they are all running out of resources, they are all doing terrible damage to their surroundings. Our surroundings. But the other thing they are all doing is making tons of money for very rich people, who share the money with politicians. So nobody, anywhere, is doing anything to fix this."

Kathryn had given him the floor, asked him to repeat the case he had made to her the previous night, asked me to listen and tell them what I thought. Then she had perched on the end stool at the breakfast bar, leaning way back, her arms crossed over her chest, little wisps of smoke curling out of her ears. I already knew what I thought. I thought I should run like hell.

Somewhat hesitantly, Brian continued. "We've talked about parts of it. Hell, everybody talks about parts of it. Industrial agriculture destroying the soil, polluting the water, squandering petroleum and synthetic fertilizer, fooling around with genetics, soaking everything with toxic chemicals. Food engineers marketing crap made from corn syrup that's making the whole country overweight and undernourished at the same time. Meat packers raising sick, miserable animals and then contaminating their meat with bacteria that poison people and can't be treated with antibiotics."

Brian was standing now, at the blunt end of the breakfast bar, facing us. The kids, to their relief, had been released to the swimming pool area out back. As Brian got into his subject, his voice took on strength, his body sort of coiled with energy.

"We're running out of oil and water and electricity and minerals and the atmosphere is heating up and the seas are rising. And the people who do write or talk about pieces of this disaster, you know what they say? Boy, it's sure going to be bad if nobody does something about it. You know how long they've been saying that? Thirty fucking years, that's how long. And you know what they know, anybody looking at this shit knows, but never ever says? Nobody is doing anything, and nobody is going to do anything. About any of it.

"So the whole system is coming down. The crash has already started. But it's like when you cut down a huge tree, you saw and saw and nothing happens. You think it's never gonna fall, and finally,when it moves, it's real slow, just an insignificant little tilt and some cracking, but once that movement has started, once that tree is on the way down, there is nothing you can do to stop it."

Kathryn was trying to keep her promise to let him talk but she couldn't. "How come you're the only one that knows this stuff? Christ, I watch the news. I talk to intelligent people. I even read a book now and then. Not once have I heard anyone say the world is coming to an end. Not once."

"Kate, I understand." He looked at her with sad eyes, and she looked back, close to tears. Two people who did not want to be fighting with each other. "The big money is doing a great job of distracting us from what's coming so they can keep making money. That blond lady who works for Exxon strolls around on Sunday TV and coos at us that we have all the gas and oil we need to keep wasting it for centuries. And then the coal industry hires some con man to rave about clean coal, as if it really existed. And they send their politicians out to get us all riled up about some wrestling match about abortion or terrorists or gay marriage. And it takes real effort to get past that.

"But they haven't been able to conceal everything, and I'm not

20

making up what you find out when you ask the questions. I'm not making up the fact that every ton of grain harvested in this country means at least three tons of topsoil destroyed. It's not my imagination that there's a dead zone, caused by fertilizer washed off of farm fields, in the Gulf of Mexico that's the size of Rhode Island. The disappearing glaciers and lakes and aquifers, the spreading deserts and rising seas, these aren't pipe dreams that I made up. They're the answers you get when you ask the questions.

"Lots of people know what I know, Kate. Climate guys know what's happening with global warming. Oil guys know what's gonna happen when we run short. Ag guys know what's up with the fertilizer and the antibiotics and the genetic engineering. But nobody puts it all together. It takes a generalist, not an expert, like a reporter for example, who looks at all these guys in their separate cubicles and realizes that when you put them together in the same room they are telling you that the whole thing is coming apart.

"Oh and one other thing. To keep their jobs, writing for an industrial newspaper or teaching at an industry-endowed college or getting their research funded by some industry – even to keep their government jobs, because that money comes from the Congress and we know who owns and operates the Congress – most of these guys have to soft-pedal what they really think, and whatever warning they do make they have to say, real quick, that bad shit might happen if we don't do something real soon. But they know, and you know, and I know, that nobody is going to do anything."

Kathryn was vibrating in place. I thought it was time to take a little pressure off her, so I weighed in. "Brian, I don't quite see how you can be so sure that no solution, no invention, no breakthrough is going to happen in any of these areas. I mean, we've had a century of stunning developments. My father was alive when the first airplane flew. How can you just ignore the possibility that we could invent our way out of trouble?"

"That's like saying when a 100-year-old man gets pneumonia, I'm not worried, he has always got well before. Things get old, Dad, problems get enormous. Hell, if you invented a potted plant tomorrow that grew a five-gallon can of gasoline every day, first you'd be in court with Exxon for about 50 years before you could ever bring it to market, and after that it would take you 50 more years just to propagate enough seeds to make a difference. I don't know how long we've got, but it ain't 100 years."

"Well, that's just it, isn't it? You don't know, nobody knows, when this disaster is going to happen. Assuming it is going to happen."

"Dad, we've had this argument before and I can't believe you are still hung up on that. You don't know when or if your house is going to catch on fire, but that doesn't stop you from spending a boatload of money on fire insurance."

"Sure. But I have seen houses burn down. I've never seen a civilization crash."

"Well if you would stop looking at the last hundred years, and look at the last hundred centuries, you will see all kinds of successful, powerful civilizations that crashed and burned. Most of them for the same reason – they abused the resources that made them successful and powerful.

"But here's the thing. It's too late to stop the crash, too late to save *every*body – but it's not too late to save *any*body. The tree's gonna fall on lots of people, but anybody who looks up and sees it coming can move out of the way.

"We – this family – can survive this. But not here. Not without making some big changes. We have to be able to grow our own food, make our own energy. For that we need land and water and equipment and know-how. We've got some time, but not much. That's where this comes in." He put his hands on the stack of pictures.

"The farm. I've been looking for this property for two years. Looking at Internet listings, talking to realtors, I went and looked at ten properties before this one."

"See, that's another thing that just fries my potatoes," Kathryn erupted. "You kept this from me for *two years?* You didn't just fail to mention it, you *concealed* it from me!" Her eyes were swimming in tears of frustration. "Makes a gal wonder, Brian. What else did you have going on during that time?"

The look he gave her was tired and sad. "The only thing going on, Kate, was me trying to find a way to keep my family safe. You. And the kids. Now I thought you were going to let me run through this, and then talk?"

"Yeah, yeah." She scrunched her arms tighter across her chest, leaned back even farther on the stool. Yikes. This was going to be a long haul for Brian.

"So we had a long list of requirements, and every property before this one fell way short."

"Tell him who 'we' is."

"Kate, goddamn it, let me tell this!" He took a breath, looked again at me. "There are two other families in this. You can't do it alone or as a small family."

"Two other families knew what was going on, for two years. I didn't."

"Sonofabitch, Kate, will you get off it? None of the kids or relatives knew, and only one of the other guys told his wife because she's been on the same page as him from the get-go. See, she listened to him, and thought things through, and she found that she agreed with him."

"Hmmph." Arms tighter. Lean farther back.

"Anyway. The farm. It's a hundred acres in a hollow between two ridges of the Allegheny Mountains just across the Virginia-West Virginia line. Two hours west of Dulles Airport, on the edge of the Lost River Valley. There's only one road into this hollow, the road dead-ends at our property, and the only way in from the back end is over a three-thousand-foot ridge. And it's National Forest back of us, so there are no houses up there at all. The road coming in is hard to spot and easy to close, and you cannot see any part of our property until you're right on top of it, so the security aspects are really, really good."

"Ask him what he means by THAT. Security aspects."

"Kate, if you do not shut the fuck up and let me explain this, I swear to God...."

"Okay, okay." She could not get the arms tighter, nor could she lean any farther back, so she just glared.

Brian took a couple of calming breaths. "Its got a house,

ramshackle but big. Five bedrooms upstairs, well water, a septic system. Lots of woods for fuel and hunting. Maybe 20 acres of pastures and a big plot with good soil for gardening. And water, a spring-fed, all-year stream called Mint Creek running all the way across it. It's damn near perfect."

Despite Kathryn's glare and my blank look, Brian was smiling. Because he wasn't seeing us now, he was seeing that farm. I hadn't seen an expression like that on his face more than two or three times in his life.

There was a pause. Each of us contemplated our respective planets.

"So," I said, the very soul of neutrality. "You want to go live there."

"I do," he said, as though taking an oath.

The sound Kathryn emitted defied description. Sort of a primordial, guttural moan of frustration. "Brian, have you completely lost your mind? You want us to go into the hills and live like cave people because you think the world is coming to an end? I mean, Jesus, Dad. Can we just have him committed, or something?" Tears of frustration, were sliding, in slow procession, down one cheek. She refused to acknowledge them.

Brian spoke softly to her, as you might to an angry grizzly you were trying to talk into having something other than you for lunch. "Kate, do you know that every steak and hamburger and chicken leg in this house is contaminated? That if you didn't handle it like a bio-hazard, and heat it to 160 degrees, it would make us all sick or even kill us?"

"Yes." She gritted out. "I know that."

"And who told you that?"

"It's been all over the news. They held hearings, they indicted those people..."

"Who told you about that danger to our family long before there was any news coverage? Back when it seemed crazy to think responsible companies would do that? Who?"

It took a long time. "You."

"Dad, who told you to get out of the stock market in 2005, months before the housing bubble took it down?"

I didn't see any point in delaying. "You."

"Crazy, huh? Kate, do you argue about spending thousands of dollars a year on fire insurance? Because it *could* happen, right? Because if it did happen, and you hadn't bought insurance, you'd be really sorry, and you'd feel stupid. So year after year, you pay it. And after a couple years with no fire, I don't hear you saying it's a waste of the money that should pay for our kids education, or our retirement.

"That's what I'm talking about, Kate. Insurance. Making sure we can survive what's coming."

She wasn't leaning back on her stool anymore, she was hunched forward as if enduring a hard rain. Like others of her gender I have known and loved, she hated it when her man used logic and facts in an argument. And she was, at least during the argument, unmoved by them.

She turned a pleading look on me. "Dad? What am I going to do?"

I held her look for a bit, and then without looking away said, "Brian. Do you know when this crash is coming?"

"It's already started, Dad."

"Yes, you've said that. You've also said it's a slow thing, like turning a battleship. When, do you think, is it going to become intolerable?"

"It could be any minute. If California has the big earthquake, if something spooks the oil markets..."

"Yes, we can imagine such things. But if you had to bet – a lot of money, or, say, your marriage – would you bet on the crash coming this year, or in five or ten years?"

"A big bet like that? I guess I'd have to say five or ten."

"Then there's some time. You talked about the house burning down. If you got everybody up in the middle of the night in a panic and whisked them away to a motel, and the house wasn't on fire, you'd feel pretty stupid, right? As dumb as the guy who didn't buy insurance?"

Now Brian got wary, and Kathryn got interested. "What are you saying?" Brian asked.

"I'm saying if you believe you need to do this, why uproot

everybody now? Get the farm. You can afford it. Make your preparations. If and when you need it, it will be there. In the meantime, Kathryn, you have a place in the country for summer vacations and weekends. Like a lot of your friends do. And it's real estate, after all. If circumstances change, it can be sold."

There was a really long silence. After a while, Brian and Kathryn made eye contact, for the first time that day seeing in each other's eyes a glimmer of possibility gradually replacing the anger. Kathryn, visibly relaxing, turned to me. "So that's why you're so damned good at politics."

"Yup. Artist of the possible. Why they pay me the big bucks."

4. APOCALYPSE NOW

June 2021

After Brian's warning call in June of 2021, I turned on the television to watch Hurricane Seven's progress, and told Google to show me the Old River Control Structure on my tablet. I learned a lot from those two screens during the next two days. Most of it, I wish I never heard of.

If you had been standing at the end of River Road, just south of Morgan City, Louisiana, looking across the Atchafalaya River toward Beers Island at about 3 pm on Friday, June 11, 2021, you would already have been dead. For six hours by then, that spot had been lashed by hurricane-force east winds that had ratcheted steadily upward from around 75 miles per hour at nine that morning to 195 miles per hour by 2 pm.

The next hour had also brought the 42-foot storm surge ashore. The storm surge is the pile of water pushed up by the hurricane winds to its right front. Why there? Because the storm is spinning counterclockwise, which means that to the right of the eye its forward speed is added to the wind speed, and subtracted from the wind speed to the left of center. So at landfall of a hurricane traveling at 20 miles per hour, the winds piling water against the land to the right front of the eye (wind speed + 20) are about 40 miles per hour stronger than the winds to the left (wind speed - 20), which are pulling water away from the land. Plus the extremely low barometric pressure at the center of the storm, relative to the water all around it, actually sucks up a mound of water in and near the eye.

When the storm surge slid in under the 35-foot surface waves, even on River Road, 10 miles inland from the open waters of the Gulf of Mexico (measured along the hurricane's path – a distance that had been cut by two-thirds since Katrina by rising sea levels) the water by now is over 20 feet deep. Along its entire length, River Road is about three feet above sea level.

But let's keep you alive for another few minutes, floundering and spitting in the 35-foot waves and trying to get your breath in the 195-mile-per-hour winds, so you can experience something marvelous. At about 3 pm, the wind, in an instant, drops to zero. The roaring that has been intensifying for more than six hours suddenly fades. The water's surface smooths, the air becomes oppressively still. If you were on dry land, or could stop trembling, you could light a match and hold it up and see, for once in your life, a perfectly shaped, undisturbed flame, its smoke rising straight as an arrow to the sky. You are in the eye of the hurricane.

But not for long. As the roaring recedes to the north – you might even bask in a shaft or two of sunlight! – it becomes audible to the south, and approaches steadily. After 15 or 20 minutes it reaches a crescendo and then the 195-mile-per-hour winds arrive, like the grill of a speeding Mack truck, now coming from the west, and sweep you to your already determined fate.

By now Morgan City is gone, along with the five thousand (or so) souls who either ignored the evacuation orders or could not comply with them. What was left of New Orleans is gone, and hundreds of square miles of refineries, tank farms and port facilities are now being destroyed, first by wind and water, then by fire. And the work of this storm is not yet half done.

Bring your newly disembodied self and fly with me, it will give you a new perspective on things. Me? I can do anything I want to, I am telling this story. Let's go high, so we can see the whole south coast of Louisiana and Mississippi, with New Orleans a little right of center. See that big fan-shaped swelling of land southward into the Gulf, marshland dotted with ponds and veined with channels? Two hundred miles from east to west, that is the Mississippi River

Delta, and it offers a major clue to what is about to happen.

See, for thousands of years, the Mississippi has been doing what big rivers do. It heads for the sea, racing down from the mountains, then jogging across the plains, all the time getting bigger and slower. When it reaches the coastal flatlands, it slows to a walk. Now it's not moving fast enough to keep suspended in the water its heavy load of silt, which now settles to the bottom, turning to mud and building up the floor of the river's bed.

Eventually, a natural river, with its bed partially filled in with its own sediment, slides on over to another channel and finds an easier way to the sea. The Mississippi has always done this, changing its course every thousand years or so, reaching the sea sometimes 100 miles or so to the east of its present mouth, sometimes to the west, and in doing so has built up this enormous, three-million-acre delta.

Then we humans came along. We put a city by the river, and a port at its mouth, and learned to use the river as a highway into the interior to bring out our crops and later, to take fuel inland. We progressed, as we humans like to do, getting richer by making everything bigger – bigger boats, buildings, factories, refineries – oblivious to the risks we were taking, ignorant of the price that one day the river would exact from us by doing what big rivers do.

We woke up to what the river was going to do in the 1950s. Look down at the delta again. There's New Orleans, at center right. Go about 100 miles west and there's Morgan City, where Hurricane Seven came ashore. Go 115 miles northwest from New Orleans, or 100 miles north-north-west from Morgan City, and there's Baton Rouge. Now go another 50 miles upriver and we come to the place of reckoning.

What we noticed in the 1950s was that the Mississippi was once again flirting with another way to get to the Gulf. Actually, it would have done so a hundred years before had it not been for an earlier human intervention.

During the 15th Century, along this stretch of river in what is now called central Louisiana, the river formed an oxbow, a horseshoe bend reaching to the west. When a river bends, the water on the outside of the curve travels faster than that on the inside. So the outside water tends to scour the bank, while the inside water tends to let silt drop out and build up the bank. At first the difference is slight, but over hundreds of years the curve is tightened until it is a horseshoe shape.

This westward oxbow of the Mississippi ran into the Red River, which until then had flowed to the Gulf of Mexico on a path roughly parallel to that of the Mississippi. Now the Red River became a tributary of the Mississippi, flowing into the north side of the horseshoe bend. What flowed out of the south side of the bend, in the former Red River bed, became known as the Atchafalaya River.

The bend was so extreme that riverboats traversing it had to navigate 20 miles of river, west and then south and back east again, to get one mile farther downstream. In 1831 an impatient river captain dug a channel across the narrow neck of the bend. At its next flood, the Mississippi followed, blasting through the channel and straightening itself out again.

Things were now as they had been, with the Red River becoming the Atchafalaya and the Mississippi doing what big rivers do. By the 1950s its lower bed was so built up with mud, its quest for a new route to the sea so insistent, that its was sending more and more of its water through the channels of the abandoned oxbow – now referred to as the Old River – and into the Atchafalaya. The Atchafalaya offered a clean, rapid transit to the Gulf, and Ole Miss was thinking seriously about making the move.

When the industrial powers realized what the river was going to do, they were appalled. Big Oil had helped build an entire economy based on cheap, plentiful fuel, and 20 per cent of the country's oil came in through the Louisiana Offshore Oil Port, much of it to be processed in 17 nearby oil refineries along the river. Big Agriculture had used the fuel and synthetic fertilizer that Big Oil made possible to bring under cultivation so much land that they had to sell their surpluses overseas in order to pay their fuel and fertilizer bills. Half of the country's exports of corn, soybeans, wheat and rice went through the Port of New Orleans. After first, of course, coming down the river.

All this business and much, much more – nearly a fifth of the country's seafood, almost all of its coffee, lots of steel, plywood, on and on – depended on the Mississippi River to carry barges, supply fresh water, and whisk away sewage. If the river decided to go to Morgan City it would leave all this infrastructure, every factory, warehouse, refinery, pipeline terminus, tank farm, container port, pier and wharf, high and dry, and bring the country to its knees.

So the Congress of the United States passed a law forbidding it. Seriously. By law, no more than 30 per cent of the Father of Water's water was to be allowed to escape into the Atchafalaya, and the US Army Corps of Engineers was told to make it so. Thus there arose, athwart the ancient channels of the Mississippi meander now called the Old River, a massive system of dams, floodgates, spillways, a lock and a hydroelectric station, most of it operational by 1964 but not complete until 1990.

The main floodgates were severely tested by the 500-year flood of 1973, in fact came within a whisker of collapsing. The engineers repaired and expanded the structures, to see it tested in 2011 by another 500-year flood that exceeded their worst-case scenarios. (The notion that there are floods and other weather events of a severity that can only be expected once in a hundred, or five hundred, years, has been abandoned now that such events occur most every year.) And now, after leveling Morgan City and New Orleans, Hurricane Seven was bearing down on Old River.

Its storm surge left behind and its winds wearing down somewhat over land (although still a healthy 100 miles per hour sustained when they got to Old River), Hurricane Seven's principal weapon now was rain. Katrina had not been a huge rain event upstream – another reason New Orleans had survived that time – dumping its maximum seven inches or so in a narrow band parallel to but well east of the Mississippi. West of the river, only about an inch fell.

This time, Seven dumped in excess of 20 inches of rain on the river and an area extending out 50 miles to either side. By the time what was left of the eye of Seven arrived at Old River, the river had reached 2011 levels and was lapping at the tops of all the Old River dams, locks and gates.

Which might have been all right. The water was going to go down as quickly as it came up, because the reach of the rain was not that far upstream. But the wind was still gusting well over 100 miles per hour, from the east until the arrival of what remained of the eye. Which meant the wind was blowing across the river and along the channel toward the main floodgate across the Old River.

This howling, demonic wind did two things that were not helpful. It created its own small but significant storm surge, piling water up against the front of the structure. But much, much worse, it seized upon the logs, the house trailers, the boats and a few runaway barges that it found in the raging river, drove them along the channel and smashed them, over and over again, into the dam.

The massive pressure of the water on the face of the structure, the vicious battering with thousands of tons of wood and metal, the undermining by the raging water released by the now-wide-open floodgates, exceeded anything the designing engineers had imagined was possible.

At 9:28pm on Friday, June 11, 2021, with a shrieking groan the likes of which had never been heard on earth before, the main floodgates of the Old River Control Structure gave way. Now a wall of water 60 feet high and soon a mile wide, the entire might of the flood-swollen Mississippi River, scoured out its new course, raging across the rubble of farms, towns and cities and eventually that of Morgan City to erupt into the Gulf of Mexico and there create what would be for the next thousand years or so the new mouth of the Mississippi.

Meanwhile, along the 150 miles of its former path from Old River through Baton Rouge to New Orleans, the majestic and immortal Father of Waters vanished, leaving behind a trickle of water in a broad ribbon of mud.

If you want to record a time of death for the American Century, 9:28 pm on June 11, 2021 would be as good as any.

5. THE DEER HUNTERS
November 2013

"Dad, I think Kathryn is going to leave me."

It was November of 2013, nearly Thanksgiving, and as usual I was in the middle of three things, had several people in the office, but I snapped to. "Why, Brian?"

"None of the four As, but thanks for suspecting," he said dryly. Years ago I had heard a radio talk show host, who called herself Dr. Laura, preach that the only legitimate reasons for divorce were the four As – abuse, addiction, abandonment or adultery. Absent one of those things, she told her callers, suck it up and make it work. It had made a lot of sense to me and I had repeated it often to my children. And to some of my friends who shed spouses like wet raincoats. "She just can't stand the Farm. Never could. And she won't accept it."

"Aw, man."

"Yeah. Listen, I know you're busy with the new job and everything, but could we go hunting? I need to talk this through."

I moaned inwardly, but this was my first-born son – only born son, actually – and he was asking for help. So I told him I would meet him at the Farm the day after Thanksgiving and stay for the weekend. We would go up into the mountains and camp, like we had in the old days.

They had done a lot of work on the Farm in three years, but not on the access road. It still looked like a spot alongside the road where you might back a truck in to grab a few fallen branches for firewood. I pulled into it a little after noon on the Friday after Thanksgiving, the big Mercedes S-Class sedan looking totally out of place, and followed the goat-track into the woods. After a few dozen yards, you could see a few signs of care. The track had been graded slightly, some holes had been filled with shale, and there was an occasional National-Forest-style water-diversion barrier like a slanted speed bump. To the right a ridge rose sharply, big timber looming over the road, old oaks mostly, with a scattering of pine. Down to the left, where a stream ran, I could see the occasional sycamore glowing ghostly white in the gloom.

Fifty yards or so in, I came to the first gate, a decrepit old wooden thing with a rusty chain for a latch. "That one's not for security," Brian had explained to me, "That one's for show. To show there's nothing special back here, no point in going any farther." I got out, opened the gate, got back in, drove through, got out, closed the gate, got back in, drove on.

After another 50 yards, around a sharp, rising bend to the right, I came to the first real security. A gate that at first glance looked like an ordinary, tubular metal farm gate, but proved on closer examination to be made of heavy gauge steel rod, not hollow tubing. It was mounted on and securely latched to steel posts set in deep concrete. Anything smaller than a Humvee or a medium tank was not going to bull through this gate if it was closed. It had a combination padlock, whose secret I knew.

So I did the gate drill again, and still had 200 yards to go before I could see anything of the Farm. By the time I could see it, I was there; the woods opened suddenly and revealed, up slope to the right, the sprawling wood-sided two-story house, its metal roof sweeping down low over a 60-foot-long front porch. At the same time I could see the huge barn, downhill to the left.

It was an old-fashioned bank barn, its lower floor opening unseen to the rear and its upper floor – what used to be the hay mow – accessible from the front via a wide ramp leading up to a pair of enormous sliding doors. I ignored the ramp and followed a driveway, down along the right side of the structure, that looped around to bring me face to face with the barn, and with a low wing bermed into the bank to my right showing five vehicle bays, two of them open. Brian's Jeep Wrangler was in one, I pulled the Mercedes into the next one. Brian was in the shop area stuffing things into his backpack.

"Hey," he yelled in greeting as I climbed out and stretched.

"Hey." It was not yet time to talk. We had a camp to make.

We had done this the first time more than 20 years ago, when Brian was 12, and probably ten times since; almost every year until the activities of his teen age and my middle age had intervened more frequently. I had hunted the farm with him three years ago, the year they bought it, but had not been able to make it since.

The routine was a familiar one, and required very little conversation. There was no need to discuss who packed the three-man tent (me) or the two gallons of water (him). Likewise, responsibility for matches, coffee, cooking pans and the various other needs of the camp had been divided between us long ago. So it was not long before we were ready to hoist packs, sling rifles and go. Except what he slung on the back of his frame was not a rifle. It was a squat, black ugly thing with a scope and curved arms.

"What is that thing?" I asked.

"Crossbow. I'll explain later."

Still it was not time to talk. By the time we had walked a hundred feet or so downhill from the back side of the barn, we picked up a trail that led along the creek flowing there. Turning right, we started a gentle ascent toward the southwest. We passed the hut containing the humming hydro generator, its two-inch black plastic supply line snaking up the stream bed to its intake high above. We were traveling, not hunting, so we were stepping out, and with 40-pound packs, going uphill, there was not much breath left over for talking. Besides, the trail was narrow and we had to go single file.

I was pleased that after an initial, panicky feeling of shortness of breath and weakness of knee, I walked through it and got into a zone, breathing deeply, striding comfortably, feeling pretty damn good for an old guy who lived behind a desk. After following the creek a half mile or so upstream, we turned right and now started to climb in earnest. At times we were reaching for branches to help haul us up, sometimes we were on all fours. After an hour of very hard work (interspersed with rest breaks every 10 minutes or so, for the old guy), we topped out on the ridge.

Like all the Allegheny ridges in the area, this one ran northeast-southwest. We had targeted a slight saddle between two higher points on the ridge, where we knew there was a small brushy meadow, with level ground – a rare commodity at this altitude – for our camp. It was also buck country, we passed two hornings – saplings shredded by bucks scraping the year's last, itchy velvet off their antlers – on the way across the meadow to our campsite.

The light of the cloudy winter afternoon was already starting to fade, so when we got to the campsite and downed packs, it was still not time to talk. I popped the tent and spread the sleeping bags inside while Brian scrounged some wood and started a fire. Not for cooking, we broke out two MREs – US Army meals, ready to eat – and used the included ration heaters to warm the mystery meat. The fire was for warmth against the quickly deepening chill. And for talking. Now, as we settled in across the fire from each other with our packets of food-like substances, it was time.

"She seeing somebody?" It's hard to ask your son that, about the mother of your grandchildren, but we had to start somewhere.

"Naw, it's not like that. Well. She thinks I'm being unfaithful, but not with another woman. With this farm."

"That's the whole issue." I said it like it was a fact, but one that I couldn't yet believe.

"I don't know if the issue is the farm, or the fact that I won't yield to her. Maybe if I took up day-trading on the stock market and she didn't approve, we'd have the same problem. But she says I'm spending way too much money and time here, for no good reason."

I set aside my meatloaf packet and eased another stick onto the fire. It was a thrifty little blaze, like you want in camp. "Are you?"

"Am I what?"

"Spending too much time and money here, for no good

reason?"

"For crying out loud, Dad, you know what I'm doing here. I'm trying to save the lives of my family. How much should I budget for that?"

"Yeah, well, that's clear to you. Not necessarily to others."

"See, that's what I don't get. You, for example. Why is it not clear to you? How'd you come out here today? Beltway? I-66? What did you see? All the way?"

"Cars. Solid lines of them, coming and going. Didn't let up until I got to Front Royal."

"Half a million of them every day on the Beltway. Three-quarters of a million every day at the I-70 merge on the Maryland side. How can you look at that and not say, wow, this can't go on?"

"But it has gone on. For a long time."

"Dad. There is only so much oil. The world is burning 80 million barrels of it every day. Are you really saying that because we haven't run out yet, we won't run out? Really?"

"Well, no. But they seem to think we have hundreds of years...."

"No they don't, Dad. No serious geologist who doesn't work for an oil company or an oil-exporting government thinks we have hundreds of years. I can give you phone numbers. But the issue isn't when we run out, but when we run short. The first time, the first day, that an order for crude oil cannot be loaded, because it just isn't there, that's the day the shit hits the fan. And we are an eyelash away from that."

"Brian, I gotta say. You're a smart guy, but Jeez. Everybody I know in the oil business or close to it is saying we got a revolution going on, we're about to pass Russia, even Saudi Arabia, maybe get to energy independence."

"Aw, man, that is such a crock. That is propaganda being put out by the frackers, the hydraulic fracturing guys, to keep the investment money coming in. They're making it up! Dad. You remember the housing bubble? No, the year before the bubble broke, 2005? I was running around with my hair on fire saying what is the matter with you people, don't you realize you're going to destroy the whole system? You remember? Remember what you said?"

"Hey. I believed you."

"Eventually. After other, more qualified people started to say the same thing. But you remember what you said at first."

"Yeah, I do. I said who are you to presume you even understand what these guys are doing, let alone that it's wrong, or going to break down? I mean, they had quants running these operations that had doctorates in advanced mathematics."

"Yup. And while the guys with the advanced degrees were putting lipstick on the pig – the pig being that the whole thing was based on making loans that would never be repaid – the guys like me who were running around yelling, that's a pig you got there, we were the idiots."

"Yeah, but..."

"Wait, Dad. You're going to tell me that this is different. Sure it's different. But we have a set of facts in front of us that anybody can look at – hell, it's the Information Age – and we have a set of laws operating on those facts. Not complicated, things like gravity, stuff always falls down, not up. Like if you have only so much of something and you use a bunch of it every day, one day it's gonna be all gone."

Finally, he had to take a breath. I waited for his breathing and facial color to return to near normal.

"Let's just stipulate all that. I imagine Kathryn's question is, and I have to say it's a reasonable question, what does that have to do with this family? These children? In particular?"

"Jesus, Dad, do you really not get it? I mean, I know she doesn't, but a man in your position, knowing what you must know? This has to do with the survival of every family, every child, on the planet. How can we go on thinking that we are exempt? When the system comes down, all the people who have not prepared are going to die. All of them. When you know that, the only question is, do I want my kids to die or not."

"Brian. If Kathryn thought that was the question, you know she would have the same answer as you. But I'm sure she and I have the same problem; you may know this is going to happen, we might even agree that it's going to happen. But there's one thing you do not know, and cannot know. And that is when."

Brian blew out a breath of frustration. "Yeah. That's true." He's the only radical I've ever known who would give you the point when you scored one. "But that is not a reason to do nothing. Yet that's where Kathryn stops. Since I don't know when, I shouldn't be wasting money getting ready. I should put it in the college fund. Even though I believe there's less chance of their getting to college than there is of the world falling apart first."

"Jesus, Brian. You're making a choice here between your theory of world events and your marriage."

"My choice? It's MY choice? Goddammit, if she all of a sudden said, I want you to cut off your right arm to show you love me, would you come here and say to me, Jeez, you gotta choose between your arm and your marriage? Come on, Dad, it's not fair. It's not even moral. What happened to that oath? You know, the one about in sickness and in health, 'til death do us part? When did that expire? My theory of world events canceled it? What?"

The food was gone, the fire had burned down to a cupful of embers, the chill had become more insistent and old bones were griping about sitting on the ground after climbing a mountain. We didn't finish our conversation, we just ran out of steam, and sat for a time in silence staring into the last of the fire glow.

I remembered something. "What is that ugly stick you're carrying?"

"Huh? Oh, the crossbow. It's a sustainable weapon. You can make bolts for it a lot easier than you can make gunpowder and cartridges. Plus it's silent. I want to get proficient on it."

"You want me to talk to Kathryn?"

"Please."

We doused the fire, shucked our boots and outer clothing and crawled into our sleeping bags in the two-man tent.

In seconds I was on my way to blessed oblivion, but just before I crossed the border I heard a sound. Tentatively, just before blankness, I identified it. It came from Brian's sleeping bag. It was a muffled sob.

And so for hours, as the night and the cold deepened, as the stars wheeled somewhere above the obscuring clouds, I stared wide-eyed at the blackness above me, suffering that unique and exquisite pain that comes only to a parent who sees a child in pain and cannot take it from him.

6. STATE OF DENIAL

December, 2013

"Hello, William. Here to practice your art of the possible?"

Oh-oh. Not "Dad" anymore, not even "Gramps" on behalf of the kids. Kathryn was smiling and her tone was light, but her words were stones.

I had called her the week after Thanksgiving, asked if I could take her out to lunch. "Are you bringing tablets down from the mountain?" she asked. She knew very well, of course, where Brian and I had been the previous weekend.

"No. I'm asking to see someone I like, to see how she is."

"Sorry. I'm feeling a little defensive these days. Of course I'll have lunch. But it always turns into an event, going out in public with you, so why don't you just come to the house? I'll fix brunch. Sunday."

So there I was, not so much because I thought I could do something, but because I couldn't just do nothing. Kathryn looked drawn. There were shadows under her eyes, her pale skin looked drum-tight over her face.

"No artistry, Kathryn. Like I said. I want to know how you are."

"Of course. Come in." Her face softened by one small degree, but what she really meant was, "Yeah, right."

As we walked from the foyer back toward the great room/kitchen, young Daniel came thundering up from the basement, down the hall and up the stairs toward his room, in the throes of some project. "Hey, gramps," he yelled, "Saw you on TV!"

"No, you didn't. That was my evil twin Billiam."

"Billiam Baldeshar? The one who wants to take over the world?"

"Exactly." A departing shriek of laughter acknowledged the standing joke, and with the slam of a distant door the water-buffalo impression was over.

I took my usual place at the granite breakfast bar and Kathryn, standing on the opposite side behind the stainless steel cook top, poured a mug of coffee and slid it to me.

"So." she said with a rueful smile. "What's new?"

"Trouble. Right here in River City."

"Yes. There's a pool table in our community. I saw *The Music Man.*"

"What are you going to do, Kathryn?"

"I don't know."

"Is there anything I can do?"

"Sure. Sure there is. Talk him into giving up this crazy obsession of his." Her voice went straight to the upper registers of strain, her eyes quickly brimmed with not-yet-shed tears.

"What if it's not crazy?"

"Not crazy? You haven't been here when he and this ex-army ranger guy that we're supposed to be partners with start talking about 'security.' Do you know they plan to shoot people who come to the farm to ask for food? Did you know that? Did you know they have enough guns and ammunition stashed up there to fight a war?"

"Yes, I did. And it's not necessarily crazy. If things happen as he expects, there will be need for self-defense. It's a first principle of anthropology – people will raid before they starve."

"I'm not that kind of person, Dad." She had slipped back into her previous, more familiar way of talking to me. "And I don't ever want to be that kind of person."

"Do you think Brian wants to be that kind of person?"

She didn't answer. She looked here and there around the room, as if seeking inspiration in the light fixtures, or the crown molding. "All he does," she said finally, "is talk about how stupid and venal everybody is who's in business or in government, how awful politics is and the weather is and the future. Jesus. All I want is to live a normal life. I want my children to live a normal life."

"I know that's what Brian wants, too. I'm sure that's what the people who lived in North Africa wanted before the famine, or west Texas before the dust bowl came back, or Bangladesh before the ocean started taking their land. What you want doesn't change what's bearing down on you. What you want and what you have to do are different, usually."

"For God's sake, do you believe him now? Are you a survivalist too?"

"First of all, he's not a survivalist. They are people who have always wanted the system to fail so they could go play with guns without restraint or consequences. They hoped the Soviet Union would invade, then they waited for jack-booted thugs from the Federal government to try to take their guns or black helicopters from the United Nations to impose world government. Now they're waiting for eco-disaster, salivating, with weapons at the ready. That's not Brian. Security at the Farm is 90 per cent passive, it's based above all on not being seen, not attracting confrontation.

"Second, I don't know whether Brian's right. I do know that he's a smart guy, that he has often – usually – been right in the past. I know the facts he cites are real, that he does not exaggerate them for effect. Whether that means that there's no hope of saving the system? I don't know. I hope not. But I do know that it's not crazy to think so."

"See, now you're doing exactly what he does." The tears came now, unacknowledged, abundant. "You're making me feel stupid and small-minded for not knowing all this stuff. For wanting to look out this kitchen window I've been looking out of for 12 years and see my kids coming home from school, through a safe neighborhood, to play basketball and watch TV and do their homework, like I did when I was a kid, like you did. Safe. With a good future.

"For wanting to talk with my husband in the evening about how was his day, and what are we going to do on summer vacation, and how are the kids doing in school. Instead we're having conversations about grubbing in the dirt growing rutabagas or something, and shooting our neighbors. And I'm the crazy one?"

She ran away then, away from all of it, the huge thing that was eating her life, that I was a part of now. She fled upstairs and slammed her bedroom door against it like she had shut her mind against it, with the faith that she could keep it out if she could just keep the door shut.

I finished my coffee, taking my time. I wondered what their lives would be like if Kathryn had more information, and Brian less. Then I called my driver, and while he was on his way from the nearby McDonald's where I had him wait while I was visiting at Brian's, I went upstairs and said goodbye to two busy, normal-sounding but very worried children.

7. CIRCLING THE WAGONS
June 13, 2021

Jackson tapped on my bedroom door a little before eight on Sunday morning. I had been up late, watching Armageddon on TV, and had slept fitfully, so it took me a minute to comprehend what he was saying: "Sir, it's your son. Brian. On the phone."

I looked stupidly at my cell phone lying on the nightstand next to the bed. "The land line, sir." Jackson said patiently, waiting for me to join the living. "He says the cell nets keep crashing." Nothing out of the ordinary there. They'd been doing that periodically for years, since they ran out of bandwidth, and power failures became so frequent and long-lasting they ran short of fuel for their backup generators. The Internet, too, was becoming more and more intermittent.

I stumbled to the analog phone and mumbled something.

"It's pretty bad, Dad."

"Hey, Brian. Yeah. I was watching."

New Orleans and Baton Rouge were gone. Morgan City was gone. No one had a handle on how many dead, but they were thinking somewhere north of 20,000. All the refineries, port facilities, barge docks, container-handlers, tank farms and factories between Baton Rouge and New Orleans – gone. The Louisiana Offshore Oil Port – destroyed. Even if they could be rebuilt, there was no point because there was no river there anymore.

Before the hurricane, the assets of the National Guard, regular Army, Coast Guard and Navy in the country had been heavily committed: to stemming the flow of climate refugees across the southern border; to facing down the Russian incursion into the virgin oil fields of the now-ice-free Arctic Ocean; and to assisting in the evacuation of the dust-bowl states – Texas, Oklahoma, Nebraska, South Dakota and chunks of the adjoining states – and Las Vegas.

(Lake Meade, the desert city's only source of water, had gone dry the previous fall. With no water to drink or flush with that didn't come in on tank trucks, and no electricity coming from the Hoover Dam, the city had become untenable. Disbelieving residents – was this not the site of the world famous water show, the Fountains at Bellagio? – had resisted evacuation fiercely, sometimes with guns. It was almost over now. One could only hope that some of the resisters had relocated to New Orleans.)

Any military units that could be scrounged up for duty on the Gulf would immediately face the problem of how to get there. After years of steadily shrinking production and inexorably rising demand, petroleum was scarce and expensive. Even military fuel reserves were razor thin, with many units having on hand enough fuel to travel maybe 150 miles. Gasoline prices had been holding in the eight-dollar-per-gallon range for a year or so, but were expected to double on Monday east of the Rockies, and rise almost as far on the West Coast.

But the rising, gut-wrenching worry was about the trucks, the 18-wheelers. If there was no fuel for them, there was no food for us. Thanks to a doctrine called Just-In-Time Inventory Management, which came in with computers and the Internet in the 1990s, there were no more food warehouses in American cities. The steak headed for a Kansas dinner plate on Friday was on Wednesday still aloft in a cargo jet over the Caribbean Sea en route from Venezuela, and the lettuce for the salad was on a truck en route from California's Central Valley. If anything stopped the trucks from running, there would be no more food to buy in three days, and for most people no more food to eat in three more.

Brian said the lines at the gas stations in the Washington area were already blocks long "I'm not sure I could get the kids home, and then get back here, even if I wanted to."

Any chance Kathryn will come out there?"

"None. She has no idea there's anything special going on. She refuses to watch the news, or read a newspaper."

They had divorced two years ago. It was before I retired, and during a time when I was pretty busy, and I had not been there with him or for him as he went through that. But I had been aware even then that it was the strangest divorce I had ever seen, each of the parties bending over backwards to accommodate the other, their negotiations not only civil but affectionate. He signed the house over to her, she insisted on fully shared joint custody for the children. They went together to all the kids' concerts and sporting events and birthdays and graduations, and seemed to have a good time together. I did not know for sure, but I suspected strongly that there were times, maybe lots of them, when he did not return to his bachelor apartment from those family gatherings until sunup. But she would not be married to him as long as he was married to the Farm. And although he did not want to divorce her, he could not leave the Farm.

"So." Brian was ready to change the subject. "You coming out?"

"Don't know. We could still ride this out."

"Yeah, well, you're only an hour from here, so if you wait a little too long you could still be all right. I didn't have that luxury. You be safe. I love you."

I grabbed some coffee, hot and fresh thanks to Jackson (I kept telling him that making coffee was not in his job description, but he kept doing it anyway), and went back to the TV. I had to turn the volume up. Rain was drumming on the roof, rattling on the windward windows, lashing the foliage in the yard. Hurricane Seven had some stuff left for us, too. Daylight had come to the Gulf states now, and a few network helicopters were incinerating precious fuel – they could not stay aloft long – to show us something of the utter devastation of southern Louisiana. It had taken them a full 24 hours to get mobilized and get into the area, they had spent the day yesterday nibbling around the edges of the story. In many of the shots there were drifts and clusters and pods of human bodies afloat and aground.

The President still had not stuck his head out of his White House bunker to make a statement. I could imagine him huddled in the Situation Room, reviewing his stock of cue cards: "No New Taxes?" No. "Government Isn't the Solution, It's the Problem?" Naw, that's not gonna work. What else we got?

The TV talkers were beginning to put together a list of things we were facing in the near future: severe shortages of gasoline, diesel fuel and natural gas east of the Rockies and skyrocketing prices everywhere; a shortage of people and assets for disaster relief and recovery; in the devastated area, a public-health and survival crisis of proportions that could not yet even be estimated. Biblical, was a word that was beginning to crop up. The talkers were beginning to sound grave and look scared.

And they hadn't even thought of the food supply yet.

By midday Saturday I had been convinced that Brian was probably right this time. It was hard to see how anyone could stop the unraveling now, hard to see where the unraveling could stop on its own. By Saturday night the hoarding had started, gas stations had begun to run out of product, and the lines at those still open often extended for miles.

And by now the talkers had caught on to the implications for the food supply. As a direct and immediate result, every supermarket east of the Rockies was under siege, and would be picked clean in hours. And as another result, the most selfish and predatory people would have the means to survive a few days longer than their neighbors.

I started to make some preparations. Waving Jackson off as he started to follow me, I went out to the garage, checked the Land Rover's gas tank, put the reserve-gas cans in the back, started to throw a little of this and that into it. Didn't stay too long, went back and watched a little more TV, then drifted around the bedroom, visited the den, thinking about things.

In mid-afternoon, a CNN crew trying to reach Baton Rouge from the east on Interstate 12, found itself blocked by a washed-out bridge over the Amite River, jammed in a relentless crush of cars and running short of fuel. The female correspondent, famous for her ineffable perkiness, ended her live report by pleading in a trembling voice for someone in their Atlanta headquarters to figure out how to rescue her and her crew.

By then I was feeling the fear, and I was not alone. I could tell because Jackson, flanked by two of the guys from the detail, burst into the house around four o'clock with the stride of a marine on a mission. I could see through the window that the doors of the garage attached to the house next door (where the guys stayed) were up, and the two black armored Chevrolet Suburbans that were kept out of sight there were being backed out. He minced no words.

"Mr. President, the security situation is deteriorating. We have authorization to move you to Mount Weather."

"I asked you not to call me that any more. Sit down, boys. We gotta talk."

PART TWO – THE ACCIDENTAL POLITICIAN

8. IN THE PUBLIC INTEREST
2008

Really? You forgot I was President? Huh. Well, it's been a long time, and it's not a credential that means much, now, here on the Farm. And it's not something I enjoy talking about. I mean, I had the chance to do something, maybe to avoid what happened. A chance like that was given to maybe a handful of people in our entire history. And I couldn't do anything. I couldn't find the words....

Can you give me a minute?

Better yet, let's break for the day. Tomorrow I'll tell you how I became the President of the United States by accident.

I was never a political guy, never had personal ambition in that way. I grew up on a dairy farm in the Shenandoah Valley, near Mount Jackson. From the age of about 10, for most of my waking, non-school hours, seven days a week, I was washing cows, chasing cows, milking cows, mucking out cow stalls, spreading cow manure and hauling calves out of their mothers' wombs with winches. I formed one, and only one, holy and consuming ambition: to never have to be around cows again.

By the time I got to college I had translated that aversion into a desire to be a writer. I had no novels in me, or passionate verse, I just wanted a trade that was practiced indoors and didn't involve dealing with a lot of shit. Well, one out of two.

I scribbled my way through college (Shenandoah University in

Winchester) and into a job at the city's daily newspaper, the Winchester *Exponent*. It was owned by the descendants of a legendary businessman and local politician, Isaac Harrier, who had founded it in the 19th Century. They say the nut doesn't fall far from the tree, but it can roll pretty far down hill, as evidenced by the third- and fourth-generation descendants who were my bosses. They reminded people of what Molly Ivins said long ago about a Texas congressman: "If his IQ slips any lower we'll have to water him twice a day."

Like most owners of unearned wealth, the Harriers saw themselves as self-made, when in fact their fortune had been made by great-grandpa, and their only achievement had been in figuring out how to live off the interest. They were profoundly conservative people who believed that government's first duty was to protect, defend and preserve their wealth. They deeply resented any attempt to tax their profits (or inheritances), regulate their activities or help the less fortunate. Because this attitude was shared not only by my employers, but also by the vast majority of the readers of the newspaper and of the residents of western Virginia, I adapted the coloration required for my survival.

My strategy worked. And my luck held. In ten years I was named editor. I hired journalists good enough to produce a paper that people would want to read, and conservative enough that their columns and enterprise stories did not bring me too many outraged early-morning calls from members of the Family. What did I think about things? I wrote editorials fervently supporting Arbor Day and Cancer Research, occasionally taking fearless stands against Godless Communism and Waste-and-Fraud-in-Government.

In those days, even after my promotion to publisher in 1992, my public persona required little more than attending frequent cocktail parties and making the occasional talk to the Chamber of Commerce or the Rotary Club. These occasions required only that I fulminate a little about how liberal Democrats were ruining the country and conservative Republicans – even when serving as President or controlling the Congress, or both – were being prevented from saving it.

This sort of rote becomes easier with each repetition when you live in an echo chamber where rote is greeted not with derision or contradiction (at least, not from anyone who matters), but with more of the same, only louder. It's also easier when your paycheck depends on it. After a few years I didn't even listen to what I was saying on these occasions, let alone think about it. It was a kind of lullaby I hummed to my employers on demand, and the notion that anyone was taking it seriously as thoughtful speech never occurred to me.

So you can imagine my surprise at what happened on a spring day in 2008. I was called to a meeting in what we called the Family Quarters – the suite of offices on the fourth (top) floor of our little building – and saw waiting for me not only Favorite Son (what everyone called Isaac III everywhere except in his presence) but one of his acolytes, who currently held the job of city chairman of the Republican Party. In addition, sitting quietly in the background looking for all the world like an undertaker prepared to clean up any bodies left after the proceedings, was the Harrier family consigliere. I don't think I ever heard him speak.

"Mr. Harrier," I said to Favorite Son, looking around the room warily, "is this a firing squad or a parole board meeting?"

Favorite Son laughed uproariously, as he always did when something resembling humor came to his attention. He wanted badly to be seen as a regular guy. He threw his skinny body around in his leather judges chair when he laughed, flopped until the silver waves of hair stuck out from his skull slightly like the wings on a Viking helmet. "Not at all Bill. I asked you to drop by because we think you can solve a problem for us."

"At your service, sir."

"Yes, of course. Harry, why don't you explain to Bill what we've been talking about?"

Harry Fielding was the party chairman for the city. Heavy set and dull eyed, he was the owner of a hamburger joint that somehow had become Favorite Son's favorite place to dine when he was not at the country club. Harry fawned over the great man at every opportunity. The great man appreciated it, and soon raised Harry to prominence in the affairs of the city. Harry became known as a connected guy, who could put you in touch, make things happen, and make lightning decisions as long as he had an open telephone line to the Favorite Son. Otherwise he did not seem to know what anyone was talking about.

"Bill," Harry wheezed – it seemed to require great effort for him to talk – "as you know, and as your paper has reported in way too much detail, our state senator stepped all over his dick in the last session."

I didn't bother to respond to the dig about the paper. Once, many years ago, Favorite Son had called me to ask whether it was necessary to publish any stories on the flagrant, public transgressions of a personal friend of his. I said, "Yes, sir. It is." After a long silence, he hung up, and had never asked me to pull or push a story again.

"It would have been better," I observed, "Given his long record as a family-values homophobe and opponent of gay marriage, if the great man had stepped on his exposed dick in the presence of a female friend, and not a professional guy."

"Yeah, well." Harry had no problem with what the guy had done, really, he was irritated that it required him to do a bunch of stuff. "He's toast, and now we got a special election. We want you to run."

I had not seen that one coming. I leaned back and stared at all of them, thinking about my comfortable life, its settled and enjoyable routines, its lack of strife.

"No."

"Well, now, Bill," said Favorite Son, "Let's at least consider this thing." Oh, shit. Somebody had talked Favorite Son into it. So I could do it, or I could quit. Either way, my comfortable life was over.

I expected most of what ensued. Dottie's despair, followed by acceptance when convinced the alternative was abject poverty, followed by depression. My own loathing for what I was going to have to do, alleviated only slightly by the realization that Favorite Son and the Chairman had taken care of the financial side of things (by making assurances, I would find out much later, about what I would vote for, and what against) and had a rather competent campaign organization all set up, ready to run whatever candidate should appear. As it turned out, I didn't actually have to be a state senate candidate, I just had to play one.

And here's what I did not expect; what happened when I stepped up to a rostrum, as I did at my inevitable victory celebration, to be greeted by several hundred cheering, stomping, clapping people. Nothing had ever felt quite that good before. The effect was way beyond martinis, into some other dimension of pleasure. After that night I thought I now understood two things: what they meant when they said that crack cocaine was instantly addictive; and why certain pathetic perennial candidates could not stop running for something, anything, just so they could from time to time stand up in front of a room and bathe in a warm shower of applause.

I had never tried cocaine, had seldom dabbled with marijuana, even in college, and had always kept myself in close check around martini pitchers. For precisely the same reasons, I made a solemn resolution that night to ration carefully my exposure to the steroid roar of the crowd.

Serving in the state senate proved to be ridiculously easy. It was a part-time job, as Thomas Jefferson had intended, and required me to be in Richmond for only two or three months of the year. I regarded the post as an extension of my job. My employer had asked me to do it, gave me the time off to do it, raised my salary because I did it, and had financed the campaign with his friends' money. I was never clear on exactly where the money came from. So when he suggested how I should vote, I took it as my duty to comply. Other than that, it was simply a matter of appearing at five or six times more lunches and dinners than before.

The speeches were easy, too. The Tea Party was on the rise, and the people who came to hear political speeches in those days were not there to learn about the candidate or the issues, they were there to yell. The more they got to yell, the better they felt. When you vowed to eliminate waste and fraud from government, they yelled. When you said government wasn't the solution, it was the problem, they yelled louder. Chant that we needed to bring God back into government, and run it like a business, nobody said, hey, wait a minute, aren't those two things mutually exclusive? They just screamed. And when you yelled about taking back the country and the Constitution, they went nuts.

Who had taken the country, from whom, where had they taken it, and what did taking it back mean? Oh, please. These people were like stoners at a rock concert, they were not interested in the words, they just wanted to move to the beat. And just the golden oldies, thank you very much, no one wants to hear your latest creations.

It was a job. I did it. When somebody asked me to vote for John Doe for the board of the University of Virginia, I did. When somebody asked me to sponsor a statewide ordinance cracking down on barking dogs, I did it. On the really important stuff, and by that I mean important to my employers, there was no partisan disagreement. For example, when word came down that we were really not to fuck around with putting any restrictions on hydraulic fracturing, the new way of blowing oil out of shale with millions of gallons of water and dozens of toxic chemicals, nobody even brought up the restrictions, on either side of the aisle. We all knew who we were working for.

Now when it came to the emotional side shows, such as preventing abortions and withholding gay rights, these were partisan affairs. Staged, in other words, for the entertainment and distraction of the voters. Our employers had no interest in the outcome of these issues, however much they appreciated the function of the endless arguments. However, the slightest misstep by any of us in the arena could expose one or another of us to lightning strikes of voter backlash. So I voted with my party, kept my mouth shut and my head down. I didn't care how anybody else voted, or whether my side carried the day – since it really did not matter to anyone who mattered – and thus I didn't make very many people mad at me. I became, well, popular.

I also became fond of martinis. I could maintain my ironic distance from the crowds, and from the content of my speeches, but there was nothing ironic about the icy tang of a cold, dry Beefeaters, up, with a twist. That iconic, angular goblet dewed with condensation, fired with the cold light of winter, exhaling a citric gust that tickled your nose just before the ice froze your gullet and the fire hit your belly. God, how I miss them.

Not that I had a drinking problem. Because I was repressing nothing, so there was nothing pent up to erupt after the the third martini, no contradictory opinions about anything, certainly nothing combative. I simply stayed happily buzzed for a few years.

Then they asked me to run for the United States Senate.

9. LEVEL OF INCOMPETENCE

2012

"So, William." Dottie was speaking to me, but not looking at me. She was looking out the glass of our sun room. "Why would you want to do this?"

We were at breakfast on a January morning in 2012. As always, she was well dressed, even for sleep, with a floral-print, lacy pajama top over filmy harem pants under a coordinated robe. Every hair was in place. She did nothing to conceal the streaks of gray advancing into the honey-blonde tresses, or the lines etching themselves into permanence at the corners of her mouth and eyes. Yet she was sailing through her 50s with the extravagant beauty of her youth seasoned, not diminished, by the years.

She had always been a classy lady, even in her 20s when I met her and began my dogged and often graceless pursuit of her. The night she first gave herself to me I had been doubly astonished: first, because I had not known for sure until that moment that she was at all interested in me; and second, that she could mutate from her habitual cool, dignified reserve to become a squealing, squirming, pleasure-seeking otter in a heartbeat. Afterward, as I had sprawled dazed and exhausted, she had carefully replaced her clothing, sat down on the edge of the bed and said, "So, William. Let's talk about the wedding."

Now, a lot of years later, she wanted to talk about the U.S. Senate. "Just a few years ago," she continued, still not looking at me "you didn't want to get into politics. You only did so, you said, because your employer required it of you. Does he want you to do this?"

"Hardly. He will be upset."

"Why?"

"Because it takes me out of his control. Beyond his reach. Into another league. The people who want me to do this are the people who run the likes of Dominion Capital, Chesapeake Resources, First Alliance and the Commonwealth Fund. Each one of those companies dwarfs the Favorite Son's little empire. What they want me to do is the same as what he asked me to do: sing the hymns and cast the votes. It means a substantial raise in pay, good and permanent healthcare insurance, and a pension. Plus, you only have to run every six years."

"Statewide."

"Well, yes." Never think for a moment that, although she participated in politics as little as possible and talked about it only when required to do so, she did not know what was going on. I had told her from the very beginning that it was going to be my job, not hers, that I did not share most candidates' belief that one must display the little woman at every rubber-chicken dinner and fire-hall rally. She took me at my word and stayed away from all but the most vital functions. But she knew very well that what I was now proposing to do involved an expenditure of time and money that was orders of magnitude greater than what I had been doing.

"And still you haven't said why. Why *you* want to do it."

"Well, Dot, we're talking about a pretty good salary, full benefits, immediate vesting in a pension. On the other hand, the future of the newspaper – any newspaper – is pretty iffy, even if it weren't for the Great Recession."

"Bullshit. That's why you think I'll buy it. I'm asking why you want to do it."

I actually experienced a moment of vertigo. I do not believe I had ever heard Dottie utter a vulgarity until then. Nor had I ever had an earnest point of mine slapped away quite so dismissively. Words failed me.

Words did not fail her. "Do you want to know what I think?" Now she looked directly at me, and the experience was not altogether pleasant. "I think you've been smoking some of the stuff you've been selling." My God. Was this Dottie? My Dottie? "I will tell you something, William, that I have not shared with you or anyone else. I do not especially like the person with your name who gets up in front of these Neanderthals and incites them."

"Aw, Dottie..."

"I know what you're going to say. That it's just a kind of Kabuki Theater, without meaning. William, you are a senator. That means something. What a senator says, means something."

"Dottie, that was true once. It is not true anymore. What the public sees of politics is Kabuki Theater, it's a distracting show about abortion and religion and gays and guns and anything else that gets people worked up. The Democrats have their talking points and we have ours. The content never changes. Nothing gets resolved, nothing gets done.

"It's a show. To be in the show you have to have tons of cash, and you get that cash from people who have tons of it to give. That means you have wealthy employers, and all I'm talking about doing is changing employers."

"William, I did not choose this life. I didn't choose to put my family and my home on public display, to spend half my time alone, another part of it on stage being stared at and whispered about, to hear vile things said about you, to hear you say vile things. It was a price we had to pay, you said, because your employer required it. Now you want to leave that employer, and double or triple the price, and I want to know why?"

I knew better than to try to slide another one past her. I needed to tell her the truth. The problem was I didn't know the truth. The best I could do was: "I suppose because I've found I'm good at it."

She regarded me balefully over her cold coffee. "So," she said at length. "You're doing it because you can. Or is it because of – what did you call it? – the steroid roar of the crowd? All right. Now answer this question. Why am I doing it?"

She got up then, and walked upstairs, and went into our bedroom, and closed the door. She did not slam it. If she had, the sound would not have been so loud.

I carried on, of course, and Dottie acquiesced, of course,

although with a level of sadness that was new, and did not go away. I could still make her laugh until she cried, but it was a lot more work than it used to be. And, of course, I had far fewer opportunities.

It was not very long after I had cut my ties with the newspaper (which required enduring a long and abusive temper tantrum by the Favorite Son) and committed to the Senate race that I knew I had made a terrible mistake. About three days afterward, actually, when I sat down with my new finance chairman, provided by my new friends. He was a pale, pudgy guy who favored tan suits that matched his tan hair and round glasses that reminded you of an SS interrogator in a bad WWII movie. He sucked constantly at a glass of ice water that was apparently his pacifier and booze replacement.

"Okay, Bill," he opened, at our first meeting, "here's how it's gonna go. You're gonna spend at least six hours a day, now to election day, on the phone, calling everybody you've ever met, done business with or heard of – former friends, ex-wives, illegitimate children, the lot – asking for money. Okay?"

I figured I needed to establish right away who was working for whom, so I hit him high and hard: "No. Not okay. I've never had to do that. I've already got pledges from a lot of heavy hitters, and they came to me. Okay?"

"No. Not okay. You got promises, which are not spendable, of about $1.8 million. You need a minimum of $10 million. Meaning we gotta raise *at least* a mil a month the rest of the campaign. Know how much that is a day? $33,333.33, that's how much. And when you get elected, you know how much money you gotta raise, on average, every day, seven days a week, for the next six years? $4,500. So, if you're not gonna do what needs to be done, let me know now so I can go work for somebody who knows what's going on."

So much for the notion that he was working for me.

What followed was, without question, the worst eight months of my life. I don't think anyone who has not run for statewide office has any idea how big a state is. To drive from Northern Virginia to Roanoke in the southwest to Norfolk in the southeast and back to northern Virginia was a 700 mile odyssey that meant 14 straight hours behind the wheel. If you didn't stop. We did the circuit over and over again.

It gave me a lot of time to make and receive phone calls. The incoming calls were to inform me that we were within anywhere from seven days to seven hours of having to suspend campaigning for lack of money. The outgoing calls were pleas for money. Making those calls, planning and scheduling fundraisers, and attending those fundraisers, consumed easily 90 per cent of my waking hours. Politics in a democratic republic.

The fun part – the set-piece speeches, the rallies, the interviews – did not go as well as I was used to. The voters who were automatically on my side – the Republicans and right wingers – were no longer content with vague blandishments about the Constitution and family values. They wanted blood and guts now, they wanted their candidates to attack and malign their opponents and all who stood with them, to cry treason! and blasphemy! and call down the judgment of a jealous god. I wasn't very good at that.

The other side, the Democrats and liberals, of course didn't show up at my events. They were much too well-mannered to try to disrupt my events with hecklers and goons, and too ethical to simply manufacture accusations out of whole cloth – to claim, for example, that I had been a child molester, or had been indicted for extortion, or something. That is why we'd been beating the crap out of them since the 1980s.

For most of modern political history, the electorate everywhere had been divided in roughly equal thirds: Republican/conservative, Democratic/liberal, and Independent/undecided. As for the other third, the independents who allegedly decided each case on its merits, who spurned simple-minded party loyalty or ideology: never saw anything of them. We had become a country with a right wing and a left wing and no head.

Winter blurred into spring; May brought the convention, at which I was nominated over token opposition. It was a weekend memorable for two treats. For one, I got a major dose of the steroid roar of the crowd from 10,000 throats, producing a high that lasted about a week. And second, Dottie put in an appearance, staying with me the weekend.

She was gracious to the crowd and warm toward me, although

there was about her a new degree of reserve. She really didn't like this stuff, and I promised her anew that I would see to it that she was exposed to it as seldom as possible. Despite her distaste for it, her unfailing poise and inner beauty made her a huge hit with the people, and I occasionally saw a bit of high color in her cheeks, a glint of reluctant pleasure in her eyes, as the accolades washed over her.

The main thing that happened after the convention was that the demands for cash intensified. Cash for television – we had to buy the insanely expensive Washington, DC stations at full price even though only about a third of their audience was in Virginia and thus able to vote for me. We were traveling now in a two-bus convoy, had a staffed office in each of the ten congressional districts, a core staff of people whom I barely recognized but who had to have paychecks every two weeks.

And it wasn't working. My crowds were lukewarm, my polling numbers (another hideously expensive necessity) were anemic. My opponent was a Northern Virginia urban liberal whose pro-choice, gay marriage, amnesty-for-illegal-aliens mantra was playing well in the suburbs, and there were a lot of suburbs. My family-values, pro-life, build-a-fence and restore-the-Constitution doctrine that had made me invincible in the Shenandoah Valley traveled well to the rural west and south, but not the metro north and east. He was staying a couple points ahead of me in all the polls.

The worst day came in mid-October. I was in Richmond for an event dreamed up by the Republican Congressional delegation and the Virginia General Assembly Republican caucus. It was a fund raising event for Lavonne Shannon, who was in what doctors said was an irreversible coma at Richmond University Medical Center. The money wasn't for her medical expenses, but to pay a company of lawyers who were petitioning every court in the system to prevent her family from taking her off life support, as they had mistakenly let it be known that that was what they wanted to do. Some genius had figured out that this was a perfect way to burnish our side's right-to-life credentials and crank up the enthusiasm of the base as the election drew near.

I was in no position to give anybody another stick to beat me with, so I showed up with skin crawling and sang a few bars about reverence for life and everything in God's hands and so on, managing to say nothing directly about, or quotable in reference to, the unhappy situation of Lavonne Shannon and her family.

So when I got on the elevator on the top floor of the Jefferson Hotel (across from the Capitol in Richmond) the next morning, headed for breakfast, last night's martini cinders lying grittily all over the surface of my brain and eyes, I was already not in top form. I did not even notice the guy standing in the back of the elevator, and jumped when he spoke.

"You have children, Senator?"

I looked at the sad-eyed, elderly man in the neatly pressed threadbare suit and drew a blank. "Excuse me. Do I know you?"

"You damn well should. You got children?"

I considered stiffing him, but although his words had an edge, his voice was gentle – either that or bone tired – and he seemed not to be whacked out or hostile. "Yes. I do."

"Boy or girl?"

"A son."

"You remember when he was little?"

"Of course I do."

"Remember when he hurt himself? Or had to get a shot? How you would have done anything to take the hurt yourself?"

"Yes."

"Then you know exactly how I feel about my little girl. Lavonne Shannon. How I would give anything in the world if I could die instead of her."

The elevator stopped on the main floor and the doors opened. I stepped outside the elevator but did not walk away from him. I couldn't.

He stepped out and faced me, at a respectful distance. He did not raise his voice. "You ever have a child die?"

"No."

"Still. You got a pretty good idea what it's like. You must have, you feel qualified to get up on television and tell me what I ought to be doing. What I ought to be believing."

"No. I...."

He wasn't interested in my denial, blew right through it.

"So I got to go back to the hospital now, like I been doing for six months, and watch my little girl hurting. And the only thing I can do for her, the only way I can take the hurt for myself and take it off her, you won't let me do. Cause you got to make a point about how much you love life." And he walked away.

I thought that was as bad as the day was going to get but I was wrong. I had not yet finished breakfast when my cell phone rang. It was Brian. "You gotta come home, Dad. Right now. Mom's sick."

10. ALL SHE WROTE

2012

"She's what? What are you doing home?" Yeah, I know, that probably wasn't the first question, but my brain had crackled into bright spinning shards and nothing was tracking right. Brian worked at *The Washington Post,* had two kids and a home in Northern Virginia, why would he be at our home in Winchester with Dottie?

"I'm not home, I'm at the hospital."

"The hos...was she in an accident?"

"No, Dad, she's sick."

"With what?"

"She asked me – no, that doesn't cover it, she made me swear – to let her tell you. When you get here. You are coming?"

"Of course. But I...I mean, sure. Yes." I hung up. Might as well, I wasn't exactly making sense. I told people I had to go, I don't even remember what I was doing when I got the call, told them to handle it, got in somebody's car, and drove, watching the flaring and rumbling in my head, like distant artillery. "Mom's sick." Ka-boom. "You gotta come home." Flare. "Right now." Ba-blam.

Got to Winchester about nine pm. Checked in at the hospital front desk, was directed to the oncology wing. Oncology. What was that? I couldn't think what it was. Found it, found her floor, and there was Brian, sitting slumped in a chair in the waiting area. His eyes looked sore. "Brian, what the hell?"

He stood and wrapped me in a hug. Damn, he was big. It was

like being gathered in by an oak tree. As usual, I had to steel myself to keep from recoiling. Hugging was not a part of what we did when I was a kid. When he unwrapped me, he said, "Go on in. She'll tell you."

Through a steel door with a window, into a soft white fluorescent glow, and there she was. Dottie. A still white form on a still white bed. She didn't look...terrible. Pale, yes. Thin. There was an IV drip into her left forearm and sensors on her right. A monitor was beeping quietly on the wall behind her. She looked to be peacefully sleeping, but then the eyes flicked open and there she was. The same deep, deep blues with the glint of a smile that was always just ready to start. It started now. "So," she said, "William. What's new?"

"Dottie?" I was so angry with her, scared for her, worried about her, guilty, ignorant, frustrated. I had no idea what to ask first.

"Now, you're not going to be dickish about this, right?" The voice was hers, all right, but feathery, without much energy behind it. "I'll tell you everything, but you have to promise not to yell at me."

"Aw, Dottie...." I couldn't talk.

"I'll take that as an 'I promise.' Pull up a chair." I did. "Now. It's ovarian cancer, dear, Stage IV, metastasized." The artillery shells in my mind were exploding closer to my position. I remembered what oncology was. I couldn't get my mouth to close. She waited a moment, then went on. "When they diagnosed it in July – you remember? I was feeling a little peckish at the convention in May, and never quite shook it? – they were pretty sure that without treatment I had at least six months to a year. So I saw no need to burden you with it until after the election, maybe even after Christmas. Well, they were wrong.

"I was feeling okay this morning, a little wobbly, nothing out of the ordinary. And then I wasn't. I was on the floor and I had to crawl to the phone and dial 911."

She sounded okay, she was clear and everything, but the talking tired her and she had to rest every few sentences. Wait a minute. Wait a minute, something she said. Not cancer, the other thing. "What do you mean...without treatment?"

"Now this is where you have to remember not to be a dick. With surgery and chemo and maybe radiation, they could assure me – not promise, just assure – of 18 months to two years of pain-wracked, nauseated, hairless life. Or if we did nothing, six months to a year of relatively pleasant life. I thought it was a no-brainer. Still do."

"But, surely to God, there's stuff we can try."

"William, darling, there are things way worse than dying. And among them are all of the things they could try on me now. Try not to make a big deal out of this."

"A big.....a big....deal? You get this diagnosis, you get a death sentence, for crying out loud, you make these decisions, and you don't tell me?" I could not help it. My voice rose.

She was quiet for a minute. She just lay there looking at me, looking like she was going to smile. She didn't have to say it. I knew. This was not about me. But it was, too. Tears started running all over my face, falling everywhere around me, hitting and flaring like artillery shells. "What am I going to do without you, Dottie?"

"You're not going to be without me, silly. We can talk anytime you want. And you don't even have to make sure your cell is charged." She was quiet for another stretch while I blubbered. "Oh, by the way," she added, "I know you don't really approve of what those Neanderthals are doing to that poor family in Richmond, interfering with the family of that little girl? In the coma? But just so you know. My living will, complete with do-not-resuscitate order, is signed, notarized and on file with the hospital and my doctors. And Brian has my power of attorney."

"Dottie! I wouldn't..."

"Well, you're a very good actor, dear. Sometimes even I can't tell what you really believe. Any more."

"How long has Brian known about this?"

"Oh, yeah, like that matters. For about 12 hours, you idiot. I do not like him more than I like you." Another long pause. "Now, if you can pull yourself together, my love, I'd like you to bring Brian in so I can see both my men for a few minutes. Then I'm going to have to sleep, I'm afraid. It turns out dying is a tiring business."

And three days later, that is exactly what she did. Just like that, it was the last day.

But it was not her last gift to me. For one thing, just as she said, we talked more often and in more depth after she died that we had before. But the other thing was that her death, and my utter inability to handle it, to talk about it without falling apart, to pick up my life and campaign and go on, engaged the sympathy of the voters who had been about to reject me. I won the election by ten points.

11. THE CHECKUP

2013

"Mr. Leader, this is a surprise." And it was. For the Minority Leader of the US Senate to visit the cramped offices of a freshman Senator was unusual. And he was alone.

"Bill," Senator Garland of California said expansively, flashing a surfer grin that was startling in its whiteness in the surfer tan under the mop of straight, surfer-blonde hair. He flopped into a visitor's chair fronting my desk, stuck his legs straight out, crossed them at the ankle. Letting me know that this was all casual, inconsequential stuff. Between the gentlemen of the club. Right.

It was late fall. It had taken me until spring that year to get fully back into the world. I finally figured out that when you abandoned hope, things got better. When I stopped wishing that Dottie were not gone, stopped hoping that she would be in the kitchen when I came home, the agony of loss receded and it was once again possible to hear birdsong and accept the existence of grace.

When I abandoned all hope of ever winning an election again, for the simple reason that I was never again going to be a candidate, I started to sort of enjoy being a senator. Of course I told no one that I intended to serve only one term. If you admit you're going to quit, no matter how far in the future, you instantly become invisible and inaudible. I was not going to do six years as a zombie.

I concealed the fact that I no longer carried the awful burden of fund raising by cheerfully helping other senators with theirs, thus earning substantial gratitude. I refused to do TV interviews. Period. I referred bookers to colleagues whom I knew had an interest – by which I mean had a major donor who had an interest – in the subject. More gratitude. I tried to appear more burdened than I was, by pretending to calculate every vote and worry about every development, but there really is nothing quite so bracing as not giving a shit. And the presence of the leader in my office probably indicated that my behavior had raised some suspicions.

"I hope I'm not interrupting anything important?" The bright grin made me want to put on sunglasses.

"No, I was just finishing up the crossword."

Garland laughed uproariously. God, I was a funny guy. A US Senator doing a crossword puzzle in the middle of the day. A great line to share with the caucus. I casually reached over and minimized the browser on the screen of my laptop. So if he came around to my side of the desk he couldn't see the crossword. "So anyway. Bill." I invited no one to call me Bill. Most people picked up the cue. "I wanted to stop in, check up, see how you're doing. See if I could get you to stop asking me for favors every day."

"I haven't asked you for any favors."

"I know. So how am I going to keep you under my thumb?" Big, surfer, I'm-just-kidding grin. The sunglasses should be wraparound. Mirrored. "Seriously, some of us were wondering how you're doing with fund raising? Some of the new members don't realize how early you have to get going if you want to stay in the game."

"Well. I guess I'm a little relaxed about that right now. I came into some money."

"Oh. When...Jeez, Bill, I was so sorry to hear about Dolores."

"Dottie. Thanks."

"So...you're okay for now."

"For now. Yeah."

"Well, good." It was a concluding remark, but he didn't move. "I was talking to Ronnie the other day." Ron Milbank, he meant, the chief lobbyist for Chesapeake Resources. "He wasn't sure you're solid on the extension of Halliburton."

Translation: Chesapeake was the largest player in the country in hydraulic fracturing, blowing natural gas out of shale rock formations using water and chemicals under high pressure. Their claim was that if left alone by government they would usher in a new era of energy independence with plentiful, cheap natural gas. The other view was that if left to their own devices they would pollute most of the country's drinking water and not make a dent in the energy problem. The Halliburton rule exempted frackers, as they were called, from the provisions of the Clean Water Act. They wanted it extended, and broadened, to include immunity from "frivolous," as they called them, lawsuits. Our side was on their side.

"My vote will be there. Why does Ronnie have the vapors?"

"Said you weren't too enthused about it."

"You want my vote, or my enthusiasm?"

"What?" Suddenly I had the leader's full attention. That had not been the question of an intimidated suck-up. Belatedly, he became aware that I was not tugging at my forelock and stirring the dust with my toe, but looking him in the eye. Sort of like an equal. He sat up in his chair. Surfer dude thought he might have seen an upright fin cutting the water.

"Mr. Leader, we can pass a bill exempting them from the laws of gravity and it's not going to save them. Those fracking wells they're drilling all over creation cost twice as much as they thought they would, and are delivering less than half the gas they expected. Meanwhile they've jawboned the price of natural gas down so far they're losing money on every single well. Their insider investors are trampling each other looking for exits. Pretty soon they'll be on *60 Minutes* and they'll be done. So they can have my vote. For all the good it will do them. It's solid."

The surfer grin was gone. He just looked at me for a long minute. "Little bit more to you than I thought." After another pause, "Solid?"

"Solid."

"Okay, then." He heaved himself to his feet, threw a hand in the air to wave farewell, headed for the door, but stopped short, turned back. "Know what else folks are saying?"

"Folks?"

"Your colleagues."

"No."

"That you seem to be the only guy in the place who isn't running for president."

"Well, that is correct, I am not running for president. And any sitting senator who does should reflect on the fact that in the history of the Republic only three have ever made it. Mr. Leader, I am sorry to have caused you concern. I am here to do a job. I think I know who my bosses are, and I think I know what the job is. Have I been wrong, yet, in any part of this?"

"No. Not once."

"So what is the problem, Senator, that brought you here today?"

He had the ability to go someplace else and think for a bit, leaving his surfer-dude face in repose in a completely neutral, semi-friendly, nonthreatening expression. It occurred to me that there was probably a little more to him than I had thought, too. "It was my problem. It was me thinking I needed a handle on you, a way to make sure. I might have to rethink that."

So he rethought it. I waited.

"There's something coming up. Wanted to give you a heads-up. Gonna need your vote, obviously, but there's an upside."

I waited some more. Wondered why he was having so much trouble, what he wanted from me. At long last he sighed and spit it out.

"The Metropolitan Council of Governments has asked the Army Corps of Engineers to dust off some plans they started working on back in the 1940s, then dropped. Metro Washington needs water. The Potomac River is drying up and what's left in it is full of shit. Gonna be critical in a couple more years.

"Out in the Shenandoah Valley, there's a place called Fort Valley, a 25-mile-long slit in Massanutten Mountain, maybe three, four miles wide at most. A creek runs the whole length of it, and the exit is so narrow and steep that it could be the cheapest water impoundment of that size, ever. Gonna have to buy out a lot of people who live there, gonna have to use eminent domain on a lot of 'em, gonna be some blowback. All that said, it's still gonna be cheap water. We're gonna do it.

"Now. We're gonna authorize generous buyouts, try to minimize the strong arm stuff. Way above market price. Gonna be six months, a year before the public finds out. So, anybody who has a chance to make some deals out there, where you live...."

He stopped talking and looked at me. I looked at him. When it got uncomfortable, I said, "Thanks for the heads-up."

He waited for more, didn't get it, so with another little wave, he left. Still without the handle on me that he wanted. But should he ever find a deed for some Fort Valley property with my name on it, dated after this day, he would have his handle. As for me, as soon as I checked the little digital recorder built in to my desk light, which activated whenever there was sound in the room, I confirmed that I now had a pretty good handle on him.

Amazing. In me he had a loyal servant, a reliable vote, somebody who was giving him no trouble. But he didn't know why I was giving him no trouble and it was driving him nuts, compelling him to take risks, big risks, just to make me compliant on his terms, rather than compliant on mine. Go figure.

I never did get to finish the crossword puzzle. My chief of staff and my press gal and my constituent-relations guy were all over me wanting to know what the Leader had been doing in my office. And right in the middle of all of that, the phone rang. It was Brian.

"Dad, I think Kathryn is going to leave me."

12. SINS OF THE FATHER

2015

"How can you do it, Dad? How can you get up in front of everybody and say the things you say?"

It was a pleasant fall afternoon in 2015. Brian had been working on the Hill, had called and said can we do lunch, as he sometimes did, and so we did. Usually we wrangled about some environmental piece he was working on. Today he had another kind of burr under his saddle. That wasn't unusual, nor was the fact that he opened the conversation with a high hard one, we sparred hard when we talked. I countered mildly.

"Apparently you have some particular things in mind." We were in the Senate dining room, and I was enjoying the warm yeasty smell and buttery taste of the crunchy dinner rolls while we waited for our bowls of the famous bean soup. Usually I spent these lunches trying to put him on the defensive about whatever crime against humanity he was going on about, but it seemed today was my day to defend.

"Yeah, I do. Yesterday, on the floor. You said, and I quote:" Oh my. He had it on his phone. "'The jury is not yet in on whether the changes in climate we are seeing are the unavoidable result of human activities, or whether there are any human activities possible that could change the climate back.' Dad. How the fuck could you say that?"

"We are in the Senate dining room. We do not recognize words such as 'fuck'."

"Yeah, yeah. How could you say that?"

"I could say it because I was asked to say it, as a talking point for the day's news cycle, by my Leader. Who, as you know, is not only my Leader in the Senate but is running to be anointed next Leader of the Free World, a.k.a. President of the United States, and whose wish is my command."

"But you can't believe it!"

"You didn't ask me if I believed it. You asked me how I could say it."

"Please. Dad. Stop with the word games. You taught me that the truth is important. I'm teaching your grandchildren not to lie. I would really like to know if you still believe that."

"Brian, I also taught you never to cross the street without holding a grownup's hand. Should I still insist on that?"

"So what are you saying? It's okay to lie if you're over 30?"

"I'm saying that one's understanding of reality becomes a bit more nuanced when one – how shall I put this – grows up."

"So the problem is not that you're mouthing mindless crap on the floor of the United States Senate. The problem is that I'm naive."

"Yes. The other problem is that when you start losing traction in an argument, you get more strenuous and upset, and thus lose the argument completely. Tell me this, Brian. What would you prefer that I say?"

"That global climate change has been set in motion by the burning of fossil fuels, by humans, that it presents a grave threat to the survival of the human race, and that every government in the world ought to have as its first priority doing whatever is necessary to mitigate its effects."

"I don't disagree with any of that. Are you going to eat that roll? No? I'll just take care of it then."

"You don't disagree with any of that. Yet you can stand up and say what you said."

"Yes. Because what I said is also true."

"You have GOT to be kidding."

"I said the jury is not in on whether climate change is the *unavoidable* result of human activity. How could we have avoided the activity that has contributed to climate change? At what point in history, exactly, do you think as a practical matter anyone could have said to the mass of humanity, forget the benefits of cheap and plentiful petroleum, forget cars and airplanes and air conditioners and plastic and cheap food. We insist that you live as peasants and draft animals for another couple of millennia so we don't pollute anything. Kind of a hard sell, don't you think?

"And as for a single human activity that can change the climate back: name one. Name one thing or one set of things that will have that effect and that has a ghost of a chance of actually being done. By anybody. Ever.

"Now. Suppose, notwithstanding all that, that I made the statement you prefer. What would happen?"

He looked at me, glumly, for a minute. The boy hated to lose. "Nothing. Nothing would happen. The industrialists would stop giving you money, they'd attack you, and you'd lose the next election."

"Exactly."

"But Dad. You're not taking their money anyway. You're not going to freaking run in the next election. So why do you care?"

It was my turn to get strenuous. "Brian, shut up. We are in the Senate dining room. Do not speak those words."

"Sorry. But answer the question. If you spoke the truth, you might enable somebody else to speak up. If a few people spoke up, something might get done. That's called leadership."

It was my turn to regard him glumly. The bean soup came. It's one of the few things in Washington that not only has a good reputation, but deserves it. I wanted to focus on it. But this son of mine.

"Gosh," I said (dialing back the sarcasm setting from "disable" to "stun," because he was family), "isn't that a direct quote from that pamphlet they hand out to grade-schoolers on the Capitol tour? For God's sake, Brian, you're a national reporter for the *Washington Post*. Oh, wait. That's the newspaper that covers presidential races as if they were horse races. As if the president "manages" the economy, and "creates" jobs. Maybe that is actually how you understand politics. Maybe you *should* be taking a grownup's hand when you cross the street.

"Leadership? You want to talk to me about leadership? Leadership today consists of one thing, Brian, running more 30-second TV spots than whoever's on the other side. You want to talk to me about speaking up? Into whose ears? The citizens of this country are fully involved watching reality television shows and vampire movies.

"Honor? You want to talk to me about honor? I am here, in this job, in the employ of people who spent millions of dollars to put me here. I owe them. I do their bidding. Does that make me somehow different from all the other employees in America?"

"Dad. You took an oath to protect and defend the Constitution."

"Oh, please. You pledge allegiance to the Republic before every Rotary Club lunch. Does that keep Rotarians from cheating on their taxes?

"Now. Could there come a time when the conditions of my employment clash with my principles? Of course, and then I would be obliged to speak up. Right after I resign my position."

"So, Dad. Let me get this straight. You honestly don't see anything out there, as you speak up for and vote for the interests of the oil companies and the hedge funds and industrial agriculture, that conflicts with your principles? Have I got that right?"

I sighed. The bean soup was gone and I hadn't really tasted it. The meatloaf was in its place, and still I couldn't concentrate on my lunch. "You talk as if my vote matters. I'm one of 100 in the Senate, one of 535 in the Congress, and the fate of just about every measure that gets to a vote here is predetermined. You talk as if debate matters. Nobody listens to anybody else unless they screw up or unless they have enough money to run 500 spots on TV. What, I'm gonna sweep my toga over my breastplate and single-handedly turn the tide with my silver tongue? I'm gonna do a Jimmy Stewart one-man filibuster? They'd throw a net over me.

"So now you're gonna say, hey, that's corrupt. That's not the way they describe it in that folder, *How a Bill Becomes a Law*. So maybe I oughtta resign over that? I guess I could. I guess I could stand becoming famous as the single most ineffective politician since Jimmy Carter. Who, by the way, was dead right about almost everything.

"What stops me is this. *It doesn't matter!* Tell me one thing – one damn thing – the Congress of the United States has done in your lifetime that has changed history for the better. That has done anything to improve the lives of ordinary Americans. That has righted a wrong.

"You tell me that, and I'll consider taking your advice on leadership and suicide."

"You are a slippery sonofagun. But it's wrong. Dad, the country is falling apart. The whole system is falling apart. Gas is seven dollars a gallon, natural gas is through the roof since that whole fracking thing collapsed, food is more expensive every day, unemployment is over 15 per cent, the Southwest has turned into a desert – my God, we have climate refugees in the United States! – and we're going to have to abandon some pretty big cities if we don't find water supplies for them.

"And not one person or institution in this country – not one! – is even working on solutions for any of this! And you, a United States Senator, tell me you are doing your job?"

"Brian. I am a legislator. I cast one vote per bill. Name a bill that has been introduced, or could be introduced, that will lower gas prices, or create jobs, or stop the desertification of the Southwest, or create water supplies for cities, and I will vote for it. Name it. Or at least describe it."

"But we have to do something!"

"Sounds like a typical Senate Resolution: 'For God's sake, do something.' I could vote for that."

Like most of our discussions, it ended like a prize fight between brothers that's declared a draw, with the tired fighters slumped on their stools in their respective corners, bleeding and grinning at each other, looking forward to the next time.

"How are things at home?" I asked after a while.

"Awful. She hates the farm, hates everything it represents. Hates it when I go there, hates it triple when I take the kids. She tried going out there a couple times at first, but now she won't even talk about it. Just hates it. But the thing is, we love each other, she doesn't want to go anywhere else. But the tension is so bad, and so constant, that I'm worried about the kids, and she is, too. That's probably going to be why we end up divorcing. To get the kids out of the pressure tank."

"And at the farm?"

Instantly, his face brightened, his shoulders came out of their slouch. "Really good. The micro hydro is up and running for electricity, the solar collectors are heating all our water, we've super-insulated the basement and enlarged it so it's a constant-temperature store room.

"We've established raised beds for gardening, although all we can do right now is soil-building and maintenance because nobody is there full time. We've cut deals with farmers in the area to host our flocks of chickens, goats and pigs; they keep all the profits and extra animals, maintain the minimum flock size and when we ask for them, turn them over to us.

"And some security stuff. If the balloon went up today it would be a scramble, but I think we could get there and get stable. Another couple years and we will really be ready."

"Well," I said, pushing back from the table. "Let's hope and pray your preparations are all in vain. Or that I'm dead before you have to use them."

"By the way," I said as we walked from the Dirksen SOB (our affectionate term for the Senate Office Buildings) to my digs in the less prestigious Hart SOB, "you've always talked as if you assume that in the event, I would be coming to the farm. But I wonder why? Everybody else has been working on it all along, and I haven't. The children, obviously, are the future. But me? I'm the past. I'm old. I'd just be in the way."

"Are you kidding? You would be the only one there – the only one – who has actually lived on a farm, taken care of animals, kept a garden. We're all city kids. We know the theory, we've read *Mother Earth News* and *Back to Basics*, but we've never done it. People who've never done it make a lot of mistakes, and if we make a lot of mistakes we're not going to survive. We need you. Big time."

I returned to the paper-shuffling and posturing of a United States Senator feeling a good deal more important than I had for a long time.

13. THE LEAST WORST OPTION
2016

The Republican National Convention of 2016 was scheduled for August in Richmond, Virginia. I had been given a nice spot in the proceedings, not to advance my career, but to end it, pretty much. It had become obvious to those who paid attention to these things that I was not going to run again in 2018, and shortly after the national convention I would have to make my intention known publicly. So they were giving me a nice opportunity for a valediction.

I was looking forward to it. The bar was set quite low; I had nothing to achieve, overcome or establish, and it would be a bracing dose of the steroid roar of the crowd. And it would have been nice, had not Iran chosen a date just two weeks before the convention to declare war on us. As if the idea itself were not brazen enough, they announced their intentions even more brazenly; by sinking the flagship of the US Fifth Fleet, the *USS John C. Stennis* – an aircraft carrier, for God's sake – smack in the middle of the Strait of Hormuz.

Who knew that those pathetic little speedboats the Iran Revolutionary Guard Navy runs around in, looking like water bugs around a walrus when they get near any of our warships, were armed with powerful missile batteries capable of blowing holes in the hull of any warship we had? Finding and destroying such boats with the world's most advanced weapons systems, as one admiral put it after the attack, was like "trying to kill flies with a hammer."

We probably should have seen it coming. For one thing, for a decade we had been discussing openly the possibility of bombing Iran to prevent its acquiring nuclear weapons. Weapons that they never seemed to acquire, but always seemed to be on the verge of acquiring, posing a threat that increasingly resembled that of Saddam Hussein's fabled weapons of mass destruction in the old days. For another, Iran had been losing control of its population.

As an oil-producing country, Iran had always seen to it that its people got cheap fuel, by selling it to them at far less than cost. And, of course, it did what it could to improve its peoples' lot. Such deeds do not go unpunished. As the Iranian middle class got larger and richer, it consumed more fuel, until the government could no longer afford the subsidies required to keep the costs down. As the subsidies came off, the costs of everything went up, and people started taking to the streets to protest and seek change. That the government decided it was time to go to war with somebody should have come as no surprise to us.

Yet the US government, like the rest of the world, was caught flat-footed by Iran's move. As an immediate tactical response, US attack helicopters, their Gatling guns churning the waters with 3,000 rounds per minute, cleaned the waters of the Strait and the nearby Persian Gulf of every moving thing within hours of the sinking, but in the meantime, farther west, other speedboats, along with missile barrages from the Iranian mainland, sank three more US cruisers and five amphibious ships. More than 10,000 US servicemen were killed, at least 30,000 wounded.

The haggard president, who had thought he could ease up during the last few months of his term, went on TV at 10pm to say what presidents say when they haven't the faintest idea what to do: "Stay calm, everything is under control." I don't think he even knew he was channeling George W. Bush when he added, "The people who did this are going to hear from us." The vice president, whose nomination to succeed the president would follow our convention by a week, went on TV to do the only thing he could do: second what the President had said.

Senator Bob Garland, our Senate Leader and presumptive presidential nominee, was on TV practically before the image of the vice president had faded. "Nuke 'em," he said, "I want Iran back in the stone age where they belong." It was pretty good politics. God-awful policy, but you have to get elected to do policy. It was the kind of red meat that got the basest of our base snarling and barking and raring to vote.

When the attacks were over and immediate retribution exacted from the attacking forces, the situation in the Gulf subsided into tense silence as our government made its diplomatic arrangements and repositioned forces, and the Iranian government and people braced for the blow they knew was coming.

But there was no silence for us. In addition to the bellowing of the politicians for retribution, there was a rising howl of protest from the citizens; not so much about the loss of life in the attack, but rather about the price of gas. It went up a dollar a gallon the day after the attack, and kept on heading north. By the time our convention started it was over $10 a gallon, gas lines were everywhere, and because of hoarding, spot shortages had started to appear here and there around the country.

I had just settled into my usual suite in the Jefferson on the Sunday evening before convention week when the phone rang. It was Brian. He sounded tense. "Dad, we're going to the Farm. All of us."

"Well, have a nice week."

"Not for the week. For the duration."

"The duration of what? High gas prices?"

"The crisis. Dad, this may well be it. We can't survive the loss of 20 per cent of the world's crude. We can't. It's been a few days, the shortages haven't even hit yet, and look. Lines, riots, closed gas stations. As soon as this bites a little deeper the 18-wheelers won't be able to run, and then we've got food riots."

"Well. I don't think we're there yet. But I've been through oil shocks before and you haven't. So enjoy. Have a good time. Wait. Is Kathryn going?"

A pause. "Yes, she is."

"How did you manage that?"

"Threats. Guilt. A stark word picture of her children growing up in a ruined world without her. That sort of thing."

"Jesus. You better be right."

"Don't I know it. And if I am, you are going to have a hell of a time getting to the Farm, because it's going to get really bad, really fast. So do your best, okay?"

"I will. But...never mind. Be well. And be wrong."

"I love you too."

He was right to be worried. We had argued about peak oil enough, and I had pursued my own lines of inquiry enough, that I knew the country had very little time to resolve this crisis and stabilize the oil markets before really serious harm set in. Right now the prices were driven by speculation, and the shortages were caused by hoarding, not by any actual deficiencies in deliveries or defaulting on contracts. But in a matter of days, maybe a week or two, we really would be in trouble. That's when the 18-wheelers would stop rolling and life as we knew it would become untenable.

So I was glad I was not the President, who instead of resting on his oars for the next four months would have to paddle like a sonofabitch to get us all out of this alive. While we were waiting for him to do that, it was great politics to complain bitterly about the pain of the gas prices and the affront to American security, to blame the President for everything bad that was happening, and to promise that the new Leader of the Free World would make all things right.

As usual, I had little to do. I had an honorary seat on the credentials committee, charged with making sure the delegates were as certifiable as they looked. So I showed up there between martinis, which at the Jefferson were very good indeed. My speech was scheduled for Wednesday night, and I had already put into it every cliche I had uttered in my political career, so no more work was needed there.

With Garland's nomination a given, the only real interest generated by the convention was how and when the identity of the vice presidential candidate would become known. Two contenders (it's up to the nominee, so you can't really be a candidate) were trying desperately to be the last woman standing. It had somehow become conventional wisdom that a woman would be best. Congresswoman Nancy Philpott had the money, experience and the right-wing credentials to bring real strength to the ticket, and she wanted the job, but she was from Garland's state of California, and it was widely thought (without a shred of empirical data, but what's new) that the ticket needed geographical balance.

That could be provided by Priscilla Givens, governor of Pennsylvania, but her politics were so far to the right, way out in the badlands of Tea Party ideology, that even raving right-wing lunatics marveled when she spoke. Faced with the prospect of alienating the right-wingers if he did not choose their candidate, and making them nervous if he did (along with the rest of the civilized world), Garland stepped up to the plate and ducked.

He would let the convention decide, he said, thus insulating himself from most of the blowback, and giving the delegates something to do besides drink and howl. Starting on Monday, they went at it with joyful abandon: Givens was a lesbian; Philpott had a child out of wedlock; Givens had used pot in the statehouse; Philpott had a criminal record; and on, and on.

By the time I gave my speech on Wednesday, with 24 hours to go before the vice-presidential decision, the entire convention was both distracted and annoyed by the wasp-like buzz of nastiness emitted by both VP camps. As a result, I did not really get the full dose of the steroid roar I was craving until I wrapped up, at which point the convention seemed to realize all at once that it was saying goodbye to me. Then I got, and thoroughly enjoyed, a standing ovation.

Thursday was the day for the selection of the vice-presidential candidate, and by Thursday morning it was obvious that leaving it up to the convention had been a mistake. Nobody knew any more how to have a low-temperature, low-stakes competition for the fun of it. The Philpott and Givens camps – and everybody was in one of them – were at war. Our 40,000 casualties in the Persian Gulf, skyrocketing gas prices, the potential crippling of the nation – all were forgotten as people screamed at each other about Givens's aborted fetus (or was it Philpott's?) and Philpott's secret rap sheet (or was it Givens's?)

The voting was scheduled for 4 pm, the assumption being that the result would be known comfortably in advance of the prime time news programs. But the first vote divided the delegates pretty evenly, with several delegations voting for favorite sons, or passing, so they could be sure to be on the winning side as soon as they could figure out which was the winning side. The result was that neither Philpott nor Givens got the majority of the delegates needed for nomination, and neither was close enough, or had momentum enough, to make any strong arguments for conversions.

By 5:30 there was still no majority, and two consecutive roll call votes had yielded no change in the tally. I was on the floor, high up in the bleachers, trying to sort out a credentials question with, of all people, the delegation from Puerto Rico. Some of their people had arrived late, just today, and had made a substitution that was being protested by someone who had been left at home.

In order to square this away I had to get the story straight, and that involved talking to some very emotional people, some of whose mastery of English decreased as the intensity of their feelings increased. Several minutes went by during which I did not notice the lack of activity on the floor, or at the podium (from up here in the nosebleed seats, the pool of light surrounding the podium and the huge video boards flanking it looked like a distant planet).

I did notice it, though, when one of Bob Garland's whips, moving fast and sweating Heavily, grabbed the shoulder of the Puerto Rican chairman, murmured in his ear for 20 seconds or so, and jogged off toward the next delegation. When I had resolved the credentials issue I wandered over to the chairman and asked him what the whip wanted.

"He say they upset about the deadlock. He say they gonna try a compromise to break it loose, and if there is any way we can see our way to go along with it, the Senator would appreciate it. And remember it. He say the VP candidate will still be the convention's choice, but if the convention won't do it he gotta move."

"Did he say what the compromise is gonna be?"

"Naw."

Just then the speakers erupted with a call of "Mister Chairman? Mister Chairman!" This would be the move they're going to try next.

"The Chair recognizes the delegation from Virginia." Virginia? What the....

"Mister Chairman. The great Commonwealth of Virginia, acting in the tradition of our forefathers who crafted the founding documents of our Republic, proposes a compromise solution to the problem before us. Mr. Chairman, I move the nominations for vice president of the United States be reopened."

"Without objection, so ordered." What? Wait a minute. You can't do that without a vote. Where's the parliamentarian? Jesus, these guys....

"Thank you, Mr. Chairman. The great Commonwealth of Virginia nominates the junior Senator from Virginia, William Trent."

Oh, fuck. The Coliseum erupted with cheers, mostly of relief that someone had showed them a way out of the trap they were in. Shit. The only way I could get this stopped was to make Don Taggart withdraw the nomination. If he refused I would kill him with my own hands. I started to power-trot down the stairs toward the surface of the earth, but they were so steep I couldn't make very good time. Still, I was halfway there when the chair got the chant of "We Want Bill" tamped down and started a roll call vote. So I had time. No way they could complete a roll call vote before I got my hands on Taggart's throat.

Some sonofabitch with a spotlight found me, and tracked me as I ran, with the sweat now running down my face, my shirt soaked through, my hair wild, and I imagine my eyes bugged out. Then somebody put the image up on one of the video boards, and the "We Want Bill" stuff started up again. The crowd was vastly amused, thinking they were seeing a superbly crafted show for their benefit. They did not understand they were about to witness a murder on HD TV.

I was about a hundred feet from the delegation, and the chair was polling the Georgia delegation, when the Georgia chairman screamed "Mr. Chairman, I move that this nomination be approved by acclamation." You can't do that either, but there was that motherfucker again with his "Without objection, so ordered." And the Coliseum went nuts, and now everything was live on prime time news and I was trapped like a bug on a windshield.

So I smiled, and I waved, and I pulled myself together and tried to get my breath back and headed for the main stage at a more stately pace. This was a steroid roar such as I had never experienced – indeed, such as few people ever experience – and I cannot say that I hated it.

When I mounted the stage they tried to usher me to the podium but I saw a knot of Garland's handlers at the back, looking smug, and I pushed my way over to them.

"Where is he?"

They were surprised by the blunt question and unsure how to respond.

"I see him now, or I don't go on." The roar from the impatient crowd was almost deafening: "We Want Bill."

One of the senior guys jerked his head and I followed him into a little hallway off of which several anterooms opened. He opened the door of one of them and there was Senator Garland, looking like he was digesting a canary.

"Hello, Bill," he said expansively. "Congratulations on being the unanimous choice of the convention."

"Yeah, bullshit. There's one thing I gotta know before I go to that podium, and I need the truth, Bob."

"Ask anything."

"Do you really intend to nuke the Iranians?"

He gazed at me a minute. Then at the handler. "Could we have the room?"

When we were alone he asked, "Between you and me? Period?"

"Yes."

"Of course I'm not going to nuke the Iranians."

I looked at him until I believed him. Then I said, "Okay. I accept your goddam nomination."

And that is what I went out and told the convention.

As it turned out, I got way better coverage for my speech than Bob Garland did the next night when he accepted the nomination for President. The reason was, he got torpedoed by the sitting President.

We knew we'd been screwed when the White House announced at 4pm that the President would address the nation from the East Room at 7pm. A couple of hours before Garland was to speak. Way to hijack the news cycle.

I was in my suite in the Jefferson, fortifying with a martini for my long evening of standing at my Leader's side looking enthralled

– how do political wives do it? – when the earnest black face of the President filled the screen.

"My fellow Americans," he said. "Tonight, at my orders, American naval forces in the Persian Gulf have deployed a tactical nuclear warhead...."

Oh, sweet Jesus. The blood drained from my head. I thought I was going to fall over, even though I was sitting down. He nuked the Iranians????"

"...to eliminate the wreckage of the USS *John C. Stennis* from the Strait of Hormuz. As of about an hour ago, the Strait is once again open for the free passage of all ships, and that free passage is being guaranteed by the United States. Our experts assure us that the radiation lingering in the area will be no more difficult to deal with, and will last no longer, than the fuel that would have leaked from the *Stennis* had she remained in place.

"At the same time, using conventional explosives, our forces have removed from the face of the earth all traces of Iran's ability to manufacture nuclear weapons.

"It is our hope that this limited response to a blatant and unilateral act of war will put an end to this matter. We do not wish to inflict any more suffering on the Iranian people. But Iran must know, and I believe does now know, that any attack on the United States, or interference with its strategic interests, will bring swift retribution."

I was slack-jawed with admiration. Who thought of using a nuke on the aircraft carrier? Brilliant! Reverse speculation would bring gas prices tumbling down, hoarding would stop, and Iran had been humbled. Now all Bob Garland had to do was stand up and say how much better he would have handled it.

Fortunately, the Vice President had the same challenge, with hobbles on. If he came up with anything that the administration could or should have done better, the immediate response would be, well, you were in the administration, so why didn't you see to it?

It was going to be a lovely campaign.

14. THE LAST BEST HOPE
2019

The day I heard my receptionist scream, saw my inner-office door crash open and my Secret Service detail charging me like the offensive line of the Washington Redskins, I had been Vice President for a little more than three years. Forty months of crushing boredom succeeded by a moment of transcendent panic.

Of course we had won the election, we outspent the other side by half. Plus, eight years of one party in executive office makes the electorate itchy for a change, any change. Sort of like a couple trying to save their marriage by buying new furniture. And, the former vice president had accidentally told the truth a couple of times, in public, about the inner workings of the machine we all served.

I saw Bob Garland one more time at the convention, and then hardly at all until Inauguration Day. Late on the night of his nomination, a night of frustration because of the way the President had hijacked the news cycle, he had drawn me aside at some reception or other.

"What would you have done," he murmured in my ear, "if I had said I *was* going to nuke Iran?"

"I would have declined the nomination. With regret."

He gave me a long look. He appeared to be experiencing a pang of something like buyer's remorse. He nodded, and moved on.

During the campaign, I went where his staff told me to go, said what they told me he wanted me to say. I was working for him now. I hardly saw him, and when I did we didn't talk. Same after the inauguration. His staff told me I would have an office suite in the Old Executive Office Building, not in the West Wing of the White House as had been recent custom for vice presidents.

My requests to be included in his agency briefings were politely declined. My requests to talk to him, likewise. When I heard from his staff, it was almost always with news of a funeral or a minor political event I needed to attend.

After a year of this I crafted a long memo to the President expressing the notion that the Republic would not be well served should I, God forbid, suddenly become President, knowing as little as I knew about what was going on. I received no answer.

Boredom reigned in our cavernous EOB digs. The really good people on my staff bailed, to find some action somewhere else, and I could not blame them. Then, on that summer day in 2019, the action came to us.

Two of the agents – one of them Ed Jackson, the chief of my detail – came around my desk, one to either side, and grabbed my arms.

"STOP RIGHT THERE!" I had been treated like a cipher for three years, but I was not one, and I had a drill instructor's voice when I needed it. They stopped. "Take your hands off of me." They did. "Now tell me what's going on."

"The President is down, sir," Jackson said. "We need to get you to the situation room on the double."

Oh, shit. "I will walk to the situation room. We will walk, calmly and without fuss. All you need to do is show me where the damn thing is."

"Sir, our protocol, when there is an unknown threat to the executive...."

I switched back to drill sergeant. "Agent Jackson, I just told you what my protocol is. Do you have any questions?"

"No, sir."

"Carry on."

We strode to the elevators, rode down to the lower level and marched into the underground corridor to the White House.

"Agent Jackson," I muttered to him as we walked, "We are in

the White House, not the streets of Baghdad. Could you please have your people take their hands off their weapons and look a little less like the Spartans at Marathon?"

"Yes, sir." He, in turn, muttered into his lapel, and the men relaxed the warrior stance about half a degree.

"It was Thermopylae, sir."

"What?"

"The Spartans. They fought at Thermopylae. Not Marathon. Marathon was the first Persian invasion."

"Oh, for God's sake. You know what I meant."

"Yes, sir." All of a sudden the men on the detail were suppressing grins, and looked a whole lot more user-friendly.

We passed offices where all work had stopped. Some people were standing mute behind their desks. Others had cell phones glued to their ears. Some of the women were weeping at their desks.

"It's apparently a heart attack, sir. Serious. No word on his condition yet."

But word came, soon enough. The President was dead. Long live the President.

"And now, from the Oval Office of the White House in Washington, D.C., the President of the United States, William Trent."

"Good evening. This is my first chance to come before you since I became the accidental president. The sudden and untimely death of my friend and colleague Robert Gordon catapulted me into an office I never sought.

"It's been three weeks now, and you may wonder why it has been so long that I have not had anything to say in public. Well, it's because, in private, I have been getting what every new president gets – briefings from every agency of the government of the United States.

"It is the first time in my political life that I have been told what is going on in the world, and in our government, by people who have no other agenda than to relate the facts (except perhaps to emphasize the importance of their agency in dealing with events). There were no conservatives in the room, no liberals, no party members of any kind. Just weary, dedicated, and capable people describing what they are dealing with, what resources they have, and their prospects for a good outcome.

"The first thing I learned was this: For decades now, you and I – and I include myself during the time I was a sitting United States Senator, and Vice President of the United States – have never been told the truth about what is happening in the world and what it implies for our futures. Your government has been concealing from you, or falsely reassuring you about, the realities of the world.

"Now, please don't jump on the wrong train here. I am not about to reveal anything about alien spacecraft from Area 54, or deals with the United Nations to unleash the black helicopters. What I am talking about is not a conspiracy of that kind. But it is a conspiracy.

"For the last three weeks, the men and women of our government have been telling me, as perhaps the only person in government with a certified need to know, exactly what is going on. I am scared to death by what I have learned. So will you be, because I'm going to tell you everything I found out. You are the citizens of a democratic republic, and you have an absolute right to know.

"Just the high points tonight, with a word or two about what I propose to do about them. Then we will have a discussion, an intense and short one, because the next presidential election is only 18 months away. I am not only an accidental president, I am already a lame duck.

"One more point about my becoming president. When I was in the Senate, I regarded myself as the employee of the people who put me there, and by that I mean the people who raised and spent millions of dollars to help me win election. An idealist will tell you that is wrong, that I should have been working for the common man. A realist knows that the common man has neither money nor time to give a political candidate. And for a very long time now, only realists have been winning elections.

"When I was vice president I regarded myself as the employee of the President. But all that has changed. When I took the oath of the office I now hold, I became your employee. I work for you now.

"Let me summarize for you the terrible news I have been given in the last three weeks.

"The gravest and most imminent threat to the life of this country has nothing to do with enemy states or terrorists. It is the increasing scarcity of petroleum. Peak oil has already occurred, by which I mean that there is not enough oil to go around and there never will be again. That has been reflected in rising prices and spreading shortages everywhere in the world.

"The people in the oil business, and the people in government who deal with the oil business, knew this was coming for many decades. Yet it was never discussed in political campaigns, and no preparations, nor any plans for preparations, were ever made. The oil business and its associated interests, intent on wringing the last dollar out of the last barrel, have spent billions on false advertising, fake science and political influence to protect their profits.

"As a result, we face the sudden loss of our means of food production and delivery, our personal transportation to and from our jobs and homes, and all the thousand other ways we depend on cheap oil for our way of life. We have no plan for dealing with this crisis and no time left. It is the worst failure of government in history.

"And that's just the beginning of what I understand today and only suspected a month ago. The next most dangerous threat to our continued existence is climate change. It is here. The seas are rising, the deserts are spreading, the storms are more frequent and destructive. A massive tide of climate refugees is gathering, not only in Africa, Asia, China, and Russia, but in the southwestern United States, that will destabilize and depopulate large sections of the world. This, too, was foreseen, its inevitability ignored by our leaders. Just seven years ago we watched a campaign for president of the United States during which the only mention of climate change was made by people – not just people, candidates for president – who denied its existence.

"Now it's here. And just as with the end of oil, we face its onslaught with no preparations, and no plan. Another catastrophic failure of government.

"There are yet more. The veins and arteries of our country's economic system – the roads, bridges, water pipes, electric lines – have been neglected to the point of failure by people who got elected by promising not to raise your taxes for any reason. Now the life of luxury and opportunity that our magnificent infrastructure enabled is about to become disabled. Our financial system, released decades ago from regulation by the only power capable of balancing greed against the common good – government – is reeling toward collapse.

"There's more. But enough for tonight. Before we get too depressed, we have to deal with two questions. How did this happen? And what can we do now?

"It happened because you and I, as citizens of what is supposed to be a democratic Republic, surrendered our sovereign power to the wealthy. We inherited the last best hope of earth, the one place on earth conceived and constituted as a place where the governors work for the governed. We gave it away. 'The government isn't the solution, it's the problem,' they said, and we let them ignore peak oil. 'Now is no time to interfere with job creators,' they said, and we let them pretend that climate change wasn't happening. 'It's not the government's money, it's your money,' they said, and we stood by while our country rotted down from neglect.

"We let them distract us with bogus arguments about reproduction and sex and race and enemies and terror and ideology while they looted the world.

"Now here we are. Our survival as a country, as a people, maybe even as a species, is in doubt. So what do we do?

"First, we take back our country. We do it by instituting as quickly as possible true campaign finance reform, which looks like this: henceforward, the only legal donation that can be made to a political candidate shall be from a human being who lives in the political jurisdiction that the candidate seeks to represent. No corporation, committee, or person who lives somewhere else should be able to determine who represents you in government.

"To be fully effective, this legislation will have to be buttressed by amendments to the Constitution – I think of them as the George Orwell Amendments – that establish that corporations are not people, and money is not speech.

"Secondly, we have to organize and direct every ounce of our energy and resources toward replacing oil as the basis of our lives and mitigating the effects of climate change. We might not be able to do these things in time, but there is no alternative to doing the very best we can.

"In order to do this, we must abandon the effort to garrison the world and maintain an American Empire. We learned, or should have learned, from the collapse of the Soviet Union among others that the weight of the world is simply not supportable by one country or union of countries, no matter how rich or powerful. All our troops and sailors and airmen must come home. We need them for the tasks ahead of us. As we need the money that our bloated Defense Department has been spending on weapons and forces that have no counterpart in the world.

"Similarly, we have to stop subsidizing industrial agriculture while it destroys our topsoil, depletes and pollutes our water, and degrades our food supply. We have to stop subsidizing the oil business.

"Here is what I am going to do. I am going to order my administration to draft the legislation I have mentioned tonight, and more. I will make it available for you to read and talk about, but I will not introduce any of it to the Congress. I have not been elected to this office, and what I propose is obviously a wrenching change of course. So I will hold off on Congressional consideration of these measures until after the next presidential election. If I am still here, then it will be full speed ahead. If I am not, then good luck to us all.

"'Fellow citizens, we cannot escape history.' Abraham Lincoln said that, in the depths of the Civil War, one of the few times before now that the future existence of this country was in doubt. He said: 'The fiery trial through which we pass will light us down, in honor or dishonor, to the latest generations. No personal significance, or insignificance, can spare one or another of us. We, even we here, have the power, and bear the responsibility. We shall nobly save, or meanly lose, the last best hope of earth."

"Good night. God save the United States of America."

Of course we lost the election. They outspent us two to one. By election day, I was variously believed by people who watched television to be a communist; suffering from manic-depressive or some other psychotic disorder; a murderer who killed his wife in order to get the sympathy vote for US Senate; a thief who systematically defrauded Favorite Son's company while I worked there; and a sleeper agent for the United Nations World Order Government. Plus, of course, all of the above.

I went on every talk show I could book, every speaking engagement I could find, held every news conference they would cover. I talked until I couldn't talk any more, rested for half a day and started talking again.

All the Democratic candidate said was that if he were elected, America would come roaring back (Yay!) it would be a New Day in America (Yay!) and that in his humble opinion people who didn't like this country should go live somewhere else. (YAAAAAY!!)

They outspent us (God Almighty could not have produced the amount of money industrial America lavished on them), and they appealed to the worst and laziest in the American psyche, and yet they only won the popular vote by two points, 51 to 49 per cent.

I wish it had been a landslide. Then I could just write off the people of this country as not being worth saving. And I would not return to those events, every black and endless night of my remaining life, to twist and sweat and ask the darkness over and over again: what could I have done, when should I have done it, where was the place and time and what the means by which I could have moved that two per cent?

The answer never comes.

PART THREE – TRIBULATION

15. RUNNING FOR THE HILLS

2021

Sunday night, June 13, 2021. Black rain sluicing down from a black sky, whipped by a fitful wind, the tattered remnants of Hurricane Seven, dying hard against the mountains. Heading north into New Market in the Land Rover, I peered anxiously out at the highway and the town through rain-smeared windows.

Nothing much seemed changed, at first. Almost no traffic, but at 10 o'clock on a Sunday night, that's normal. New Market's only traffic light was swinging in the wind, blinking though the sheets of rain with only me there to obey it. Left turn, toward the Interstate, along the little town's Great White Way. All the gas stations and fast-food joints clumped around the Interstate exit ramps, all six of them, closed. One of the little food mart places was boarded up, one of its plate-glass windows shattered. Otherwise, Sunday-night normal. Deserted.

Under the Interstate. Sunday night on the Interstate is always busy, 18-wheelers rolling nose to tail to make their Monday morning Boston/Philly/DC/New York deliveries. And they were there, but not in their usual numbers. Fewer than half of them. And no cars among them, no college students/lake travelers/ weekenders headed back to base. Everybody hunkered down, I guessed, waiting to see.

West toward Timberville across the flat farmland, between two lines of ranch-style houses on quarter-acre lots sitting cheek by jowl along the road. They looked normal. Lights on in some of the rooms, other windows showing the electric blue flicker of the TV screen. Some buttoned up for the night.

I felt an ache when I thought of the innocents and the ignorants who were soundly sleeping in their snug homes, not understanding the events bearing down on them, secure in the knowledge that someone somewhere would keep them from harm. Part of the ache was envy. Part, shame. I was one of the ones who had been supposed to keep them from harm.

Still, they were part of the problem that was about to overtake us all. Collectively, in their innocence and ignorance, they were the ones who had decreed that the highest and best use of land was a building lot. They were the ones who never bothered to face their windows south, to put in insulation, to live somewhere near where they worked, to buy a car with decent gas mileage. And now, in brick boxes about to become ovens in the southern summer heat, with SUVs parked outside that were about to become inert steel sculptures with no fuel, they were soundly sleeping in their snug homes.

I turned on the radio, entered the familiar wasteland of mindless ear-stimulation. The only all-news or public radio stations that might be informative were in DC, too far away for me to pick up. A strong signal from West Virginia Public Radio, but of course they were playing classical music. I never figured that one out. Here and there I could get a "Dum. Da-Dum" beat, or animal screams behind over-amped guitars, but no information about the end of the world. I switched it off.

The last I had seen before I shut off the TV, took a long look around my comfortable little cottage and wondered if I would be back next week, or ever, was remarkably bad, when you considered that we were only 48 hours into the crisis. It was the hoarding that was making everything worse, and the worse it got the more frantic the hoarders became. It was bad enough at the gas stations, but it was really bad at the grocery stores.

We had seen gas lines before, and price spikes, and spot

shortages, and all of them had constituted serious inconveniences. And in a coddled population that felt entitled to whatever it wanted, let alone needed, inconvenience could lead quickly to lawlessness. But this was the first time that there had been a serious question raised about where the next meal was coming from, about whether there would even be a next meal. The result: rapidly escalating, open-throated, pistol-packing panic.

Most grocery stores east of the Mississippi River and north of the area devastated by Hurricane Seven had been picked clean by mid-day Sunday, by jostling, angry, self-centered and often violent crowds. Full scale rioting had been averted in most places only by the promise that the stores would be restocked by Monday morning. If that happened, things might ease for a while. That's why it was so worrisome to see only half the usual truck traffic on Interstate 81.

As for southern Louisiana, it had become a watery hell from which nothing came, and into which no one willingly went. The National Guard, the Coast Guard, the Red Cross, all the many brigades that had always rushed to the aid of the stricken in America, were crippled by lack of money and fuel. Those who had survived the worst now faced even worse, and they faced it alone.

The President still had not come out of his bunker to speak to the country. My lip curled at the thought, and then I thought again: Whoa, that could have been me! If I had been elected, had started everything I intended to start, nothing would have changed the impact of Hurricane Seven. The sneer vanished. Maybe I would stay in the bunker too.

Timberville's traffic light, like New Market's, was stubbornly policing its empty intersection despite the gusty winds, driving rain and the absence of anyone to police. I stopped on the red, marveling at my vestigial obedience, and waited for the green before I turned left and proceeded up the gentle hill that flanked the town.

Looking down to the left, into the parking lot of a shopping center anchored by a supermarket, I saw the first discordant thing. A knot of pickup trucks clumped in the parking lot, and next to it a little swarm of people. One of them was standing on a tailgate, lit up by headlights, apparently haranguing the rest of them, his body jerking, his long hair and arms flailing with the spasms of his passion. His audience couldn't stand still, it vibrated in place, its members taking little strides here and there, the whole group seeming to convulse with agitation.

The road continued to climb the hill. At the far end of the shopping-center parking lot, it provided an overlook. There, on the shoulder across the road from me as I passed, sat a town police car containing a lonely man facing a difficult decision. When the first window broke down there, whether tonight or tomorrow or the next day, what would he do? Touch off his light bar, goose his siren, and go home as fast as he could? If he was smart, he would.

Another right, and I'm on the road to Brocks Gap, the Lost River Valley and in about 45 more minutes, the Farm. A few more miles hemmed in by ranchers, then the houses are fewer, and farther from the road, more of them are the typical Shenandoah Valley two-story, tee-shaped clapboard farm houses. The rain is easing. Looks like I'm going to make it with no worries except for the headlights that have been in my rear view mirror since New Market.

I had driven part of it fast and part of it slow, and the headlights had stayed the same distance back. Way back.

As soon as I was through Brock's Gap (the notch in North Mountain, the first range of the Alleghenies along the western border of Virginia), miles before the Farm, I started looking for a pull off that wasn't an entry to someone's yard. Pretty soon I found one that snaked to the left through a couple of ranks of trees and down to a little flat by the river, big enough to turn around in.

I parked the Land Rover with its ass toward the road, killed the lights and the engine, opened the door and removed the interior light bulbs. Just for the hell of it I reached in back and got the Remington 12-Gauge tactical pump shotgun, but I didn't jack it.

It took a while. He had lost sight of my taillights, and was wary, coming on dead slow, no doubt hyper-alert. When he was almost abreast of the little turnoff, I tapped the brakes on the Land Rover, dove out of the vehicle and scrambled away ten yards or so and took cover behind a bush.

In the misty air, it was as if a pair of red searchlights had switched on to seek out bombers passing overhead. He did not pause, nor did he hit his own brakes, he just kept going at the same pace. The wind had backed off some more, and I have pretty good hearing, so I knew that he had eased to a stop a hundred yards on down the road.

I waited. I knew I wouldn't hear him coming.

"You made me, huh?" The voice, when it came, was unbelievably close.

"Yeah. You needed more traffic."

"I'm a hell of a lot better at this shit when I got a team, and communications, and a helicopter." Ed Jackson came around the Land Rover and leaned against the tailgate, showing me his hands. I came out of the bush, the shotgun over my shoulder. I saw him looking at it.

"I was pretty sure it was you. But not completely sure. What are you doing out here, Ed?"

"Sir, I been looking after you a long time now. It's kind of become a habit."

"I appreciate it, Ed. But that's over. I e-mailed the letter declining protection to Washington this afternoon. Come morning, that's going to put you off the reservation, isn't it?"

"Yeah. I suppose." He just leaned against the Land Rover, letting the drizzle ooze off his head and shoulders and soak into his blazer, regarding me in the wet gloom.

"Plus," I went on, ignoring the sick feeling I had that I knew what was coming next, "You should probably be with your family."

"No family. Ex-wife's in California, no kids, thank God. Folks're dead."

"Well. There's the Service, then."

"Service gave me a job protecting you. I'd like to keep doing that job, sir. You're going to need protecting."

I knew that if I waited long enough, he would say please, and I didn't want to make him do that. "Ed, I have a place to go. With people who have been expecting this for a long time. They're prepared, and it's safe. The other thing is, I don't have the right, and I don't have the ability, to bring anybody else in. Not anybody. No matter how well qualified, or how much I like him."

We stood in the mist a few more minutes while he processed it. The he sort of stood to attention. "Yes, sir. Good luck sir. And good night."

He disappeared then, and after a while his headlights whipped by, headed back east toward New Market. I waited a while after they had gone. Couldn't have driven very well anyway. It was the first time I had cried since Dottie died.

Fifteen minutes later I passed the lane into the Farm. Impossible to see the damn thing coming. Muttering, I made a U-turn, came back, turned in. My lights punching a yellow tunnel through the blackness – at least the rain had stopped – I got out, unlatched the first gate, pulled through, got out, re-latched it, got back in, drove on.

Around the rising turn to the fortified gate. I stopped, thinking this would never do if one was going to commute every day, got out of the Land Rover, leaving the door opened, and went to key in the combination.

An apparition stepped into the light, a giant in woodland camouflage, his face blackened, an AR-15 across his chest, an enormous KA-BAR knife strapped to his thigh and a big grin on his face. "I'll get it, Mr. Trent."

My brain locked, and had not yet registered his presence when a voice from the vicinity of my left elbow said, "It's okay, Dad. We were just running a little exercise on you. You lost."

"Big time!" said a chorus of voices from the woods uphill to the right.

"Jesus Christ, Brian. Don't you know I have a heart condition?"

"No, I didn't know that."

"Well, I didn't have one till just now. I called to let you know I was coming. Couldn't you have said something about meeting me?"

"We wanted you to act natural. We'll see you up at the house, get you settled in." And with that they were gone. I was alone in the dark, looking at an open gate. I decided they had probably done this before.

Lacking any directions on where to put the car, I pulled around back of the barn, as I had done when Brian and I had gone hunting – my God, eight years ago? – grabbed my overnight stuff from the back seat and trudged up the hill to the house. A great weariness, a slowness, was settling over me. This couldn't be real. This couldn't be me, doing this.

From the outside the house was completely dark, it looked abandoned. But when I opened the side door into the great room, it was brightly lit with a profusion of LEDs, and the residents were gathered at the huge table. Some of them, at least, I had no idea how many were here, or who they were, or what the hell I was doing here.

"Come on in and sit down, Dad. Have a drink while the booze lasts. We're just wrapping up our after-action on your ambush."

The table was round, so I didn't know if Brian was sitting at the head of it or not, but he was apparently conducting the meeting.

"So, Daniel," he continued. (Daniel? That sober-faced young man in the cammo, with green and brown streaks on his face, that was *Daniel*?) "The thing to remember on OP duty is that you ring us the second your ears go up, not when you've checked and assured yourself it's a problem. Don't worry about false alarms. If it is a problem, we need every second of prep time. If it's not, we can always use practice. Right?"

"Yes, sir." (Yes, sir? What had they done to Daniel?)

Brian turned to me. "OP is observation post, Dad. You'll be on the roster, everybody takes six hours every three days or so, watching the road and the entrance. You've met George McInerny?" The giant who had materialized in front of me at the gate raised a hand and flashed the amazing grin. "He's our security guy, and he runs that roster, so tomorrow check with him. George, anything more about tonight?"

"Yeah, one thing. I'm hearing a lot of metal-to-metal rattling when you guys are hauling ass down to the gate. Some time tomorrow I'd like to see each one of you in your combat gear, the ones on offense, so we can do a little doctoring for noise control. Other than that, we did great."

"OK. Dad, we'll introduce you to everybody and get you oriented tomorrow. Until you're briefed, a couple things. We are under smoke and light security. We show no smoke in the daytime, or for that matter on a moonlit night, and no light at night. Make sure a blackout curtain – they're rolled up over every window – is in place before you light up anything in any room.

And don't throw any wood on any fire tomorrow morning. George's wife Patsy is our provisioner, she schedules cooking for smoke security and apportions food. If you want to eat well, be nice to Patsy. Sleep well. As well as you can. And we'll talk tomorrow. I'm glad you're here."

He came around the table then, and gave me one of his carbon-steel hugs before leading me toward my bedroom upstairs. On the way I gripped Daniel's hand and shoulder – he was as solid as his Dad – and gave Julie a hug. they were a young man and a young woman, both looking subdued and sad on account of their absent mother, but focused and resolute nevertheless. No hint of teenage angst or boredom.

My room was a monk's cell, room for a narrow bed, a small chest of drawers, and a wooden chair. The window was covered by a blackout curtain. Another roll of something that looked like rope hung above the window. Under the window was a pile of sandbags from floor to sill. Lord, it was a firing position.

Everything came to me now from far away, in slow motion, as if I were dreaming. This was a good thing. If I had been capable of grasping the reality of where I was and why, I would not have slept that night. As it was, I don't even remember Brian shutting the door.

16. MORNING IN AMERICA

Daylight. I could sense it on my eyelids. If I didn't open them, I would not have to admit it. Would not have to start living the next day of the rest of my life. As long as I did not open them, or move a muscle, I could pretend that I was in my bedroom in our old house in Winchester, that Dottie was in the kitchen frying bacon, the newspaper was waiting on the front stoop, the sprinklers were spritzing the lawn, the TV in the kitchen was muttering boring news about boring celebrities.

Okay, fallback position. Maybe when I went out into the day, things would not be so bad, maybe the gas and the food would be where it needed to be and people would calm down and go back to their homes and their jobs and this terrible wound to the country would start to heal. Maybe I could go back to my comfortable retirement cottage on the golf course and wait there quietly for a good and gentle death.

The catch was, if I went out into the day, and things were not as I wished, I would still be out in the day. Oh well. No way around it. I clawed myself to an upright position, got both eyes looking the same direction, shrugged into yesterday's clothes and made my way downstairs.

A bunch of people were seated at the huge oak table in the great room, staring at a laptop screen streaming an all-news channel. Brian was among them. He raised a hand, called out "Morning, Dad," and there was a chorus of "Morning, sir," and I mumbled something and headed for the end of the room designated kitchen, where there was a row of insulated carafes I took to be coffee containers.

Between me and them was a petite lady with long brown hair pulled into a ponytail, wearing rimless glasses and an attitude of focused efficiency. "You're Patsy," I said, "and I have to bribe you to get coffee."

She laughed, shortly, to let me know she got the joke and didn't feel especially lighthearted. "Oh, no, let me get you some, Mr., uh, gosh." She stopped, flustered. "I've never had anybody famous in my kitchen. Am I supposed to call you Mr. President?"

"God, no. Anything but that. I've always answered to William."

"Oh, okay. Here's coffee. Stuff to put in it is over there."

I took it to the table. George McInerney, the grinning warrior I had met at the gate last night, was seated to Brian's left, and kicked out a chair to his left for me. He wasn't grinning this morning.

"Dad, this is Carlos." Indicating a wiry guy with a Viva Zapata mustache seated to his right. "Carlos Juan Ramirez. We call him CJ. He's a firefighter and EMT with Fairfax County, he's our medic. The lady over there on the couch is Juanita." A beautiful Latina with long black hair playing with a toddler, a miniature of herself.

Juanita flashed a grin and held up the toddler. "Hi. This is Carla."

Daniel was seated next to Carlos, looking grim. "Morning, Gramps." Next to him, a sullen 14-year old – I would find out later it was George's son, Jacob – who was communicating with his body language that he didn't want to be there and didn't want to talk to anybody. Julie was over in an armchair in the living-room area. Her eyes were puffy. She'd been crying. She was staring at her cell phone, punching it over and over, obviously not getting the result she wanted. She ignored us.

I looked at Brian. "She trying to get her mother?"

"Yep. Circuits are busy almost all the time now."

I waved a hand at the laptop. "What's the situation?"

"Awful," Brian answered. "They're trying to resupply the grocery stores but there are crowds waiting at every one. It makes no sense. Nobody's going hungry yet, if they let the supplies on the trucks get distributed, everybody would be okay for a while. But they're going nuts. Looting the trucks before anything gets in the store. Just taking it. One driver tried to pull his truck away and two or three guys pulled pieces and blazed away. Killed him."

"Whoa." I really had not thought it would get that bad, that fast.

"Yeah. It's almost as bad at the gas stations. At least people aren't hijacking the gas trucks, if only because they can't fill their cars from them. But the stations are so jammed with lines all around them the trucks are having a hell of a time getting through. And there aren't enough trucks. A lot of those stations will not be opening again. For the foreseeable future."

"Jesus."

"Yeah. We're trying to decide when to call it. I mean, if we're really here for the duration there's a ton of stuff to do, but most of it is kind of irrevocable. You now, like losing our day jobs. We're all AWOL today, kind of hiding behind the cell nets being down. But we have to decide. Probably today."

He exchanged grim looks of agreement with George and Carlos. "Oh by the way, you haven't met Red yet, he's on OP duty. And his wife, Sarah, is expecting. Not at her best in the morning, these days. She'll be down in a bit."

"How are you going to do it? Decide, I mean. Take a vote?"

"No. We've decided that all our decisions, as a community, have to be unanimous."

"Really? How long you think that's gonna work?" I was too surprised, and it was too early, to be diplomatic.

"Well, as I remember somebody telling me about a hundred times when I was a kid, the Iroquois Confederacy did okay with it for about a thousand years. We thought we'd give it a few weeks."

"Oh, yeah." I had long forgotten my private passion for Native American history, way back when there was time for a private passion, when I was constantly being amazed by the wisdom of Black Elk, or the Anasazi, or the Iroquois Constitution. I never suspected that Brian had actually listened to my various rants of discovery, let alone that he was trying to put the ancient wisdom to use.

We turned back to the laptop then as a particularly shrill

reporter yelled at us that the plume of smoke we were seeing on the screen was a WalMart super-sized shopping center going up in flames somewhere in New Jersey. Firefighters were trying to fight their way through the traffic jam and mobs surrounding the store, in order to save it.

"Don't you wish you were there, CJ?" George asked.

"Really."

There was a glum silence. Punctuated by an odd sound, a kind of a warble. From over in the living area. Julie shrieked at her cell phone. "Omigod! It's Mom!" She slapped the phone to her ear. "Mom? You got through! Are you okay? Yeah, sure, we're good. We're still at the farm. I know, but Dad didn't think....yeah, I know, he tried to call you but......sure. Hold on."

She brought the phone to Brian, holding it out from her body like it might sting her. "She's pretty mad," she told him as she handed it over.

"Kathryn." He said it levelly, without inflection. Then he didn't have to say anything more for quite a while. George and CJ thought of things they had to do elsewhere and left the room. Patsy got busy in a far corner of the kitchen area. Daniel stared fixedly at the tabletop in front of him. I figured, hell, I'm family, and I stayed put.

After a while Brian said, with obvious effort to keep his voice flat, "Kathryn. Are you at all aware of what's going on out there? I know it's against your principles to watch the news, but given the fact that the government told you not to come to work today, are you at all curious about why?"

Her response was brief.

"So you do know. And you seriously think the kids should be out in that instead of safe here at the farm? Really?"

And then he didn't have to talk for a while. After which he sighed, and said, "Kathryn. If you are right and the government restores order in a day or two, I will bring the kids back immediately. If not, I will ask them what they want to do. They know why we're here, and why you're there. I am not *making* them do anything, I'm not taking them or keeping them from you. I am, however, going to keep them as safe as I can. I would keep you safe, too, if I could. How are you doing? You know you're welcome here if you can get here.

"Yeah, I know where you stand on that. And there was a time when that was a reasonable disagreement to have. Not now. You have to look around, and see what's happening, and save yourself. Turn on the goddam TV.

"All right. Here she is." And he gave the phone back to Julie. She and Daniel went over to the living area to continue the conversation. Brian gave me a bleak look. "That is one stubborn woman."

George and CJ drifted back in with fresh coffee and sat down again. Brian picked the stubby little two-way radio off his belt and thumbed a switch. "Hey, Red." He said when he got an answer. "Come on in. We can leave the OP for a while, We gotta make some decisions, or at least decide when we're gonna make some decisions."

Red arrived a few minutes later, his hair and freckles and milk-white skin proclaiming him to be a son of Ireland, while his 20 or so extra pounds and generally soft appearance made me wonder how he had become a part of this group. When I found out he was an advertising executive, I wondered even more. (The answer, when I got it, was simple. He was Brian's next-door neighbor.) His wife Sarah came down shortly, looking out at the world with a wan and queasy expression from a riot of spectacularly red hair.

CJ motioned Juanita over (little Carla was asleep on the couch now) and Brian indicated with a twist of his head that Daniel and Julie should join us. And there we were, 11 people at a 12-seat table, staring at the laptop with its fragile link to the ether as if it were a crystal ball that could tell us our future.

At length, Brian closed it. Took a deep breath. "Well. Here we are. We said yesterday we'd see how things looked today. And here we are. The question is do we declare Mayday, activate the Farm and settle in for the duration? I think we have to. The country is completely unprepared for this food crisis, mentally and logistically."

Nobody seems to have realized that using computers and the Internet to fine-tune deliveries to food markets, what they call Just-in-Time inventory management, had a downside. It worked fine for the industry, let them cut back on warehouse space, made sure the stuff didn't stay long on their shelves. But it stretched the supply lines so long, and so thin, that a serious break meant instant shortages, and a prolonged break meant famine.

"When people realize there's no food where they are," Brian continued, "and no way to get it to them, they're going to want to move, and that's when the gas crisis is going to bite them in the ass. When gas means life itself, and there's not enough for me and you, then to hell with you. That's where we're going, and fast. I say we activate, and button up. What do you say? Dad?"

"Me!? I'm a guest here. You all have been working on this for years, I just dropped in."

"Nobody's a guest here. This is going to take maximum effort from every one of us if we're going to get through it. And that effort requires maximum commitment. So you vote like all the rest of us vote, because we need you to."

"I didn't think I'd have to make that kind of decision today. I'm not ready."

"None of us did, and none of us is. But here we are."

But I wasn't where he was. Not yet. "This is the United States of America. I know this is serious, but the government has tremendous resources. Given a little time, I've got to think they could..." I hesitated. Brian didn't.

"Could what? Rebuild the New Orleans ports and refineries at Morgan City? That would take 20 years if we could find the money. Restore order with the National Guard? Where are the personnel, and how do you move them without fuel? FEMA's broke. The national flood insurance program, the one that kept everybody rebuilding over and over again on the same old flood plains and water fronts, is broke. The crop insurance fund is empty. This country HAD tremendous resources. There's a reason the President, your successor, hasn't come out of the situation room to talk about the situation. There is nothing he can say."

"I hear you. Let me abstain for a few minutes. Is everybody else convinced?"

"Well, see..." Sarah Mulaney's voice was tentative, and she wasn't making eye contact, and you could tell she was still nauseated, but she carried on. "I'm like Mr. Trent, a little? I mean this is a crisis in *this part* of the country, isn't it? Not everywhere.

West of the Rockies, is fine. There are lots of refineries in Texas? On the Gulf?" Her Irish heritage sounded loud and clear in the lilt at the end of sentences that made them all sound like questions.

"Sarah, love, that's like thinking it's only our end of the boat that's sinking, so we'll all run to the other end." Red's voice had an echo of Ireland to it, as well, much fainter than Sarah's, and overlaid with the harsher memory of whiskey and cigarettes. "Remember the New Dust Bowl? There's a desert between us and the Rocky Mountains now. Remember Las Vegas abandoned, and Phoenix next? The West can't take on any more refugees. And those refineries? Their product is for export, they're not set up to bring it inland. There are no pipelines for it.

"All along, people been saying, we've got enough oil and water and food and whatever to last for hundreds of years. But it was never about when we would run out. It was about when we would run short. Now we have, and there's never going to be enough for everybody again. I say we burn our bridges."

"Noooo!" The word was torn from Julie's heart. "Dad, we can't!" she said with a pleading look at Brian. "What about Mom?"

He looked stricken. "Sweetie, we can't kidnap her. She won't come. It's her choice."

"But, Dad! She could die out there!"

There was a long silence around the table. There was no adequate response to that.

"Julie, honey," CJ offered at last, "We've all got people out there. We all decided a long time ago to build a lifeboat, baby, and some people are getting into the lifeboats and some people are taking their chances staying on the Titanic. And the only decisions we get to make, are our own. I think it's time we called it. We wait much longer, we're going to have trouble moving the animals, and we can't have that."

Brian looked over at the giant to his left, who turned out to be not much for speeches. "George?"

"Lock and load." End of that conversation.

The faces around the table were serious, engaged, and generally in agreement – with allowances for Julie's distress and Sarah's nausea – with one exception. George and Patsy's son Jacob sat sullenly, slouched in his chair, staring at his hands interlaced in front of him on the table.

"Jacob?" Brian asked, in a neutral tone of voice, "how do you vote?"

Jesus, I thought, 14 years old and he has a vote?

Reluctantly, Jacob brought his eyes into focus and regarded Brian. He delayed his answer right to the edge of insolence. "Whatever."

George's eyes blazed and his mouth opened, but Brian's quickly raised hand stopped him. "Jacob, you haven't spent a whole lot of time with us, and I get that you don't want to be here, but here we are. We're talking about whether we're going to live, or die. I'm afraid 'whatever' isn't going to get it."

"What do you care what I say? You'll do what you want anyway."

"No, actually, we can't. Because the first rule we all agreed on when we started this was that we have to be unanimous in every decision we make. You weren't here for most of the calls we've made along the way, but you're here now."

Right, I thought, and this is where that rule gets thrown out.

Brian went on. "My father doesn't get a pass just because he's new to the group. And you don't get a pass because you're 14, and you don't want to be here. You know why? Some night you're going to be in the Observation Post on duty, because we need everybody to take a shift, and if all you're thinking about is how you don't want to be here, and you aren't a part of this, and somebody made you do it, you know what? You're not going to be paying attention, and maybe you're going to fall asleep, because it's all bullshit anyway, and you're going to get us all killed."

Jacob's eyes widened. He sat up straighter.

"Jacob, we have to be able to trust you with our lives. All our lives. And you have to be able to trust us, that we will do anything to keep you safe. If you can't do that, or if we can't rely on you, then vote no and we'll have to rethink this."

Jacob's eyes stayed wide. "Seriously. You'd let me stop the whole thing."

"It's not a matter of letting you. We are all in, or we're not. So it's not 'whatever.' It's yes or no."

Jacob was a young man whose eyes were seeing a world he had

never thought of. Brian gave him time to absorb it. A long time.

"Hell, yeah," Jacob said at long last. "I'm in."

Everybody looked at everybody else, and it was obvious. Everybody was in.

The room erupted with activity. Obviously the eventuality had been discussed, and prepared for, and everyone appeared to have urgent work to do. Except me. I looked around in some confusion until Brian caught my eye. "Hang in for a minute, Dad. I'll get you briefed."

In seconds the room was empty, except for Brian and me, and Patsy at work in the kitchen area. It was as if you had jumped a covey of quail, and they had whirred off in all directions. Brian was grim, but energized. The world might be coming apart, but there was a light in his eyes that said two things. One was, "We can do this." The other was, "I was right, goddammit."

But that wasn't what he said. "We worked all this out, obviously, and practiced it. CJ and I are going for the animals. Red and George will be planting the garden. Mid-June is a little late to get started, but we should be okay, Red brought a bunch of flats with started plants. Look, Dad, we've all sorted out what we want to specialize in. I'm the energy guy, Red's the gardener, Patsy's the provisioner, and so on. You're the only one of us who has ever cared for farm animals. How'd you like to be our animal husband?"

Wow. Talk about coming full circle. At least there would be no dairy cows. "Sure, but tell me something. What were you going to do if Jacob voted no, or stuck with 'whatever'?"

He gave me a long, veiled look. "Well, that would have been a test, wouldn't it?"

"Nice evasion. But seriously. How far are you going to take this unanimous thing?"

"First of all, it's not me. I have no special authority here. We make our decisions together. But if you want my opinion, I think we take it all the way. Two reasons. One, I don't think 50-per-cent-plus-one is any way to make a life-and-death decision, and all the decisions we make right now are life and death. I think our history shows it's a bloody awful way to make any decisions, dividing everybody into winners and losers.

"Second. Young people. There have been a lot of studies of the attractions gangs and cults have for young people, and of the way young combat veterans who served in places like Iraq and Afghanistan, despite all the violence and horror and loss, long to go back and spend more time in hell. Why? It turns out the attraction is that when they are with the gang, or in the cult, or with a platoon in the field, they matter. The people they are with value them, depend on them, and are always there for them no matter what. It's what families used to do.

"Our whole culture now is a winner/loser, richer/poorer, boss/employee, top-down, chain-of-command, yes-or-no deal. We're so used to it we've come to think it's the only way to do things. But it's not. Most of humanity, most of the time, has done it way different.

"Remember when you used to tell us about the Native American clans, the way they were matrilineal? People were born into their mother's clan, and it was a person's uncles or aunts who spent the most time with them, teaching them the ways of the clan? That the biological father was almost irrelevant to their lives? No way you can wrap your head around that, yet it worked fine for them."

He stopped, thought a minute, then looked around him at the new day waiting. "Whatever." And there was the flash of the Brian grin of old. He stood up. "It's not a day for philosophy, sir, it's a day for action. Let me have Daniel start to get you up to speed so you can prepare for incoming: 50 chickens, 20 goats and five pigs, and you're their new Daddy."

"And when you get a minute," George interjected, "I need to brief you on security, get you up to speed on the radios, armaments, OP duty – Daniel, why don't you take him by the OP on the way to the barn? – and the defensive drill. Okay, sir? Uh, Mr. Trent?" He turned to the others at the table. "Dammit, he needs a handle. We can't be calling him up and saying Gramps, or Daddy, or Mr. President, kindly get your head out of your ass and open fire. We need clarity on the coms."

"What was your Secret Service codename?" Brian knew what it was, he was needling me.

"Never mind."

"Aw, come on. It's history. We can learn from it, they had the same reasons we have for assigning it."

"Ap." I mumbled.

"What? Didn't hear you?" Brian was grinning.

"It was APPLE. People think Winchester, Virginia, they think apples. All the apple orchards are subdivisions now, but that's what they think."

"The Apple has landed." George pronounced it as if he had just bitten into a lemon. "Not what I had in mind."

"Good thing you didn't hail from Iowa," Brian muttered.

"I got it," Daniel chimed in. "What we call him sometimes. One syllable, easy to say."

"No, Daniel." I tried to head him off.

"Pops."

"No, I said, " I said.

"Perfect," said Brian.

"Just the thing," said George.

"Great," said everybody else.

"No," I said. "Do not call me Pops. I won't stand for it. Didn't you say all decisions have to be unanimous? I'm exercising my veto."

"So, what was it that guy said at the convention, the one that made you vice president?" Brian was actually laughing. "Hearing no objection, so ordered." And he hit the table with his hand and everybody stood up to get on with the day, and everybody was laughing.

So that went pretty well.

17. ANIMAL FARM

The agony of the world receded from our consciousness for the rest of that day, and on many of the days that followed. Real life, it turns out, is lived where you are standing, within sight of your eyes and the reach of your hands. Everything else, all the "news" of the wars and riots and famines and disasters that are happening to other people, recedes to irrelevance. When your survival is in question, maintaining your life requires all your attention and energy, every waking minute. Knowing what other people are doing beyond your horizons has little value.

Now that we had made the commitment to stay at the farm, and depend on our own resources, our survival was of course in question. We had enough food stored on site to get us through the winter. Not comfortably, but alive. Our comfort in the coming year, and our survival beyond that, would depend on our gardens and our flocks. Any serious mistakes, or accidents, or setbacks, would jeopardize our lives. As would any breach of our security.

Brian and CJ left immediately after our meeting, pulling a 16-foot stock trailer with an elderly Ford F-150 four-wheel-drive pickup truck, to get the goats. Like the chickens and pigs, the goats had been literally farmed out, each flock to a farmer willing to care for the animals in return for their production. The deal was that on demand, the farmer would hand over the original number of animals that had been put in his care.

Meanwhile Daniel took me out to the observation post. A well-worn and -cleared trail led from the back of the house obliquely up and along the rise of the ridge that hulked between the house and the road. He said it would be a five-minute walk, or a two-minute run, to the OP. We chose to walk.

"How are you doing, Danny Boy?" The happy, chatty, often silly boy and youth that I had known was gone, and in his place a tightly wound and grim young man.

"Ah, I don't know, Gramps," he said, with an exhalation that spoke of the high pressure within. "I mean, we've been talking about this for years, as long as I can remember. Well, Dad and I have been talking, Dad and Mom have been arguing. It doesn't seem real that it's actually happening. And I'm worried about Mom."

"Yeah, I know. Maybe she'll change her mind and come here."

"How, Gramps? You've seen what's going on out there. How could the world be coming apart so fast? I mean, you were the President. Can you explain it?"

"No, I can't. I'm as amazed as you are. But it's like your Dad has been telling us for years, and like I found out when I got into office. It didn't just come apart now. Everything has been coming apart for a long time, but so many people have been making so much money from it that they didn't want anybody messing with it. "

"But, Gramps, people are going crazy and they're not even hungry yet!"

"I know. We used to say that any country was only three missed meals away from a revolution. But what we didn't realize is that if people think they're going to miss a meal, they get just as desperate as if they already have."

We walked in silence for a while, Daniel under a very dark cloud. "It's ugly, Gramps," he said at length. "It makes you wonder what's the point of being the last people alive in a world like this."

I was groping around for an inspiring, or at least comforting, answer to a question I had not yet answered for myself when we arrived at the OP.

The ridge between the house and the main road, like all ridges in the Appalachians and most in the country, was oriented southwest to northeast. They were wrinkles raised in the bedrock eons ago by the titanic force of a collision between continent-sized chunks of the earth's crust. In our area, the slow-motion crash had warped and fractured the floor of an ancient sea, and in places had snapped apart the ridges after they had been raised, as for instance where the stream flowed through the gap in our ridge. On each exposed end of the fractured ridge you could see distinct, slightly upended layers, where sediments on the sea floor had been pressed into rock. Each layer, different from the next in color and texture, showed how normal life had persisted for hundreds of thousands of years, then had abruptly changed to an entirely new normal.

The layers had eroded, during the millennia they had been exposed, at slightly different rates, and where we were now, the effect was a sort of giant's staircase up the nose of the ridge to the crest a hundred feet above the stream. Except that in a few cases the layers, each between four and eight feet thick, did not regress but jutted out over the one below. Under one of these overhangs, tucked under its rock roof, was the OP.

Standing front and center in the OP, facing across the gap and along the continuation of the ridge to the northeast, I could see, down and slightly to my left, the first ramshackle gate on our lane. Looking 80 degrees or so to my right, I could see the second, fortified gate. If I turned left, 90 degrees, I could see several spots along the main road. Looking more closely, I could tell that the guys had carefully cleared underbrush from sight lines through the woods in a way that left few signs and created no obvious corridors.

Daniel stood behind me and pointed all this out. "You'll bring a two-way radio with you, like the one I have on my belt, when you're on duty. They're in a charging rack by the back door. Later on, when the batteries don't work any more, we have this." He opened a metal ammunition box tucked into a crevice in the back of the OP and showed me the counterpart of the ancient, voice-powered army field telephone that was hanging in the great room. "When things, um, ramp up, we'll be manning the OP 24/7. George will brief you on that. Issue you some weapons, and all."

He stared glumly down the hill for a time while we both took it all in. "It's so weird talking to you like this," he continued. "Gramps, do you really think we're going to have to fight? A lot?"

"I don't know, Danny Boy. Your Dad has always said that this place was all about passive defense. If nobody knows we're here, nobody's going to attack us. So I guess the rule is, hope for the best and prepare for the worst."

We headed back then, to inspect the barn and get ready to receive our new guests. We were rounding the house when the radio on Daniel's belt crackled. "George? Brian, over."

"George here. Go, Brian."

"We have a tail."

"On my way. Where are you?"

"Five miles out. South."

"See you at the intercept. Out."

Brian explained it to me. "We figured that when we went to get the animals, one of the farmers, or somebody connected with them, would probably want to find out where we are and what we're doing. They probably wouldn't be a threat right now, but later on, if they know where we are and what we've got? Anyway, Dad and George have a plan."

The next thing we heard was a stampede. But it was only George, thundering in from the garden area, slamming through the house, snatching up an AR-15 from the weapons rack, slapping a boonie hat on his head (he was always dressed in cammo and boots, apparently) and running full tilt to the equipment shed next to the barn. Sixty seconds later we heard a muted hum, sort of like a distant electrical transformer, and George shot up the drive next to the barn, and out the lane, on a nearly silent black motorcycle. It was a 1200cc BMW sport-touring bike, and I could not hear it. "Is that an electric bike?" I asked Daniel.

"Naw. Super-muffled. George said he rigged it for night reconnaissance. He can kill all the lights on it, even the brake lights. Has a set of night-vision glasses on board."

What George did, we all heard later, was blaze out onto the main road before Brian, who was coming from the south, reached the turnoff to the farm. George sped north nearly ten miles, to a spot they had selected where a sizable farm lane turned sharply right into some woods. George pulled in, got the motorcycle out of sight, and waited in the trees near the main road. Brian sped past the turnoff to our farm without slowing down, and when he neared the one where George was waiting he sped up, to increase the distance between him and the elderly farm pickup that was on his tail.

At the lane Brian braked hard, turned into the lane and, a few yards in, stopped and backed up, jackknifing the trailer so it completely blocked the lane. By the time the driver of the farm truck had realized Brian had turned off, he barely had time to stomp on his brakes and make the turn, so he did not realize the situation he was in until he had slammed to a stop to avoid smashing into the trailer. By the time he recognized the trap, his door had been flung open, a large hand had gripped him by the throat, the muzzle of an AR-15 was jammed under his chin, and a giant was growling into his left ear:

"You were told to make no effort to find us. We did not say on pain of death, but that's what we meant. Are you ready to die today?"

"No, sir. Please, sir. I was just curious, sir. I didn't mean no harm. Please don't hurt me."

The kid, in his 20s, cultivated the shit-kicker look favored by West Virginia dudes. Steel-toed construction boots, jeans, plaid shirt, tractor cap. Would have been wearing a brown Carhart work jacket if it was cold. Tough guy, normally, but now tears were leaking out of his terrified eyes.

"You got one chance to see the sun set, boy." George really went over the top with the Hulk Hogan growl. "You turn that truck around, you go home, and you never again even drive in this *direction*. This is *my* road, I see you on it again I'm going to turn you into a red mist. Do you read me?" The last was screamed.

"Yes, sir!"

"Then get out of here!" George flung him back in the seat and leaped back from the truck, slamming the door and at the same time releasing a couple of three-round bursts into the air. The kid tried to get his truck backed up and turned around but he couldn't get his feet and hands to work right. He stalled the engine going back (it was a stick shift), then burned rubber jerking forward, then slammed to a halt, then stalled it again. Eventually, he careened onto the road and disappeared back the way he had come.

Brian straightened out the trailer and George retrieved the motorcycle. He pulled up next to the driver's side of Brian's truck. "I'll make sure he goes home and stays there. I'll give you the all clear when we're past the lane, and you can head back."

So the goats didn't get to the barn until mid-afternoon. The lower level of the bank barn, the part that was bermed with earth on three sides, was divided into four large pens, each about 18 feet square. We put the goats in two of them, and I spent the next couple of hours hanging out with them, getting them used to me and their new quarters. At first they just bawled and ran around, some of them getting up enough speed to run part of a circuit three feet up the block back wall of the barn. They were, in fact, climbing the walls.

I took a five-gallon pail into each of the pens in turn, upended it and sat there for a while, letting the goats calm down and get curious about me. Eventually, girls first, they started to come over, nuzzle at my back, lip my shirt and tug at my gloves sticking out of my back pocket. After a while a few extended their muzzles toward my face and we exchanged breaths, and soon I had several new best friends. Hey, it had worked pretty well with Members of Congress, back in the day.

By the time Brian and CJ arrived with the chickens, this time without any incidents, and had them apportioned to the chicken tractors out in the corral, it was late afternoon. We thought about not getting the pigs until the next day but because of our encounter with the young man from the goat farm, and the worsening news from the outside, figured we'd better not wait for people to start talking and thinking about us. By the time we got the squealing pigs unloaded and secured it was dark, past 9 pm, and we were tired people. We straggled in for supper, and to find out what was going on in the world.

The satellite Internet service was still functional, so it did not take us long to find out that things had gone from bad to worse to unimaginable in a very short time. There was almost no news from the devastated areas of south Louisiana, the news organizations simply could not get in there. Occasionally someone who was still alive there got a phone call through, or somehow managed a computer connection, to plead for help. But there was no help.

It wasn't just that FEMA, and the Red Cross, and the National Guard, and all the organizations that would have helped, were broke, and had no fuel. It was much more than that. The rapidly deteriorating food situation threatened the life of every man woman and child in the eastern United States. No one who lived there had ever imagined, let alone experienced, such a threat. Moreover, it was a threat that money could not solve. It didn't matter how fat your bank account was if there was no food to buy. And if your family's life was under threat, and money didn't matter, then why go to work?

There were fires in many of the cities now, most of them in supermarkets or shopping centers, ignited by incredulous mobs when they learned there was no food there to buy, or to take. But firefighters were staying home, and more than half the blazes roared on unattended. Cops were staying home, and the mobs – some consisting of desperate people looking for food to take home, others bands of criminals celebrating the descent into anarchy – roamed freely. But the really surprising thing about the mobs, to us, was that they were relatively small and relatively few. Apparently, the great mass of people were waiting in their homes for someone, somewhere, to fix this, to make it go away.

TV news reporters and anchors and camera people were staying home, so the news was getting more fragmentary, less reliable, consisting more and more of scraps of rumor reported by a scared-looking anchor sitting in a bare room. (The chirpy blonde women who used to show a bit of leg and giggle with the anchormen were gone. I guess they were staying home too.) The engineers who toiled in the big regional centers maintaining the precious and precarious balance of the electric grid were staying home, and with the enormous hole torn in the southern grid, and the random destabilizing impacts of the fires in the urban centers, the edifice was creaking and tilting and the lights were flickering everywhere east of the Rocky Mountains. Blackouts and brownouts – variations in voltage that were anathema to electronics – were afflicting the big data farms that provided the backbone of the

Internet, forcing them to go to their ranks of diesel generators, that had maybe three days worth of fuel, assuming they were properly tended to, but the tenders were staying home. Nobody was going hungry yet, nobody was out of fuel yet, and the country was coming apart.

We watched a half an hour of it while we ate, and then closed the laptop. No one had anything to say for a long while.

"Well," Brian ventured with a sigh, eventually. "I guess we'd better go to maximum security right now. Noise security, light security, smoke security. The OP manned 24/7, someone sleeping with a radio in here, George has the rosters. George, have you got with Dad....I mean with Pops" – a wan smile – "to get him briefed on the radios, weapons, so forth?"

"Naw, not yet. First thing in the AM?" George lifted an inquiring eyebrow to me.

"Sure."

"Remember, everybody. There's a radio receiver audible in the great room here, but if you go anyplace else, you go armed and with a radio. Don't forget. Anything else before we go to bed?"

"Well," said Patsy, from her usual place, standing with her back to the kitchen counter, leaning on it and facing the table. "Couple of things. We'll have coffee for a few weeks yet, but if you're a heavy drinker like George is, you want to start cutting back. To a cup a day or less. Otherwise the headaches, when we run out, um...." She choked off a sob, and tears began streaming down her cheeks. She stood there, rigid, her arms tightly folded across her chest, trying to get herself back. George went to her side, put a massive arm around her shoulders. "I'm sorry," she said, to him and to us. "It's just – I can't believe this is really happening." And then she just wailed.

So we all went to her, and we all hugged her, and she wasn't the only one crying, or the only one comforted by the hugs. And then we all (except Jacob, who had the next watch in the OP) went to bed. But not for long.

18. Order of Battle

"AWK. AWK. AWK. AWK." I came out of a deep sleep having no idea where I was, aware only of the raucous klaxon sound blaring through the house. Then I heard running feet, and remembered where I was, and leaped into jeans, boots and shirt before dashing downstairs. People were snatching weapons out of the rack and heading out the door. I hesitated. I didn't know what to do, or why.

George's meaty hand clapped onto my shoulder. "Pops, you haven't trained with us, so you need to stay here. The OP has called a Mayday, we have intruders at the lane. When we're out, grab a 30-30 – you've hunted with them, right? – and keep watch from the sandbags on the porch."

And with that they were all gone, and the only sound in the house was little Carla's fitful crying from back in the west bedroom wing. I grabbed a lever-action Winchester 94 from the rack, levered a round into the chamber, thumbed the hammer to safety and went out onto the porch. It was a clear night with no moon, and after a minute or so I could see pretty well.

Jacob had sounded the alarm about midnight, when he saw a pickup truck easing along the main road at about 10 miles per hour, two figures standing in the bed casting flashlight beams along the shoulders of the road. When they saw the turnoff to the lane, the truck stopped, they dismounted, and two more got out of the cab. By the dome light Jacob saw they were all men, and all armed, rifles slung over their shoulders. They were loose, relaxed, a couple of them stopped to light cigarettes, they wisecracked a little, snorted a few laughs. So by the time they started inspecting the surface of the turnoff with their flashlights, George and his team were hitting the trail to the OP, coming hard.

Jacob murmured the target count and the targets' positions into his radio. The four were walking toward the first gate – not purposefully, more like strolling, casting their lights here and there. After the last trip in, as always, Brian had raked the approach to the gate and scattered pine straw and leaves. Beyond the first gate, however, the tracks of the heavily-laden stock trailer would be visible here and there. And there was always the chance a spot had been missed closer to the road.

They expressed no special interest, even when they caught sight of the ramshackle gate. By the time they approached it, George had eased into his position, between them and the OP, and had rested the cross hairs of his night-vision scope on the forehead of the leader. As he had suspected, it was the kid they had ambushed and run off earlier that day, now nursing a grudge in addition to his curiosity about what they had and where they were.

The intruders bunched up at the gate. The lead kid fingered the rusty chain that held it shut. A few of them flicked their flashlight beams over the trail on the other side. Clearly, they were as far from their truck and into dark woods as they cared to be, even without knowing that they were now in the sights of six rifles. Number one shitkicker hesitated, looking up the lane. Along the ridge, safeties eased off. At length, he spoke. "Naw. Ain't been nothing on this lane for years." And they ambled back toward their truck, laughing and snorting.

When they were well gone, every member of the team made a point of finding Jacob (whose OP shift was now over) and giving him a vigorous high five. No one remembered ever having seen such an incandescent grin on his face as he responded to the accolades.

I thought we would be up for hours recapping the events, but once the story was told to those of us who had stayed at the house, and the weapons had been cleared and re-racked, weariness overtook everyone at once and we all went back to bed.

Everyone told it again from his or her point of view over breakfast. Sarah Mulaney, who had not attended the festivities because of her pregnancy, listened with increasing agitation.

Finally, she burst out: "Really? You were going to kill those boys?"

That was a conversation stopper. "Sarah," Red said with a placating tone, "We all talked about this. Many times."

"I know we did. But now it's real. You were on the point of killing four young men because they were looking at our gate."

"No, Sarah," George put in. "First, we did not kill anybody. Because the way we've set this up we shouldn't have to, and we set it up that way because we don't want to. However. If those four young men found out where we are, and what we have, and went back to their homes, we would have become famous in these parts. And before things got very much worse we would have had people with guns pouring over these ridges from every direction. We would have been outnumbered, and very likely killed."

"But you don't know that would have happened. You just threatened him the first time?"

"Right. And you see what happened. The very same day he's back, with backup, and guns."

"But, I mean, to kill them. You could all go to prison."

George snorted. "There's no law left, Sarah. Even if there was, it would have been a missing persons case, and what law officer left standing out there is going to have time for that?"

"I just think it would have been a terrible thing. For them and for us. I don't think the Commandment, 'thou shalt not kill,' is there to keep people from being killed. I think it's there to keep people from killing, and losing their souls."

Now Brian jumped in. "No question killing is hard on you. George knows that, and I know that, from our military experience. But dying is hard, too, and we're here because we have all decided we are not going to die in this collapse. Millions are going to die, Sarah, we've known that for a long time. We have decided that we are not. That is going to mean being hard, and doing some hard things.

"There's a difference between killing somebody out of greed or jealousy, and killing somebody who's trying to kill you. George Patton told his soldiers that their job was not to die for their country, it was to make the other sonofabitch die for his country. Those nice young men did not bring their guns with them last night because they were going to go squirrel hunting later."

Red was impatient. "We've been through all this many times, back when it wasn't important. Why do we have to go through it all again?"

"Because," Brian intercepted Sarah's hot reply before she could make it, "that is the way we've chosen. Everybody agrees, or we don't do it. No matter how long it takes. Sarah, are you satisfied?"

There was a long pause.

"I understand what you're saying," she said after a while. "I guess I accept the necessity, and I won't make an issue of it. But satisfied? Not by a long shot."

"Me neither," said Brian. "But remember, this will not go on forever. There's going to be a starving time, for the next few months, and during that time there are going to be bands of desperate people trying to find and take other peoples' food. But of all the unsustainable ways to live, that is the least sustainable. Their victims will die first, but the predators will be a close second because they will very quickly run out of victims with full pantries. So you see, after these folks have removed themselves from the gene pool, we won't have to be automatically hostile toward everyone we see. Right now, we do."

Sarah nodded, unhappy but on board, and we turned to the laptop to see what was going on Out There, before we went back to work in real life.

"I found something last night," Brian said, "Before the kerfuffle. I was looking for a better source of information, and I tried some of the European websites. Figured they'd have power, their people would still be going to work. And....Bingo."

With a flourish he turned the laptop so we could all see it.

"This is the BBC. The crisis triggered by the destructive Hurricane Seven in the southern United States continues to spread around the world. The destruction of New Orleans and the widespread devastation in the state of Louisiana have found the United States government virtually incapable of responding due to fuel shortages, multiple international crises and a lack of funds. Meanwhile the interruption in the movement of fuel and food – both into and out of the United States – caused by the relocation of the mouth of the Mississippi River has precipitated a spreading humanitarian crisis.

"Virtually all major American cities east of the Mississippi River are experiencing food riots, the severity and violence of which has surprised international observers. The expectation of deprivation, in advance of actual deprivation, along with hoarding, have led to riots, often including gun play. Widespread absenteeism, again caused by the fear of deprivation and an unwillingness to leave threatened families, is hampering the ability of public agencies, utilities and businesses to operate.

"Now there are troubling manifestations in international markets and relations. Speculators, again in the absence of actual shortfalls but in the expectation of them, have sent the prices of commodities skyrocketing, with devastating effect on the ability of people in the poorer nations to feed themselves.

"Moreover, there is news today of multiple oil-delivery contracts that are coming due at major export terminals being 'unilaterally renegotiated.' In other words, oil exporters are either unable to deliver promised crude, or are willing to withstand severe breach-of-contract penalties in order to wait for markedly higher prices ahead. In either case, refineries around the world expecting tankers to arrive with crude oil a few weeks from now will not be seeing them.

"Sovereign nations are reacting quickly to the indications that signed contracts will no longer assure delivery of oil. The British government reports that Russian Navy warships are now escorting drilling rigs toward the Arctic Ocean, and according to Israeli intelligence, a Chinese Navy Battle Group including an aircraft carrier is approaching the Persian Gulf, where a few of the Emirates and Iraq, unlike Saudi Arabia and Iran, are still able to export oil. "

Brian stopped the feed. "My," he said. "How time flies."

We went to work.

19. THE INTERLOPER

First, my security briefing from George. He assigned me a tactical shotgun from the rack and went through its operation with me, then a Ruger 9mm sidearm. It was too late for target practice, the shots would attract attention from miles around. But the weapons, he made clear, were to be with me at all times as long as the danger of intruders persisted. In the event of another Mayday, I was to do what I had done the night before, take up a defensive position on the porch and concentrate on not shooting any of our guys coming back in.

Then for me it was out to the animals, whose panic level was down from the day before. Still, they were spooky and easily upset. At the moment my objective was to get them used to me, get them accustomed to where they were to find their feed and water. After a few days of calm, and the re-emergence of routine, their squeals and bleats and squawks would change from complaints to comments, the upheaval would be forgot and life would become normal again.

Which is what started to happen for all of us during the ensuing days. We would get up, watch the world burn for a few minutes, have breakfast, discuss our agenda for the day and go to work until dark. Whereupon we would have supper, watch the world burn for a few minutes, talk for a while and go to bed.

What was happening out there was unthinkable. So we pretty much stopped thinking about it. The people we knew out there were unreachable – the cell net was down all the time now – so we stopped trying to reach them. The need to grow and accumulate food before the killing frosts of October, to secure our flocks against predators and disease and mishap, these priorities swelled until they occupied almost all of our lives, almost all of the time. We settled. We found a rhythm, found ways to avoid thinking some things and concentrate on other things, and we carried on.

A few days in we lost the electric grid, and thanks to the years of preparations it was no big deal. We had more than two kilowatts available from solar panels, another two from hydro, a substantial battery bank and enough solar collectors to heat our water. "The thing is, though," Brian told us the night the lights went out (and then, after he threw a couple of switches, came right back on again), "Now we have to be as mindful about using energy as we are about our food. We always have to be thinking, do we have enough left, is this a good time to use some. It's going to be hard to do, because for a hundred years everybody has been schooled NOT to think about it, to regard it as so cheap and plentiful we can waste it. Think about phantom loads, for example. If you have a radio or DVD player that has a remote control, you have to unplug it or put it on a switchable outlet. Any battery chargers you use have to come out of the wall unless they're actually being used. Things like that. We have enough electricity to use, but not enough to waste."

Morning coffee was replaced with a glass of cold spring water. Breakfast consisted of our own eggs, with ham or bacon from the sides hanging in the basement, soon to be replenished from our barn. Lunch and supper were ham and beans, sometimes catfish from the stocked pond on the stream below the barn. Sarah Mulaney took on the duties of milkmaid. I helped her train to the milking stand the few goats that were fresh, and soon there was milk, cheese and yogurt available, not yet enough for everybody, but soon there would be. As soon as our flocks were stable and growing as they should, the menu would include goat chili and roasted chicken. The after-dinner drink was another cold glass of spring water, although CJ was working on his first batch of fermented potatoes from which he was going to distill some dual-purpose elixir: it would be fuel for the pickup truck, or vodka for medicinal and celebratory occasions, whichever need was greater.

The appearance of the women did not change much, but that of the men did. Shaving had become an unsupportable luxury without a point, and was abandoned. As our beards grew, so did our hair, and we just tied it back out of our way, forming a queue with a bit of twine.

The days began to slide into one another so easily that it was an effort to recall their names. The agony of the outside world receded even further. I imagine the enormity of it was its own anesthetic, that the mind numbs itself when necessary for its survival. It was as if we were adrift in a lifeboat, from which we could hear no sirens, could see no smoke, and our memories of the great ship that had gone down with its crystal chandeliers and all-you-can-eat buffets were replaced by thoughts of catching the next fish or weeding the next bed of vegetables.

I was musing along these lines on a blazing hot afternoon, probably in late June but it could have become July. I was in the pasture across the creek from the barn. I had moved the chicken tractors, checked their water and was helping some of the goats explore territory that was still unfamiliar to them. An elder billy was strutting around, striking poses and checking on the status of all his female friends. One of the young females that had bonded strongly with me kept coming over to me and rearing on her hind legs to place her forelegs on my chest and exchange sniffs. I was leaning dreamily on a walking stick I had picked up at the edge of the woods.

"What kind of cows are those?"

"SONOFABITCH! Where did you come from?"

"Over there." He gestured over his shoulder toward the mountain that rose behind the stream. He was a lean young man, at least he struck the eye as a young man but on closer inspection could have been 30 or 50. He wore bib overalls, faded by many washings, over a plaid short-sleeved shirt buttoned firmly to the top. His round face was leather brown, his pale blue eyes slightly bulbous, his hair a roughly trimmed thatch. "My Momma used to tell Daddy he would go straight to hell if he used words like that."

"Yeah, well, I'll look forward to meeting him. How long have you been watching me?"

"I've been watching y'all since you came here." He was leaning against a tree not ten feet from me, and I had had no clue he was there. I realized that my shotgun was leaning against a tree about 20 feet in the other direction.

"Really. Have you talked to any of the others?"

"Naw. They always seemed real busy. In a hurry. You're the first one slowed down enough to say hey."

"Huh. What's your name?"

"Billy."

"Well, we have something in common. My name's William."

He looked as though I had said something strange. "Said Billy."

"Yeah, it's the same as William."

"No it ain't either. It's Billy." His face darkened, and he stood erect, away from the tree. "You mocking me?"

"No. no, not at all. I must have heard wrong. Where do you live?"

He relaxed a little. "Over there, I said," gesturing over his shoulder again.

"Up on the mountain?"

"Naw, across it. In the holler on the other side."

"You walked all that way? Today, in this heat?"

"Sure. I generally check on what y'all are doin' every day."

Jesus. This was not going to be welcome news. I wondered if I should be using the radio to raise an alarm, but I didn't feel alarmed. Yet.

"Really. Who do you live with?"

"My momma. She's real sick. She don't leave the house no more, hardly gets out of bed. My Daddy, he died three, four years ago. We buried him out back. I asked you about them cows."

"Oh. Yeah. Well, they're not cows, they're goats."

He looked at them thoughtfully. "They eat leaves and vines and stuff, even stickers. Like deer do."

"Exactly. They're browsers, like deer, not grazers like cows are."

"Why don't you have cows? Can't you afford 'em?"

"Well, we prefer the goats. Because of what they eat, and because they breed faster. A nanny can have two sets of kids, usually twins, every year."

"Huh. I didn't know that. I think I saw a picture of one a them once, in a Bible story book."

"Yeah, they've always had a lot of goats in the Holy Land. Say, do you have a lot of neighbors?"

"Naw, nobody else lives in that holler. Couple city fellers have what they call hunting cabins, but whenever they come they just get drunk and walk around in circles. I seen 'em walk by bucks as close as I am to you and never know it."

"Get to town often?"

"Couple times a year. If you wanna know whether I told anybody about what y'all are doin here whyn't you ask me? I ain't. I seen y'all sneakin around, putting blankets over your windows, raking the road, I figured out you wanted to be left alone. Besides, only other person I talk to anyway is Momma. And Rex, there."

"Where?" Somebody else? Now I was feeling alarm. I found the radio on my belt with my left hand, eased my right toward the holster of my Ruger. But I didn't see anybody else.

"There." Billy pointed low. I looked down. Into a pair of pale blue eyes over a black muzzle surrounded by a halo of frost-colored hair.

"Oh," I said weakly, "Your dog."

"Yep. He's a Malamute. They use em as sled dogs up north. He's not too bright, but he's a good listener."

When my heart rate was back down below the stratosphere, I asked him again about going to town. "You said only a couple of times a year. What do you do about groceries?"

"Don't know about groceries. We eat what we raise. Always have. Nuts and roots and mushrooms and stuff from the woods. Deer and squirrel and possum. Mama's garden. Well, my garden, now."

"Really. You've always lived that way." I pondered this for a minute. "Did you go to school?"

"Naw. Momma said I was too smart, knew too much about the woods and the deer and all, they'd be jealous and want to put me in a hospital and find out how I knew all that stuff. So I stayed home. I gotta go."

And with that he was gone, and the dog was gone, and I was alone and wondering if I had fallen asleep and dreamed him.

As I had suspected, the news about Billy, when I shared it at the supper table, did not go down that well with my fellow farmers.

"God damn," was George's comment, "You let the sonofabitch go?"

"I did. He's no threat to us. In my opinion."

"Your opinion?" George was livid, having a hard time restraining himself from just pounding me into the floor. "You staked all our lives on your opinion? Sweet Jesus, Pops, he knows all about us!"

"And he has, for years." I didn't get excited. When you've been screamed at by the Chairman of the Joint Chiefs of Staff, a four-star with special ops on his resume, you can handle ordinary anger. "Doesn't seem to have told anybody, yet."

"Didn't much matter, before. Now it's life or death. Our life. Our death. Pops, we got to take him out."

"No," I said, "We don't."

"I'm with George on this, Dad," said Brian. "We can't afford to take a chance. You see him again, you need to take him down."

"No," I said, "I won't."

"And if you don't see him again, we'll have to mount up a patrol and go find him."

"You going to shoot his Momma, too? Just to be sure? Better shoot the dog, for all we know he might talk. We gotta be sure." I took a deep breath. "Can we just give a thought, here, to what we are turning into?"

CJ came in to it now, leaning forward over his plate, jabbing his fork. "It's the same issue, Pops, that we had with the four young men. If we get soft about our security, we're gonna be dead."

"It is not the same issue. The young men were trying to find out about us. If they had, they would have spread the word to everybody they know. Billy has known all about us – everything – for years. And nobody, not those four young men, apparently not anybody but Momma, knows what Billy knows."

"In your opinion." Brian was giving me a hard, level look. "It's like George said. You're betting all our lives on your opinion."

"Yes," I said, "I am." I gave him a level look back.

"Pops," Red Mulaney sighed, "I gotta say, I'm with them on this. Things are so desperate out there, you don't know what people are gonna do. We can't afford the exposure."

"Things aren't desperate in Billy's hollow, Red. Things haven't

144

changed there, at all, except his Daddy died and his Momma is sick. He has no idea what's going on in the world. Never has had. So how's it going to change his behavior? If he was in the habit of talking to people, how come Social Services or some such agency hasn't grabbed him up and put him in an institution, years ago? You think keeping secrets is a new idea to him?"

There was a long silence around the table. Really long. George and Brian were glowering, the others looking uncomfortable.

"We are not unanimous, Brian." I said it quietly.

"Okay," he said at long last. "Okay. But we discuss any and all contact with him, right? No secrets."

"Right."

And with that we stepped away from it, and called it a day.

20. THE DYING TIME

In the second week of June, the dying began in earnest.

Jim and Ruth Porter, retired, lived on the 6th floor of a ten-story apartment building in Queens, New York. They had no food, no water, infrequent power, no car and no hope. They still had an Internet connection, on which they indulged, to the last, their recently acquired passion for posting the details of their lives and thoughts on Twitter. In the second week of June they sent what they intended to be their final tweet:

"All done now. Going up to the roof, where we will hold hands and step off to a better place. Goodbye."

But 15 minutes later, there was one more, from Ruth's smartphone (as hope had faded and batteries had expired, cell phone traffic had decreased, allowing occasional calls to get through on the dwindling number of functioning towers). Their actual, final tweet read:

"Wouldn't you know it. There's a line."

We got the story from Al-Jazeera, which along with the BBC was one of the few active websites left that was doing any actual reporting on what was happening in America. Most domestic websites had gone dark, or static, and most of the foreign sites' content was fact-free tabloid-style ranting about how Americans did, or did not, deserve what was happening to them.

The Porters had a lot of company in their decision to leave the premises. The vast majority of people, it appeared, when the last hope of salvation evaporated and the hunger became unbearable, quietly ended their lives in their own homes. They used pills, ropes, guns, plastic bags or razor blades, according to their predispositions, comforting each other as best they could, helping each other through it, able adults dispatching the young and the elderly and the sick as mercifully and quickly as possible before ministering to themselves. Some made use of their gas ovens, and the resulting explosions set more fires raging unchecked that took the lives of scores of people before they were quite ready to give them up.

Some got in their cars and made a last-ditch run for someplace, anyplace where there might be food and water and peace. But mostly what they found was traffic jams, endless gridlocked superhighways stretching to the horizon from New York and Philadelphia and Boston and Washington and Atlanta and everywhere else. When they ran out of gas, and realized that the traffic jams were permanent, most of the trapped people committed suicide in their cars.

Such was the fate of people who were in families, or at least still with someone. The strangers – the criminals, the disaffected, the drug-crazed, the permanently angry outliers of a society in which they had never seen a place for themselves – were quite a different matter. They were at first exhilarated by the disappearance of order. Like the looters in New Orleans after Katrina, they expended a lot of energy stealing stuff – TV sets, for example – for which they soon discovered they had no use. When they got hungry they took someone's food and exulted in their power to do so. Having no ties to a home, they did what they had always wanted to do; they banded together and roamed the streets, smashing their way into homes and businesses, taking what they wanted from victims whom they beat or killed at their whim. They were at last, in their view, living large, with no retribution at hand. Or so they thought.

They could not go far because they did not have cars. So they stole cars, but the cars didn't have any gas, or just enough to get them into a traffic jam. So they contented themselves with looting their own turf, and protecting it from invaders from other turf. Increasingly, the victims they could find and the homes they could loot had no food. Retribution, it seemed was at hand after all.

All this we learned, or divined, from what was now the only direct source of news about the cities and suburbs of the Northeast – aerial footage taken on the infrequent, high-speed and high-altitude helicopter flights for which fuel and pilots could be found. Some of them were military. There were functioning military enclaves at several of the major airports and military bases, but except for the occasional information- gathering foray, they dared not come out of their fortresses. The flights had to be high and fast because the only two things that seemed to be in endless supply among the desperate population were guns and ammunition. Just as the well-heeled were learning that their money could not buy them what they most needed now, the well-armed were finding that guns could not get it either. So they shot at the helicopters.

As profound as the horror was, we had little time for it. Those who were not with us were presumed to be dead. Daniel and Julie grieved for their mother, of course, but were moving through it to the life beyond her. All of us grieved for someone, aunts or uncles or cousins or friends, and all of us felt the horror when we looked out at the world, briefly in the morning and again briefly at night. But what stayed foremost in our minds was that every day brought us closer to the killing frosts of the fall and the dead days of winter; that every meal we took depleted our precious stores, every use of energy – every bath, hot beverage, lighted book and computer screen – had implications for our limited supplies, implications that had to be thought through, and reconciled.

Red and CJ, with everyone's help as needed, had set out the started plants, the tomatoes and cabbage and cauliflower that Red had brought with him, had got the seed potatoes in the ground and has planted the *milpas* – the three-sisters combination of corn, beans and squash that had sustained Native Americans for millennia – along with plots of wheat, barley and oats. Now it was a matter of waiting and watching for rain, for insect infestations, for funguses, for hailstorms, for all the thousand things that could threaten our gardens.

My chickens were thriving in their tractors, visibly enjoying the freedom of the range (they had been cooped by the farmer who had kept them for us, the idea of letting chickens do what they wanted to do was foreign to him) and producing a wealth of eggs.

A couple of the goats had had twins and had joined the milking herd, so the flow of milk, cheese and yogurt was steadily increasing. We were free-ranging the pigs as well, and they were ecstatic about the variety in their diet and, yes, the cleanliness.

In the third week of June I was wrestling with a chicken tractor – they were relatively light, A-frame structures but they could hang up on a rock or even a clump of grass. I moved them every day with a long pull rope attached at the front to both skids to form a loop. When the going was tough I would get inside the loop, position the rope across my shoulders and heave backwards. Which is what I was doing on this particular morning, using my back instead of my head to horse the thing over whatever it was caught on. Just as I put maximum torque to it, the coop sprang loose and dumped me on my ass.

"Wouldn't have to work so hard if you just moved the rock," said Billy, stepping out from behind the A-frame with a rock in his hand.

"Dammit, Billy, you have got to stop sneaking up on me. You're gonna get shot."

"Naw. You put that gun down in the morning and you don't even think about it again till you go home."

"I got another one, on me."

"Yeah? Where?"

I pawed a couple of places and then found it. Billy smiled. I noticed that he did not carry a weapon of any kind. I decided not to threaten him any more, and clambered to my feet. "Where's Rex?"

"He's around. You folks are gonna have a problem with your garden."

That got my full attention. We could not afford to have a problem with our garden. "What do you mean?"

"You're just about 50 feet from the tree line with some of those beds."

"I know. They get plenty of sun."

"Sure. But there's two black walnuts right there at the edge of the trees."

"So what?"

"Walnut roots put out poison. Your tomatoes are going to get about halfway up and then quit. You can't grow anything within 150 feet of a black walnut."

"Jesus. What should we do?"

"Griddle 'em."

"Do what?"

"Griddle 'em. Cut the bark all the way around. Kill 'em."

"Oh, girdle."

"Yeah. What I said. You need to do it right away. Might already be too late for this year."

"Really." I did not delay sharing this piece of information with everyone as soon as we gathered for the evening meal. At first, their annoyance at Billy's presence kept them from hearing what I was saying.

"It sounds like that little fucker is watching us around the clock," George fumed. "How come none of us ever see him?"

"Because he doesn't want you to see him, George." I knew he would be even more irritated that someone was besting him in the woods. "But can we focus, here. please? Red, you're the garden guy, do you know anything about this?"

"Never heard of it. Let me check some reference books." He came back from his room a few minutes later. "I see some references to the toxicity of black walnut roots. But I don't have anything as strong as what he said."

"So what do you think we should do?" I asked. "Ignore him?"

Red thought about it a minute. "He lives here. He gardens. He would know. We're not going to miss two trees, but we sure as hell would miss our garden."

"What I was thinking."

There was a sudden, alarm-like sound. A buzzing sort of ring. Everybody flinched, George leaped to his feet. I checked my two-way, but it wasn't the OP. Our cell phones had been turned off for weeks. We all looked wildly around the room.

Brian got it first, and stared at the source, gaping. On the kitchen counter, back in a corner, never used, long forgotten. The land-line telephone. Ringing.

21. BRIAN'S RUN

I think Brian knew, before he got across the room, before he snatched up the old-fashioned receiver and said, "Hello?"

He heard the echo of his voice ricocheting away into a hollow, galactic hissing, across impossible distances. Far away, in the buzz, in the star-noise, he heard what sounded like a kitten mewing. And then he heard his name. "Brian?"

It was just a breath, really, almost not there at all. Then the kitten started up again.

"Kathryn! Jesus! Where are you?"

There was a long wait for a response. Across the room, we could see Brian's knuckles turn white as he gripped the phone. Julie shrieked. Daniel stood up, knocking his chair over. Eventually, Kathryn's voice came again, thin as a cobweb.

"I just...just wanted to say...I'm sorry. Sorry I didn't believe. To say...goodbye."

"Kathryn! Where are you?"

"Doesn't matter." Every phrase required an effort that left her gasping, required her to gather herself to get the next one out. "Dying now."

"Tell me where you are." He was almost screaming.

"Um... the house."

"Are you hurt?"

"Doesn't matter. People came. Took everything. Me too. No time now. Tell Julie and Daniel..."

"Tell them yourself. I am coming to get you."

"Noooooo. You can't...."

"Listen to me. You are not going to die there. You are going to be safe, and with your children again. Do you hear me?"

Just the kitten, mewing again.

"Julie!" Brian held the phone out to her. "Talk to her. Tell her I'm coming. Tell her to hang on. To go into the basement if she can. To hang on!"

He gave her the phone and headed for the door. But he ran into a solid wall consisting of me, George, CJ and Red.

"You cannot do this, Brian." I used my most fatherly voice, put into it every ounce of authority I had. He was the one who had seen this collapse coming, had made it possible for us to get away clean, and I was damned if I was going to lose him to it now.

"Let's take it on the porch."

We backed through the door. As soon as it closed behind him, Brian turned on me. "I can't do it? You want to go in there and tell your granddaughter to hang up on her mother? Let her die?"

"No. I also don't want to go back in there and tell her to get ready to lose her father, too. Because that's what you're talking about."

"Dude," CJ put in, "what about our vote? When do we get to vote?"

"This isn't a group decision. It's personal."

"Personal? You're endangering the whole family!"

"Number one, I intend to come back. Two, if I don't, you all can carry on."

George was anguished. "Man, you can't try this without backup! I gotta go too! I'm trained for this shit. I could ride shotgun."

"Then we *would* be risking the whole group, and the group would have to vote. Vote yes to take a terrible risk, vote no to sentence Kathryn to death. You really want to do that? No, I didn't think so. Besides, George, there's no place to ride shotgun. I'm taking the motorcycle. That is, if it's okay with you." At that, Brian gave him a weak grin.

George suddenly went dead quiet. "Brian," I tried, "you cannot seriously be considering going out there alone. Not just out there, but into the worst of it. It's suicide." I kept looking over at George,

154

a little distracted by his silence and the odd look he was giving Brian.

"Not suicide, Dad. I have a plan."

"That weekend you borrowed the bike," George said. "Last fall. And a couple weekends later you stowed that tube steel rig with the weird wheels in the shop. You sonofabitch. I know what you're going to do!" He was actually smiling.

"What! What are you going to do?" I just hated being the last one to figure things out.

"I haven't got time to explain it, Dad, if I'm going to get there before dawn. And I have to. I'll hunker down at the house and head back tomorrow after dark. But I have to go NOW."

George, still grinning, stepped back out of Brian's way. "You go Dude," he said, "I think you might just make it."

Brian ran for the shop. I turned on George. "Tell me, dammit! What's he going to do?"

By the time George had explained it to me, the sounds of frantic activity from the shop had ceased, and the motorcycle thrummed up the driveway into the yard. It showed no lights. Brian was all in black, from his boots to his windbreaker to the balaclava pulled over his head. He wore no helmet, but a strap head-mount held what looked like a small pair of binoculars at his forehead. His crossbow was slung over his back and a tactical pump shotgun was in the cycle's scabbard. A couple of small, tubular-steel trusses, one about four feet long, the other shorter, were lashed diagonally from under his right ankle to over the right rear saddlebag.

He gave us a wave, and then my only son rode into hell.

Which is where I stayed until, eventually, we were able to piece together the story.

It was around 11pm, just over an hour after full dark. In six hours it would be light again. The night was clear and warm, with no moon. Most people think the night is always black, because most people look out at the night only from lighted places, or from behind flashlights. Submerge yourself in virtually any night, and after a few minutes you will see well enough to do almost anything.

And so Brian ran the main road north toward Baker at pretty high speed, with no lights, able to see the empty highway ahead by starlight. If a car had come the other way with its lights on, he would have had to pull over, or turn on his own lights, to avoid being blinded, but there were no cars. Many of the houses he could see from the road were dark, but a few showed lamplight at the windows. Bad idea. Obviously the people who lived there had resources for this kind of situation, probably including stores of food, and they were advertising the fact to all who passed. These were probably good people, hard-working and self-reliant, unable to grasp what was happening to their world, incapable of imagining where it might lead. They would be wiped out very soon.

In 30 minutes or so, pretty much the normal travel time, he hit Route 55 at Baker, took it east toward the Virginia line and Strasburg, a town of 6,000 on Interstate 81. Still no cars moving, the houses he could see looking closed up and empty. Dark mountains folded away in every direction, hunched under the starlight. He wished fervently that he could stay in their quiet embrace, but he did not slow. His cycle humming, he shot through the glowing night, with no obstructions in his path.

Just east of Baker he took the interchange onto the benighted superhighway called Corridor H. It was a four-lane, median-strip chunk of highway that arrowed from somewhere in West Virginia to somewhere else in West Virginia, connecting nothing much to nothing at all. (It had been part of someone's vision to join the Interstate systems in the two states, but Virginia's effort had dead-ended at the border 40 miles north of the dead end of West Virginia's effort.) It carried little traffic in good times, so Brian figured there would be nothing at all on it now, and he was right. Unfortunately, after about seven miles, the superhighway morphed back into a two-lane trail passing through the village of Wardensville.

Now Brian got a little hinky. There were no lights showing in the village at all, the grid was well down now, especially after a couple of fierce thunderstorms in early July. As Route 55, as the old highway was designated, entered the town it bore left 45 degrees to become Main Street. An old, abandoned white clapboard house stood at the junction, with a triangular side yard onto which Brian eased his lightless motorcycle, easing just far enough past the edge of the house to give him a view along Main Street. It was, of course, in shadow, and unlike the open road could not be seen clearly in starlight.

Brian raised his hand to the binoculars mounted on his headgear and flipped them down in front of his eyes. They were night-vision goggles, and they showed him at once that his caution had been justified. About halfway down Main, where two large, two-story, wood-sided mercantile buildings faced each other, the one on the left a general store (its front plate-glass windows broken out, obviously looted) and the one on the right long empty, two pickup trucks were parked diagonally across their respective lanes, nose to nose, barring the passage of any vehicle. He could see movement in one of the cabs, a pinpoint of bright light. Smoking! The guy still had cigarettes! As he watched, another form detached itself from the trucks and walked to the gutter to relieve himself.

Brian thought about the level of desperation, the number of other options played out, that would keep men on a blockade of an abandoned street in a remote town in the middle of the night, hoping for luck. And he wondered: how in the hell could that guy still have cigarettes? He walked the bike back behind the house and considered his options. He could make a run at them and pass them on the sidewalk, be gone before they heard him. Maybe. From the store on the left a porch roof extended over the sidewalk, with posts at the edge of the sidewalk to support it, reducing the width of the passageway. The building on the right had a raised porch that butted partway into the sidewalk, reducing it on that side as well. Not good odds.

He reached back into the left saddlebag and got out a hand-held GPS unit. Neither the unit nor the positioning satellite needed the grid, nor any maintenance or human supervision (other than charging the unit), and thus were still working fine. He called up a map of the town and saw what he needed to see. He shut the unit down, replaced it, and eased the cycle across Main Street to take the right fork in the road he had been on, a cross street that led one block to an alley that traversed the town parallel to, but a full block away from, Main. He turned off the night-vision goggles and flipped them out of his way – if while looking through them he were struck by a sudden light, as from a spotlight or headlights, he would be blinded for too long to get off his motorcycle without falling or to get out of whatever situation he was in. But he could see well enough without them. He slowly ran the alley to the other end of town, turned left back to Main and then right again to resume his eastward journey without the highwaymen of Main Street ever suspecting his presence.

As he raced eastward in the glowing night he soon began to climb the flank of North Mountain. The 1200-cc engine took it without strain. He sailed down the other side, the road empty, the countryside dark, past the edge of the hamlet of Lebanon Church, then across the flats of the Shenandoah Valley with the Blue Ridge undulating along the far horizon ahead of him, Massanutten Mountain rearing up, closer, to his right front. At about half-past midnight, more or less on his mental schedule, he came in sight of Interstate 81, cleaving the Valley north to south. When he came to the overpass that carried Route 55 over the Interstate, he eased the bike to a stop so he could survey the highway below.

There was a burned-out 18-wheeler rig a half mile to the north in a southbound lane. Must have been carrying food, Brian speculated, got jammed up and looted. He could see four cars, dark and still, abandoned along the highway, one of them squarely in the left lane. Must have run out of gas, he figured, and the drivers left them where they quit. Or were still in them.

Brian eased the bike forward, looking for the first right turn. It wasn't much of a street, just a lane leading into dark woods, but he took it. He had found it in his earlier studies of the GPS maps, when he had been thinking about the possibility of having to make this very run. A half mile in he came to an industrial building with a large parking lot, which he passed. Another half mile to a T, left across a set of railroad tracks and almost immediately a second set. He pulled onto the second crossing and stopped. It was time to deploy his secret weapon.

He backed the bike around, then walked it forward, until both its tires were on the right hand track. He kicked the stand down, dismounted, and unshipped the masts from where they had been lashed to the cycle. The larger one was a long, thin tripod with a small, rubber-tired wheel mounted at the point. He took it to the left side of the motorcycle and laid it across the tracks. He stood quiet for a few minutes, turning slowly to sweep the area for any signs of activity. He was exposed to view from a couple of houses, in this otherwise industrial area, but they were dark and silent. If there were any occupants, they did not want to be noticed.

He flipped open the right rear saddlebag, took out a small headlamp on an elastic band and fitted it to his forehead, under the night vision goggles. Its light was red, so that he could see what he was doing without sacrificing his night vision. He switched it on, grabbed a small, battery-operated driver and a sack of parts, and removed the left fairing that covered the motorcycle's battery and engine compartment. He located three bolts, the points of a triangle with the apex at the top, that appeared to be integral to the bike's chassis, but had in fact been installed by a welder at his direction on that long-ago summer weekend when he had borrowed the bike. Using the driver he spun the nuts off, fitted a cup to each bolt and replaced the nuts, tightening them securely on their lock washers. Now he inserted the ends of the three members of the mast into the cups, securing each one with a steel pin through aligned holes in the cup and the frame, and securing the pin with an attached spring clip.

The other, smaller mast was a bipod, whose legs he attached the same way to cup-like receivers that he clamped to the handlebars. After adjusting the angle, he was ready to travel again. The tire on the left mast would run along the left-hand rail, stabilizing the motorcycle, while the two small tires on the front mast, mounted in a V shape, would guide on the right-hand rail and hold the motorcycle's front wheel steady. All he had to do now was operate the throttle and keep his center of gravity slightly to the left.

He was on a railroad that led directly to the town of Clifton, where his home was, where Kathryn was. It did not go through the centers of most of the towns it passed, but off to the side, through the industrial areas, and was not subject to traffic jams. To most people, railroads were invisible, not thought of, and not only was it extremely unlikely that any of the desperate people between Brian and his goal would be on the railroad, the chances that any of them would even know it was there if asked were vanishingly small.

He started the engine and applied power gently. He had experimented with this, and knew he could cruise at 40-50 miles per hour but could not make any sudden starts or stops. Any faster than that and the outrigger tended to become airborne at the slightest change in the relative elevation of the tracks. But it was virtually a straight-line course, with no significant mountain grades, and he reckoned he would be in Clifton in about an hour and a half, three hours before daylight.

He sailed the curving tracks to eastward – he had mounted them at the junction where one line headed north to Winchester, the other east to Manassas. At first there was forest to his left, a scattering of houses to his right. Massanutten Mountain, the 50-miles-long spine of the Shenandoah Valley, rising halfway between the Alleghenies he had just left and the Blue Ridge to the east, loomed to his right front, stretching away southward. On a starlit night like this, a century and a half ago, the weary, haggard men of Jubal Early's Confederate Army of the Valley had traveled all night, as he was doing now, toward a desperate fight at Cedar Creek, a last chance to save something they believed in, to stave off the end of their world. They had scrabbled along game trails over precipitous ridges and through bramble thickets, sweating and gasping, no time to imagine the fight they were facing; he was sitting on leather with nothing to do but listen to a powerful engine whisk him through the night. Nothing to do but ride, and think about what was coming.

Brian had been an MP in Iraq, trained and equipped for sudden violence, but not for a long march into battle. In Iraq the problems, whether from his own people or the other side, came out of nowhere, swinging fists or spitting metal or an exploding street, and after a few minutes you were either in a body bag, on a medevac flight to Germany or wondering what you were going to have for dinner. Not like this, all this time to worry about what he was going to find, what he was going to have to do, whether he was prepared.

The rails ran parallel to Main Street in Strasburg, a block and a half to the west, yet passed few residences, and they were all dark. At the end of the main business district, where the main street as Route 55 continued east toward Front Royal, Route 11 angled off to the left to pursue its northward course along the floor of the Valley. One of the oldest highways in America, it had been etched in mid-Valley by buffalo, had been trod by Shawnee and Catawba and Iroquois, then traversed by the wagons of Scotch-Irish and German settlers, by British troops and colonial militia, by Stonewall Jackson's Confederates and Phil Sheridan's Federals, followed by the gleaming cars of tourists and the hulking 18-wheelers of commerce. It was and always had been the aorta of the Valley's circulation of goods and services and people.

Brian slowed to a cautionary stop where the railroad track crossed Route 11. No lights anywhere. Nothing moving on the street. Not surprising, really. There was no more gasoline available, therefore any travel had to hold out the prospect of a reward worth the expenditure of one's final gallons. And where would that be at 2 am in a dark and unmoving world? There was a 7-11 convenience store to the left, and he eased forward a bit so he could see its parking lot – empty except for the shards from its shattered plate-glass doors and windows, and discarded packaging from its former contents.

He resumed his journey, rolling swiftly through another industrial district, surprisingly large for so small a town, then out along the curving Shenandoah River around the nose of Massanutten, through the flat river bottom where Jubal Early's exhausted men had lain shivering in the predawn chill, waiting to rise up and charge Phil Sheridan's guns. No chill to trouble Brian now, just the simmering aftertaste of the day's searing heat, both a memory and a forecast.

Through another vast expanse of warehouses, this one attached to Front Royal, one collection of them the so-called Inland Port, whose christening had signified that where America had once depended upon ships and railroads to move its commerce, it had now turned to 18-wheelers. Only the big trucks could put the stuff in the stores, just in time to replace the old stuff that was sold out.

Brian sailed across the wide South Fork of the Shenandoah, just upstream, or south, from where it joined the smaller North Fork to form the main river, on a 500-foot, three-span trestle. It was a thrill to look down through the bones of the structure and see the black water glimmering below, and a thrill to think that if a fast train was coming – yes, sure, it was impossible, but *if* – then he would be afoot a long way from home, because there would be no way to get the motorcycle out of the way, he would be lucky to get himself out of the way. The tracks skirted the north end of the Front Royal settlements. He could see the glow of fires in the town center off to the right, but nothing impeded him as he rolled on through a gap in the Blue Ridge and out into the Piedmont country.

The tracks ran roughly parallel to Interstate 66, the main east-west connection between the Washington DC area and Virginia's hunt country, Blue Ridge and Shenandoah Valley. Now each time the highway came within view, he could see a few more useless cars, just a scattering at first, with some nose-down in the ditch or median strip, others stopped dead in their lane. After a while he was seeing clumps of them, 10 or 12 at a time. He raced past the villages of Linden, Markham, Delaplane, Marshall and The Plains without seeing a sign of life. He was approaching the fringe of the densely populated, sprawling DC suburbs around Haymarket and Manassas when he saw the first sign of trouble. Not the fires burning over the horizon where Manassas was. The shape, ahead, squarely on the railroad tracks.

He killed the throttle, gently applied brakes, and when he had slowed to a crawl flipped down the night vision goggles. He was looking at a caboose. It was the back end of a train, of indeterminate length, stopped in the track ahead.

Brian sighed. He had known there was a chance that a train had been abandoned outside of a yard, on the main line, but had hoped not. He had worked out how to deal with it; unship the stabilizers, strap them on as he had before, and pass the train on the right-of-way. Dicey, but doable. The large gravel the railroad used for fill shifted around under a motorcycle's tire, and it was level only out to the end of the tie, after which it sloped sharply downward, but if he took his time he could do this.

Provided. He grabbed the GPS unit out of the saddlebag and switched it on. Found his location. Zoomed in.

"Shit." His luck was worse than he thought. Two hundred yards ahead of him, the tracks crossed a small stream. On a trestle. Probably only 50 feet long or so, but no matter, there was no way to get a cycle across that bridge if the train was on it. The track ahead of him was straight, so he could not see, even with night vision, how long the train was. But he had to assume the train was on the trestle, because if he proceeded, and found the train on it, his chances of getting the bike turned around were slim. He had to find another way.

It was 2am. Three hours until daylight, at least another hour of travel time. His margin of safety was still there, but shrinking. He consulted the GPS unit again. Where was the last road crossing he had passed? There, where there was some kind of fill – timbers, or pavement – between the rails and level with them, it would be easy to dismount the bike from the tracks. Elsewhere, it was a six-inch drop from the top of the rail to the ties, a drop that could easily damage the outriggers, would interfere with their removal, and play havoc with any attempt to get the cycle turned around. Better to find a road crossing, push the bike backward to it, and get off that way.

Except there was no such crossing, not for miles behind him, and he did not have time to push the cycle for miles. However, 150 yards or so back, a large industrial yard of some kind, a level, open expanse on the GPS, extended almost all the way from the tracks to a state road that ran parallel; to them. There was a line of trees along the edge of the tracks, so he had not noted the yard when he passed it, nor could he have seen that it fronted on a state road. A mile to the east, the state road intersected Route 15, which crossed the railroad tracks a few hundred yards south. Maybe he could make that work. As long as the train was not long enough to block Route 15.

Since there was no alternative, he started pushing. It was easier than he thought it was going to be. And faster. He had hardly had time to get drenched with sweat and start gasping for breath when he saw the open field off to his right, through the line of trees. The railroad fill dropped off to a shallow ditch along the edge of the field. He picked a spot where there was an adequate space between trees, and stopped.

He caught his breath, and got the flow of sweat down to a torrent. He reached back over his shoulder and grabbed the crossbow resting against his back, brought it forward over his head, and unslung it, laying it carefully aside on the ground, checking as he did so that the safety was secure. Then he unclamped the front guide mast, laid it aside, and as gently as possible, with the side stabilizer elevated as high as he could hold it, eased the cycle off the left side of the rail. Then he detached the stabilizer boom, laying the cycle down against the rail on its right side as he did so. When the boom was clear he righted the cycle, put it on its kickstand, and lashed the stabilizers in their position.

He horsed the front wheel over the right rail, whereupon, as he knew it would, the cycle hung up on the engine. With one hand on the left handlebar and one on the rear cargo mount, he hauled with every ounce of his strength and dragged it two inches. Gasping, he did it again, got the rear tire to the edge of the rail. Rested a minute, then heaved with everything he had. The rear tire came up, the front tire went down, twisted to the right, and then the bike came down. On him.

He did not lose consciousness, but he saw a lot of stars, and decided to rest a minute. The fireworks in his head didn't last long, all his extremities wiggled on command, he figured his only problem was that he was laying on loose gravel under about 500 pounds of motorcycle, and was experiencing sharp pain from a couple of pressure points. He could work this out. In a minute.

He looked up at the stars. They looked weak and smeared through the smoke in the air, but were beautiful still. He felt a slight breeze against his sweaty skin, and thought what a great thing it would be to take a nap. Then he remembered the mewing sounds on the phone, thought of Kathryn lying beaten in their home, and he surged upward, prying the motorcycle off him, scrambling out from under it, heaving it upright, running it down the incline into the little ditch with enough momentum to get him through it and up on the flat ground without falling over again.

He swung aboard and was about to hit the starter when he muttered, "Crap," dropped the kickstand, got off, and went back for the crossbow.

Then it was relatively straightforward. He ran the mile, made the turn, and saw to his relief that the locomotive of the abandoned train was a hundred feet back from the Route 15 crossing. He reconfigured the bike again, and was soon on his way toward the glowing sky over Manassas, into the belly of the beast.

He had lost 45 minutes. It was nearing 3 am. The sky would start getting lighter in a little over an hour and a half. He had 20 miles to go. He would make it, if nothing else went wrong.

He could see the Interstate to his left, at times less than 100 yards away, and as the railroad left Haymarket it passed under Lee Highway, a major commuter route headed south. Both roads were littered with ranks of abandoned cars, jammed hood to trunk in all lanes. Most of the cars' doors were gaping open, the trunk lids up, debris scattered around them; some of them had been carrying supplies for their owners' imagined new start in the West, and they had been looted. And now he could see the bodies. In the ditches, in the median strips, next to the cars, alone and in groups, some dead by their own hands, some no doubt at the hands of looters. Then came the smell, the sweet, fetid stench of human death that, once learned, can never be forgotten or mistaken for anything else. Brian had learned it in Iraq, and he knew it now.

He spotted movement among the cars at one point and stopped to check it out. The night vision goggles showed him a human form, lurching from car to car, staggering, falling down, crawling into one car after another, apparently oblivious to the stench – a human nose accustoms itself to anything, given enough time. A gleaner, Brian realized, searching for something that could keep him alive another day. An overlooked can of beans, perhaps. Maybe a body that was not completely ripe. Unable to stop and sleep, knowing he would not wake up. And very soon now, he would be unable to continue, and sleep would come.

The smell did not leave Brian as the railroad track wound through the dense settlements around Manassas, where it was less pungent, but was sharpened by the acrid stench of smoke and old ashes. Nausea flipped in Brian's gut like a landed fish. Horror seared his mind like napalm, burning everything, obscuring everything with its fierce light.

And then, remarkably, the track entered a deep, long wood, with a stream to the left, and now Brian smelled pine on the air and the horror receded, he was able to think once again. He thought of all the zombie movies that had been so popular for years, people flocking to watch the disfigured undead stumble through streets just like the gleaner he had just seen. Did they all know at some level what was coming, what was inevitable? Did they embrace the movies not to experience horror, but to vent it?

Brian shook himself, cleared his head of shock and pointless musing. He had arrived at Clifton.

22. HEALING

Then pavement of Clifton's Main Street where it intersected the tracks was level with the top of the rails, so all Brian had to do was steer to the right and his out-rigged motorcycle obediently made the turn onto the road. He stopped, looked carefully around, dismounted and was removing the left stabilizer when he heard the sound of running feet, coming toward him.

Many feet. He grabbed the crossbow and brought it over his head, while turning to face the noise and moving closer to the shotgun scabbard, all the while trying to identify the sound. There was a long-abandoned gas station to his right, its old-fashioned Texaco sign sticking out of a sea of weeds. Nothing there.

Across the street, a vacant lot, and a dark mass speeding toward him. Thirty yards and closing. He flipped down the goggles.

A pack of feral, emaciated dogs, slavering, yipping, panting, headed straight toward him. A Rottweiler, two or three pit bulls, a couple of German Shepherds, and a half dozen large mongrels. No small dogs. In a nanosecond he got it; they had been pets, regularly fed and cared for, who had been on their own for weeks, with no food except what they could find on their own. There was no doubt that much of that found food had been human, and that he now represented to them not a potential master or pack leader, but a meal.

Before he had completed the thought he had slipped the safety off the crossbow and loosed a bolt at the lead dog, a Rottweiler. Taking the bolt full in the chest, the dog yelped and fell, rolling, to the ground. Before his body had come to a stop the entire pack was on it, ripping and snarling, gorging on its former leader.

Brian figured he had about 60 seconds. If they came at him again he would have to use the shotgun, and risk drawing a lot of attention. As quickly as he could, desperate to hurry but just as desperate not to lose any of the essential parts, he finished detaching the two masts and then, not having the time to lash them in place, simply held them balanced across his lap and pushed off down Main Street, getting distance and he hoped forgetfulness between him and the dog pack.

The village of Clifton, still a remarkably rural place for all its proximity to the population centers of suburban Washington DC, was, like the villages he had passed in the Valley, dark and silent. If there were desperate people in the homes, hungering and watching fearfully, he did not know. Or if there were desperate gangs sheltering somewhere, their sentinels marking his passage carefully, he did not know. But he knew what he had to do, and the closer he got to his objective the more urgency he felt.

About 500 yards on, Brian took the familiar leafy turn onto Clifton Heights Road, idling past two large Victorian McMansions on his right, and two on his left, to the third and last on the right, at the cul-de-sac. His former home.

He surveyed the area as well as he could for signs of activity or surveillance, saw none. He took the driveway along the left side of the house to the side-facing three-car garage at the back of the lot. He left the cycle running on its kickstand and ran, awkwardly lugging the two masts, to the garage's side entry. The door was still there, and still locked. He leaned the masts against the side of the garage and fished his house keys out of his pocket. Inside, he ran to the lanyard that released the hold of the electric opener on the main door, and hauled the door up.

He backed the cycle in, killed the engine, closed the main door and re-engaged the electric motor so the door could not be raised from outside. He felt a fearful anxiety now, about what he would find in the house, but he nevertheless took the time not only to bring the masts in and secure the side door, but to lash the masts to the motorcycle so that it would be ready for a fast departure. He leaned the crossbow against the bike, grabbed the shotgun from its scabbard and the bulky medical kit from its saddlebag, flipped down the night vision goggles and headed inside.

He went through the interior door that connected the garage and the kitchen. The house smelled, but more of sewage than of death. He saw that the front door was both ajar and askew, splintered and broken off two of its three hinges. The living and dining areas of the great room were undisturbed. The kitchen had been trashed; the cabinet doors were open, many of them broken, scraps of packaging and containers of things that could not be eaten, spices and flour and the like, littered the counter tops and the floor. But the signs were of looting, not of violent conflict. They must have come in the night, Brian figured, caught her upstairs, looted afterward.

He ran to the second floor, resisting the urge to call her name, not knowing who or what might be in the house. The bedroom was where it had happened. It was a shambles, blood was everywhere, but smears of it, not puddles. He had seen enough crime scenes in Iraq to know that the human body contains an unbelievable amount of blood, and that what he was looking at was not evidence of mortal wounds.

The door to the bathroom off their – her – bedroom was shattered. She had locked herself in there and they had gone in and got her. Brian shook his head; modern doors, made of a frame of two-by-twos and a couple of pressed fiber panels, offered about as much security as a sheet draped over the opening.

So this was where it had happened. Where was she? Brian remembered telling her to go to the basement, so he headed there on the run.

She was there, in the recreation room, curled unmoving in a fetal position on the carpet, the old land line telephone lying near her. She was filthy, almost naked. She had nothing at all on below the waist and only the torn remnants of a shirt, maybe one of his old shirts, above. Crusts of blood were everywhere, massive yellow contusions all over her body, her left eye was swollen shut, her lower lip the size of a sausage.

"Aw, Jesus, Katie. Son of a BITCH!" He ran to her, dropped to his knees, grabbed her throat to feel for a pulse, exhaling a gust of relief when he felt it. It was fluttering like a bird's, weak and rapid, but it was there. He felt tears welling but he slapped them away, there was no time for that. No time. Not only was she beaten, and dehydrated, and starving, but she had fouled herself, and lay in a stinking puddle. He had to get her cleaned up.

Apparently she had already been in the basement when he told her to go there, it was the only place in the house there was a phone physically connected to a land line. For years they had used it only for an Internet connection, it was surprising she even thought of it. And from where did she summon the memory, or find a record, of the phone number at the Farm? As these thoughts skittered through his mind he was rushing into the rec room bath to check the faucets, but of course there was no water. The toilet had been used several times without flushing, which explained the odor in the house. He stood still for a minute, letting his mind range over the problem, poke around outside the box.

Then he had it. He ran up to the garage, snatched a length of garden hose from its reel, and ran down to the basement utility room. He fastened the garden hose to the drain of the water heater, a 60-gallon reservoir that doesn't get depleted when the water pressure is off (the only exit from a water heater, aside from its drain, is from the top; it takes water pressure to get hot water out).

He picked Kathryn up and brought her into the utility room, laying her down near the floor drain. The tile was cold, but she wouldn't be there long. He opened the water heater drain – since the power was off, the water was not hot, of course, but it was water – and washed her thoroughly, sluicing the filth down the drain. Then he carried her upstairs to their – her – bedroom.

He found towels and dried her; found warm sweats and put them on her; straightened up the bed and put her on it; and bundled her in blankets.

He ran down and got the medical kit from where he had left it in the rec room, grabbed a push broom from the garage, and his headlamp from the motorcycle's saddlebag. Back in the bedroom he made sure the drapes were closed, turned on his headlamp with maximum, white-LED light. He leaned the push broom against the wall next to the head of the bed, extracted a bladder containing a couple of liters of saline solution from the kit and hung it from the push-broom handle. He inserted a six-foot-long flexible tube into the bottom fixture on the bag, secured it, primed it and clamped it.

Then, visualizing the practice sessions they had had with CJ, cross-training everybody at the Farm to be medics if they had to be, he extended Kathryn's right arm, palm up, next to her on top of the bed clothes. He used a disinfectant swab from the kit to clean his hands, then another to sterilize her skin on the inside of her elbow. He ripped off a couple lengths of surgical tape and laid them, tacky side up, on Kathryn's midriff. He got a syringe with attached catheter port from the kit, opened and fitted a sterile needle, then while holding it in his right hand clamped down with his left thumb on Kathryn's skin at the fold of her elbow. It took a few seconds, but that raised the vein in her forearm just enough that he could see it.

Gingerly, he inserted the needle, slanted toward her upper body. Got it to where he thought it should be. No blood appeared in the syringe. Kathryn moaned softly. Shit. He didn't want to dig around, he withdrew the needle and tried again. Still no blood. On the third try, he got it. Taped the catheter port securely in place, withdrew the syringe, fitted the IV tube to the port, unclamped it, and taped it down as well.

Sweat was running down his back, over his forehead and into his eyes. He grabbed a dry washcloth and wiped some of it away, sitting back on a side chair near the bed and decompressing. He switched off his headlamp, saw around the edges of the drapes that it was starting to get light outside. It was time for him to secure the perimeter.

But first Kathryn needed water. In her mouth. He didn't like the idea of giving her water from the water heater. It had been warm and still for days, and thus was a perfect Petri dish for the growth of microbes. People who moved into unoccupied houses without draining the water heaters often had severe intestinal problems. But he couldn't think of another...

Yes, he could. He went to the kitchen, opened the freezer side of the refrigerator, pulled out the ice-cube bin. There were a couple of quarts of cool, filtered water that had been ice cubes when the power went off. He took a glass of it up and moistened Kathryn's lips with it, got a little bit of it into her mouth. She made a sound, but her eyes did not open. He held his wrist against her forehead to check for fever. She was warmer than she should be, but not seriously. He moistened a washcloth in the ice-cube water, folded it and lay it on her forehead. He checked her IV, then left her to make his rounds.

He considered re-closing the front door of the house, maybe even nailing it shut, but decided against it. The looters might – in fact they probably did – live nearby, might pass the house often or even be able to see it from where they were. No sense advertising that things had changed.

He went from room to room, the rooms where he had lived his life for so many years, looked out every window at his familiar neighborhood. There was the Mulaney's house next door, looking normal from where he stood, but probably looted and wrecked. Across the way the Patterson's. He should go over there, check on them, but of course he couldn't. What would he do, could he do, if he found someone alive? What if he found a bunch of people, alive and hostile?

He went into his old office. Kathryn had left it pretty much as it was, hadn't turned it into a sewing room or anything after they split up, his desk was still there. He sat in his high-backed leather chair, sank back and then snapped erect – he could be sound asleep in a heartbeat. He tried to remember what it had been like, sitting here, worried about stories and deadlines and childrens' plays and soccer games. Watching CNN and arguing about the presidential race and having the Mulaneys over to watch a Redskins game.

Sure, he had figured out what was probably going to happen, had argued the case fiercely for years, but he knew now that he had never really deeply believed it, had never actually grasped that he would one day see what he had seen last night or be where he was today. Back in the day, that constant blizzard of distractions, the TV shows, the overheated, content-free political arguments, the buzzing of the gigantic sports industry analyzing what huge people were able to do with little round or oblong objects, had worked on him as it had on everyone else to turn his mind away from the stern dictates of logic and arithmetic and physics, and direct it instead to the dreamy acceptance of the notion that people could live in extravagant, unsupportable luxury – huge air-conditioned homes, big air-conditioned vehicles, trivial, paper-pushing jobs all day, constant entertainment all night, with power shopping on weekends – forever and ever, world without end, amen.

What was it his Dad said: you get up every day, expecting it to be just like the last one, and then one day, just like that, it is the last one.

So here he was, distracting himself with pointless musing. He checked on Kathryn's IV, moistened her mouth with water again, went to the garage and replenished the motorcycle's gas tank from the two one-gallon cans he had stowed in the saddlebags, gathered some clothes for Kathryn from her closet and dresser and stuffed them in the space thus freed up, every few minutes going to the windows and surveying the neighborhood for any movement. He saw none, but he kept the stubby 12-gauge at hand anyway.

By mid-morning the house was already hot. And it smelled bad, but at least it was not the stench that rose from the corpse-strewn Interstate 66. He filled a pail with water from the water heater and flushed the toilet in the master bedroom's bath. After a while he took a straight-backed kitchen chair into the bedroom and sat watching Kathryn, allowing himself to doze a little because if he fell deeply asleep he would fall off the chair and, he hoped, awaken. The day wore on.

He was in that lovely country between waking and sleeping, between living and dying, where thoughts shed their usual constraints, where ordinary musings and typical scenarios veer suddenly into rich fantasy, where he could meet old friends, encounter himself younger and older, visit a past that never happened, without regret, and explore a future that could never happen, without fear. It is a country where nothing that occurs requires an explanation, it just is. So for a few moments the blap! blap!blap! of an approaching Harley engine simply was. Then the alarms went off in his head and he leaped from his chair, shotgun in hand.

He ran to the front of the house and peered out carefully between two curtains. There were two of them on the Harley, which idled up the street and without hesitation veered into his driveway and stopped. Two men, wearing leathers and stubby-toed shifter boots. No helmets, those had disappeared when the cops did. They had do rags over greasy strands of hair that hung to their shoulders. Big guy in front, a huge Colt .45 pistol jammed in his belt, smaller guy behind cradling a sawed off double barrel 12 gauge shotgun. They dismounted and looked the house over as if they owned it. They tried for swagger, but they were haggard and sick, gray of face, thin, and were more likely to stagger.

Brian knew immediately who they were, and what they were here for.

"Oh, sweetie," he heard the big man call, "We're back."

Brian ran, as light-footedly as he could, to the bedroom. From the walk-in closet set into the left wall he grabbed a robe and draped it over the IV bag. He turned the covers back over the line and her taped forearm. Looked at her, shook his head, he needed...

He heard a crash as the remains of the door got kicked in downstairs. "Where are you darlin'?" the big man called in a singsong tone, "We come back to see you. For a little more lovin'. And we forgot our manners before. We was supposed to ask you over for dinner." He tried to laugh, but it turned into a gargling cough.

Brian snatched his multitool from his belt, snapped open the blade, reached up under Kathryn's sweat shirt and slit it open, laying bare her breasts. Satisfied now, he stepped into the closet and slid the folding doors almost closed, leaving just a crack.

The assholes didn't waste much time downstairs. Headed straight for the bedroom.

"I don't smell nothin dead," the smaller guy said. "Just shit and all. Could be she's still with us."

"Better be," his leader growled. "We need her to be fresh."

Then they were at the bedroom door.

"Well! Looka here," the chief greaseball said. Brian couldn't see him yet, but could picture the grin, the wide eyes focused on, seeing nothing but, her chest. "She made it into bed, and she's all ready for us! Mmmm-mm."

Brian fervently hoped that deputy dog was snuggled up close to his pack leader, getting a good look at Kathryn, firing himself up. And when they came level with Brian's little slit in the door that's where the number two perp was, looking over his buddy's shoulder, mouth and eyes hanging open.

Brian knocked the closet door aside and discharged the Remington twice in less than a second. Everything above the shoulders of the two would-be attackers turned into either a red mist hanging in the air or a red-gray pulp, laced with bright slivers of bone, oozing down the far wall. Their trunks flopped to the floor, twitching and kicking.

Brian waited for the ringing in his ears to ease. But it didn't. Then he realized someone was screaming. Confused, because he was pretty sure the perps didn't have the wherewithal, he checked to see if it was him, but it wasn't. That left Kathryn.

She was sitting upright, the eye that could open bugged out, hands pressed to her ruined face, howling like a banshee.

Brian went to her and gathered her into his arms, holding her close, rocking her gently, murmuring to her, "It's alright, Katie, it's me, I've got you, we're going to be okay." Slowly, she quieted, leaned against him, eyes tight shut. He eased her back on the pillow, checked to make sure she hadn't pulled her IV out, gave her a few swallows of water that she took eagerly.

She tried to say something, but all she could produce was a croak.

"Don't talk, Kate, just rest. You're gonna feel better."

She croaked again, more insistently. She was getting a little agitated.

"Okay, okay. What?" He leaned down, turned an ear to her mouth. She whispered.

"Gotta pee."

"Excellent! Kidney function!" Delighted, he grabbed the broom with its IV bag in his right hand, got his left arm around her back and gripped her under her armpit. She helped a little, but she had the coordination of a newborn colt and he basically just dragged her into the bathroom and got her seated.

When she was back in bed again she took all the water he would give her, plus a swallow of fresh goat's milk from its bottle in the medical kit. Something to gently start her digestive system, to add a little fuel to the glucose she was getting in the saline solution.

"Tired," she murmured, and fell back to sleep.

He covered the mess on the floor with a sheet, tried to ignore the thickening odor of blood and feces, and went back to his chair, to wait for dark. Then he started to his feet again. The Harley! In the driveway! He went down to the garage, surveyed the street, and, seeing nothing, raised the overhead door and ran the intruders' motorcycle inside. He closed the door and watched the street for several minutes. He saw nothing move.

Sweating hard from his brief exertion, he went back to his vigil over Kathryn, willing her strength to gather so she could withstand what he was going to put her through. Through the long, sweltering, putrid afternoon he sat with her, patrolled the windows, sat with her some more, saw her swim into hazy wakefulness a few times, gave her water often and a few swallows of goat's milk, dozed and hallucinated in his chair, seeing hordes of zombies coming down his street, sailing the sky to a safe landing at the farm with his arms outspread, jerking awake and waiting some more.

Hours later, or days, maybe weeks, darkness came at last. He waited another hour, then took out the IV, stowed it, got Kathryn dressed, carried her down to the motorcycle, got her onto the buddy seat, opened the garage door, mounted up, strapped her to him with a nylon strap that encircled them both under the armpits, kicked the engine to life and headed for home.

He reckoned he had saved her life. He wondered for what.

PART FOUR – BRAVE NEW WORLD

23. BREAKING UP IS EASY

We started to come apart the night Brian went on his odyssey. It wasn't his fault, it was just that the anxiety he added to the mix seemed to bring the pressure on us to a critical level. It was as if a distant earthquake were causing the ground to shift and crack beneath our feet, opening fissures between us.

I don't think any of us slept the night he left. I know I didn't. I tried to stop my mind from following him, tried not to imagine the thousand horrors he might encounter. But when I managed to wrestle my squirming imagination to stillness, started to drift toward the quiet world on the other side of sleep, a great hairy arm would shoot out of the ground, reaching for my throat, and I would jerk upward in bed with a sucking gasp of terror. Each adrenaline overdose made sleep impossible for another hour.

It could not have been any better for Daniel or Julie, or really for any of the others. We had been, or at least had imagined ourselves to be, fairly secure, but now the collapsing world had reached its great hairy arm into the center of us, had taken a part of us away, and might not give it back.

Breakfast was a miserable affair. No one wanted to talk, or even make eye contact. Julie kept checking the land line, in vain – she had tried to keep talking to her mother as Brian was leaving, but Kathryn had said nothing more, and eventually the connection was lost. Now there was not even a dial tone. We went about our tasks, but without focus, without giving them our full attention, so there was no satisfaction in them.

At mid-morning, I was in the barn forking hay to the goats while Sarah Mulaney was milking the nannies. The goat being milked stood on a raised platform, its head locked in a stanchion, while Sarah sat on a stool to the side and filled her pail. One of the nannies decided time was up, took a kind of a sideways jump, and her hind quarters fell off the milking stand, putting her full weight on her neck, still held fast in the stanchion. Her cries were those of a young woman being murdered slowly with a dull knife. I ran over as Sarah was awkwardly trying to get around to the other side of the nanny. I grasped the goat by the tail and heaved her hindquarters back up on the stand. And then for some reason I gave voice to my simmering frustration.

"You need to be careful, Sarah." I knew as I said it that it was a gratuitous and hurtful remark.

"Tell the damn goat to be careful." She snatched up her milking pail, slammed open the stanchion to release the goat, and stamped away to the house.

Later in the day I heard Red Mulaney and Patsy McInerny arguing in back of the house, outside the kitchen door.

"Red, you have got to give them more water. I'm telling you, those tomatoes are not where they should be."

"And I'm telling you they've had plenty of water. Too much and we'll have fungus everywhere. We can't let that happen."

"Don't you think I know that?"

It went on for a while. And later, CJ went stamping through the yard as I was passing, muttering to himself. "Got a damn alarm in the generator house. No damn water at the wheel. Guess I'll climb up the stream to the diverter and see what I can see. I don't know anything about this shit. We need Brian back here."

It went like that all day, grievances and irritations piling up, until by suppertime everyone was in a black mood. Which wasn't helped when I told them that two more chickens had died and a couple more looked sick and I had no idea why.

There was a long, dark silence. I wanted to go to my room and curl up into as small an area as possible and wait for my son to return safe. But I was, after all, the elder.

"I think we have to talk about this."

It was as if I had pulled a cork from Juanita's mouth. "It's just not fair, you know? I mean, I love Brian, we all love Brian, and oh please God nothing has happened to him, and I feel awful being mad at him while he's out there, with God-knows-what going on. but if something does happen to him we're in terrible trouble here, and he's doing this to go get a woman – I am so sorry to say this in front of you, Julie and Danny, I know she's your mother and I know she's been hurt, but she could have been here, she could have helped us all the years we've worked on this place but she said no, she divorced your Dad because she did not want anything to do with this, with us. And now we're all in danger because Brian wants to save her from herself. And with her hurt like she is, and Brian in danger, I just feel like such a bitch for thinking these things." Then she gave up and just wept bitterly.

Daniel and Julie looked as if they were about to erupt. I gave them a small shake of the head and a look that willed them to hold their tongues.

"Don't feel bad about yourself," Patsy called from her usual place back in the kitchen, "You're not the only one thinking those thoughts."

"I gotta say, guys," Pat Mulaney weighed in with a sigh, "He kinda blew that unanimous- decision thing away."

"You remember how he was, when she divorced him?" CJ was scowling at his plate. "Man, he was a basket case."

Everybody sat there looking as if they were drinking vinegar, having thoughts they didn't want to have. It was time for the elder to fix this, and the elder did not have a clue about how to do it. I figured, if I started talking, I might say something useful.

"Do you know what this is? What we're all feeling here?"

"Yeah," George shot back, "It's being pissed off."

"Well, sure. I mean, the first thing I want to do, when Brian walks in that door..." I tilted my head at the front door, and had to pause a second to get the quaver out of my voice, "is slap him upside the head. Not so much for what he did – Daniel, Julie, don't take this the wrong way, okay, it's not against your dad or mom – as for how he made me feel. Scared. Being scared pisses me off.

"But look. This is more than Brian. This is about what we've lost, and how much more we're going to lose. We were the folks who lived in the neighborhood, and the neighborhood is gone. We were the people who were our jobs. Cop, firefighter, accountant, whatever, that's who we were, and now the jobs are gone. So who are we now? We chose our clothes, our cars, our houses and furniture, to let people know who we were, and now all the stuff is gone, and the people, too. So who are we?

"All this effort, the farm, getting it ready, going through what we all had to go through to get here. If we're not who we were anymore, what's the point?"

"Survival, man," CJ barked, "That's the point. I don't care about keeping my identity, I care about staying alive, and keeping the kids alive."

"Sure, I get that. But we're human, and it has never been enough for us to just have a day, and enjoy it, roll around on our back in the grass like a happy dog. When we get a day, we want to know; what's it for, what am I supposed to be doing with it?"

"Maybe that's part of what was wrong with the world before, why it broke down," Patsy yelled from the kitchen.

"Maybe. But my point is that we have all these habits, all these attitudes, all these reactions to things that are so basic we don't even think about them, and now all the things those habits and reactions were based on, are gone. It's like we're in space, beyond gravity, and nothing works like it's supposed to."

"We're alive. That's the point." George, like CJ, sounded annoyed and defensive, like I was attacking him for something.

"At first, it is, sure. Until the shock starts to wear off. And then we start looking around and saying to ourselves, whoa, I'm not a politician anymore, so what am I? When I want to feel good about who I am, I can't look at my stuff, so how can I feel good again? If I want to feel secure, I can't pull up my bank account or my social security, so how do I feel secure? So I'm alive. Now what?"

There was a long silence. I had touched something. Red Mulaney had pushed his chair back from the table, was sitting bent over with his elbows on his knees, staring at the floor. After a bit he looked up at us.

"We talked about that, some, while we were working on stuff. What we wanted to be, afterward. How we could do things better. Maybe we didn't talk enough. But it was awful to think about, we kind of shied away from it."

"And now here we are." I said. "We're alive, but what are we going to do now? We're alive, but what kind of people are we going to be? Kathryn never supported the Farm, and now Brian has risked everything to try to save her. Was that the right thing to do? Was it wrong? Who decides?"

"Do you have any answers to those questions? Sir?" Daniel was haggard and red-eyed with anxiety for his parents, but he was bearing it all with an impressive stoicism, a combination of dignity and alertness that was beyond his years.

"No, I don't, Daniel. We're going to have to work them all out as we go along. We're going to have to invent all the things that the next generations will take for granted. But I have a thought about what's tearing us up right now – your Dad's decision to go after your mother.

"One of the really bad ideas that got drilled into us, over and over, was 'survival of the fittest.' That's what we thought evolution was, the replacement of the weak and unprepared with the strong and the smart. You know, Darwin never used that phrase, and didn't like it when he heard it. He knew that evolution was a string of accidents, volcanoes, meteors, climate changes, whatever, that killed almost everything except a few outliers, mutants, who by chance had the attributes the new age needed.

"He also knew that groups did not survive these catastrophes just because they were strong and fitted for the new conditions. People who studied evolution learned that intangible things like compassion and mercy could provide the group with a critical advantage, too. So the quality that a member of an endangered group demonstrates by risking everything to save another member could be the very quality that makes the difference between making it and not making it."

That earned several minutes of silence in the room, ended by CJ's mutter: "She's not a member."

"Yeah, she is," I responded. "She's human, and she's alive."

And that's how we left it, and straggled off to bed knowing we were not going to sleep, not happy, any of us, but thinking forward now, maybe wondering about things that had just made us mad before. So that was something.

I did not intend to sleep. I did not think I could sleep. And yet, when the raucous "Awk! Awk! Awk!" of the alarm filled the house, I lunged up in bed, not knowing where I was or what the sound was. Until, faintly, I heard the metallic voice of Red Mulaney, who was on duty at the observation post: "We have a motorcycle incoming!"

The tremendous crashing wave of relief disabled me for a minute, sapping my ability to move or think. I had not realized how clenched I had been until everything let go at once.

"He has a passenger! Lashed to him, looks like. He's going to need help with the gate. I'm going down."

I was trying to fling my boots on with rubbery arms – I had laid down fully clothed otherwise – when I heard George shout a reply. How in the hell he could already be at the radio I did not know.

"Negative Red, negative! You need to keep eyes on that road, make sure he hasn't attracted any flies. Watch the road! I'll get the gate!"

"Right. I knew that."

George had galloped out the front door before I got to the stairs, which I had to be careful about because I had all the muscle coordination of a newborn foal. By the time I negotiated them, and got across the great room to the door, and crossed the porch and got out into the yard, the black motorcycle hummed into view and I saw with my overflowing eyes that my son was alive and grinning. Even in the dark I could see that he was drawn and pale, that his eyes were sunken in his head with fatigue, but he was grinning. Kathryn was unconscious, her head lolling on his right shoulder. She looked awful.

George trotted up behind Brian, steadied him as he kicked the stand down, killed the bike engine and eased its weight onto the stand. As George started to untie the belts with which Brian had bound Kathryn to him, CJ and Juanita ran up with a litter and his medical kit. Julie, sobbing in the agony of her relief, and Daniel, trying to keep a stone face and failing, rushed up, and together they eased Kathryn off the bike and onto the litter, and hustled her into the house.

Slowly and with great effort, Brian dismounted, and stood

shakily by the bike.

"You did it, son," was all I could manage.

The grin widened just a little. "Piece a cake," he said, and then his eyes closed and he toppled forward into my arms and for the first and last time in a very long time I had the privilege of carrying my son to his bed to sleep. Me and two other guys.

August brought searing heat and no rain. Most days the temperature was over 100 degrees Fahrenheit, and most nights it did not get below 80. I had expected to suffer greatly from the lack of air conditioning, but it was not so bad. In the absence of periodic refrigeration, our bodies acclimated to the heat, and soon we paid it little attention. Often in the late afternoon I would shed my sweat-soaked clothes and lie in a pool in the stream back of the barn. It was much reduced by lack of rain but was still running, and although there were some long stretches of dry rock in the stream bed, there were also many basins brim full of trickling water, suffused with green forest light. To ease my hot and smelly old body down into that blessedly cool water was to go to a better place than I had ever been on this earth. After the initial gasp of shock I would stretch out, face up, to let the chuckling water lave my skin while I gazed up through the overhanging trees, watching clouds sail silent by, seeing high red-tailed hawks wheeling in their airy gyres, listening to crows shouting distant insults and pileated woodpeckers screaming bloody murder from tree to tree. No church had ever offered me such peace, no act of mine had ever been infused with such reverence. It was possible, lying there bobbing gently on the undulating universe, to believe that the world had barely noticed the convulsion that had wracked our poor selves. In a half hour or so my body would be chilled to the core, and would stay comfortable long into the steamy evening. The comfort bestowed upon my soul lasted for days.

We had run out of coffee and alcohol, and had pretty much forgot we ever used them. We drank water, and with the heat and the sweating work, we drank plenty of it. I suspect we had never been so well hydrated. Breakfast was eggs – all you care to eat – and bacon, of which we had enough to last until fall butchering. We got used to our food being room temperature, because Patsy and whoever was assisting her had to do all the cooking before dawn to maintain smoke security (when the moon was full we got cold cuts, period). We had to saw her stove-wood with crossbuck hand saws because we did not dare fire up a chain saw, which could be heard for miles. Lunch was a ham sandwich (there were plenty of sealed, five-gallon plastic pails of flour in storage, and hams in the cold room) with a glass of goat's milk, and dinner usually featured chicken, or goat chili, and a green salad from the garden. The daily work accelerated our metabolism, melted our fat, hardened our muscles and deepened our sleep. The exposure to the sun bronzed us. We had never been in better shape in our caffeinated, alcohol-sedated, carbohydrated lives.

The exception of course was Kathryn. She came back to health slowly, and out of her silence even more slowly. She was ashamed of what had happened to her, of being wrong about the Farm, and of now living on the charity of the people she had spurned. But for all the resentment that had been expressed the night Brian returned, everyone was gentle with her, and took pains to show her that the past was past, that she was forgiven and – this was the kindest part – that she ought to get the hell to work. Soon she was helping in the kitchen, and before long demanded to be added to the OP roster.

There was no more news of the outside. We spent long evenings debriefing Brian and trying to divine what conditions were, and were becoming. It seemed clear from what he had seen that the dying of the lambs had nearly run its course. The lambs, of course, were the people whose faith in industrial prosperity had never wavered, had never allowed them to think about the signs of collapse growing like a jungle on the margins of their bright neon world, had continuously promised them that technology would find a way, long after there was no way. Even Brian, who had argued for years that collapse was at hand, was stunned by its speed. In a matter of days, untold millions had begun to starve, to die of thirst, and there was no help for them.

The criminals, as we had expected, were hanging on a bit longer. But no food was no food. It wasn't that there was a place they could find that would have everything they needed. When they had run through the meager leavings of the lambs, and then had fought over the slight hoards of their rival gangs, they, too would be gone. That left us, and perhaps – no, surely – others like us, in our scattered enclaves. Maybe next year we could start to reach out, to make contact, and see what would happen then.

24. CONTACT

A goat standing shoulder deep in sweet grass and clover had seen something on the other side of the wire field fence so attractive that it had forced its horned head through a four-inch square of 12 gauge wire and could not get out. It was mid-afternoon of another scorching, late-August day. I was trying to stay in the shade, and was looking forward to my end-of-shift soak in the stream. I had been drawn to its situation, maybe 100 yards north of the barn and on the far side of the stream, by its piteous screams, more of outrage than of pain at this point, consisting of four- and five-syllable renditions of the phoneme "ma." It's something only goats, two-year-old children and Mandarin speakers can do.

As these things do, it was turning rapidly from a situation into a debacle. I leaned my "street-sweeper" shotgun against a fencepost, climbed the fence, and tried to maneuver the goat's head back through the fence, but succeeded only in making his eyes bug out and cutting the hell out of my hand by getting it between his frantically plunging horn and the wire. While I was cursing and nursing my hand he managed to kick my shotgun over.

I was going to have to cut the wire to get him out, which pissed me off because it was about the sixth time I had had to cut that same stretch of fence, and because I had trotted out to investigate without fence pliers. So I had to trudge back to the barn to get the pliers while the goat told me, in ever louder and more emphatic terms, what he thought about being abandoned in his predicament.

By the time I got back I was sweating freely and short of breath. I knelt next to the goat, clipped the vertical stay next to the idiot's head, and watched him bolt toward the rest of the flock, shaking his head in annoyance, not a word of thanks. I stayed on my knees for a minute to get my breath and that's when I heard another sound. A distant wailing, upstream. I thought for a second it was yet another goat caught in wire, but this was different. A high keening that sounded like grief, not pain, but did not sound human. And it was moving downstream toward me.

I grabbed the shotgun and moved toward the stream to intercept whatever it was. I keyed the radio on my belt: "Attention at the house. I have incoming of some kind, moving down the stream toward the barn, making a lot of noise. I'm moving to intercept. Be aware, over."

I climbed the fence out of the pasture and took up a position behind a large sycamore that leaned out over the stream. The wailer kept coming, I could hear it thrashing through underbrush now, and I released the safety on the shotgun. I did not want to fire it in the middle of the day and advertise our presence to a large chunk of the country. I was a little tense. I wished I had specifically asked for help when I radioed the house.

Then the creature shambled into view. It was Billy, stumbling forward, howling, tears and snot running down his face, his face and hands raked bloody by stickers. I snicked the safety back on, held the shotgun at port arms and stepped into his view. "Billy! What on earth is the matter."

"Aaawww!" he groaned, his tone changing as he saw me, and he ran to me, collapsed into my arms as I hastily leaned the shotgun against a tree so I could hold him up.

"What's the matter, Billy?"

He had to say it three times before I could make out the words. Then I wished I hadn't. "They killed my momma! They killed my dog!"

Oh, shit. I keyed my radio. "Attention at the house. I have a situation here. I need backup, and we need to go on defense."

I turned Billy and eased him into a seated position against the sycamore. He was still weeping miserably. I knelt in front of him, made eye contact, spoke firmly. "Billy, I need you to pull yourself together now. We might be in danger here. Tell me what happened, and when."

It took him a few minutes, but he did it. "This morning. Rex and I was out, like always, before daylight, lookin' around, and when I was comin back in for breakfast I saw 'em, all around the house, and Momma lyin' on the porch." Here he had to stop and wail again, and I just had to wait a minute until he could talk. "Rex, he took out after 'em, like a rocket, and when he was on 'em he started to bark, and they just shot him."

I had to wait again for him to stop howling his grief, but I did not think I could wait much longer. I tapped him gently on the cheek. "Billy, stay with me here. Focus! How many were there?"

"Plenty."

The answer didn't come from Billy. It came from behind me.

All I could see when I turned my head was the enormous black muzzle of the 45-caliber pistol aimed at my face. It was held by a scrawny young man dressed in filthy bib overalls with no shirt. I stood slowly to face him and to screen Billy. I know, that made no sense, I just did it. The gunman's next comment was flung over his left shoulder.

"I told you he was headin for somebody's place. Can I shoot 'em?"

My breathing was getting fast and shallow. I swiveled eyes right to see another apparition, an older version of the first, skinny as a sapling, bent by age, cradling a deer rifle, a Winchester or Marlin lever action, in his arms. "Naw," he said, "Cut they throats. And be quiet. Then we can tell the others."

"Awright. Cover me." The young man, grinning, holstered his .45 and unsheathed a wicked hunting knife as the older man swung the muzzle of his 30-30 in our direction.

I imagined then that a baseball bat smashed into my left chest. I groaned explosively, clutched my chest and started to sink to my knees.

"Look, Paw," said the younger man, his grin widening. "The old dude's havin the big one. Gonna do our work for us." He whinnied a laugh, and the older man stepped out so he could see better.

"Well, I'll be," he said, his rifle swinging away from us as he gawked.

I reached back with my left hand for the support of the sycamore tree. I turned to it as my legs gave out, sliding down the trunk until I was lying on the ground facing away from them. Then I rolled right, came up with the shotgun in my hands and shot the younger man just below his grin, which vaporized.

Simultaneously, as I was swinging the muzzle toward the older guy, I heard a sharp double crack from downstream and saw him throw his gun away and pitch forward onto his face.

I looked over my shoulder and saw George at the edge of the trees downstream lowering his AR-15 and trotting toward us. As he checked the younger man's body he said, "Pops, I did not know you had that in you."

"Me either." I rolled over so I was face down and threw up my lunch.

Brian appeared and gathered up the interlopers' weapons. He and George dragged the bodies into the brush and threw some branches over them. Then they helped me to my feet and leaned me against the sycamore. "That was good, Dad," said Brian. "I really thought you were having a heart attack."

"I'm not sure I didn't."

Billy had been stone silent since the gunmen appeared. He was sitting braced against the tree, staring off into the woods. "I brought them here," he said faintly. "I'm sorry. I didn't think they saw me."

Brian and George looked a question at me and I told them what had happened at Billy's home, and how the men had appeared.

"That's what he said?" George asked when I was through, "That after they killed you two, *then* they could tell the others?"

"Yes."

"So maybe we have a little time. They'll have heard the shots, but they may not have missed these two yet, and even if they have, it'll take 'em a while to figure out what to do. How many of them are there, Billy?"

"I don't know. I think I saw 10 or 12."

"Awright let's go. We got to move!"

I was surprised to see George go to Billy and help him to his feet. "Come on, Billy, you're with us now."

With Billy shambling along, his arm in George's firm grasp, we trotted for the house. Brian was barking into his radio. "Everybody! Arm up! Go to defense! Now!!"

Now all the drills they had conducted – many more than I had been involved in-- paid off. By the time we got to the house everybody was armed and on their way to their places. The cargo nets had been deployed over all the downstairs windows and doors except the main door onto the porch. We held a quick huddle in the great room. For this, George was in command.

"OK, listen up," he said, reverting to his Special Forces persona. "We have 10 or 12 hostiles incoming, most likely from the north and west. We know they are hostile, and we know they are killers. We have to put them down. Remember the drill. Remember what to do with the fear. And remember to make sure of your target. I'm going out to locate them, and I don't want to get shot coming back in. We should have a few hours before they engage, but be ready! I'll see you in a few."

As he spoke he had been stepping into a full ghillie suit and smearing dark cammo paint on his face. When he had finished he snatched up his AR-15 and was gone. We all looked at each other, acknowledged the fear in each others' eyes – this was, after all, the worst-case scenario – and, there being nothing more to say, went to our places.

Mine was on the northwest corner of the porch, behind an L of sandbags, banister height, each leg about four feet long. Someone had already placed a couple of boxes of double-ought shotgun shells there, along with a rolled up sleeping mat so that I could stretch out on the floor and keep watch around the ends of the sandbag emplacement. I had a clear view westward over the front yard, the barn, and of the approach from the north that our enemies were likely to use. I unrolled the mat, stretched out and settled in.

My hands were no longer shaking but I was still trembling internally from shock and horror at what had happened. Now that I was alone and still, it washed over me again. I really don't know which was worse to think about; that I had been moments from a violent death, or that I had killed another human being. I had never done such a thing, had never contemplated doing such a thing, I had always assumed that committing homicide would do incalculable damage to the soul. Now I was about to find out.

A thunderstorm muttered darkly to itself off to the west as the afternoon waned. I lay drenched in sweat, pining for the blessed cool of the stream. As time passed, my distress over the events of the afternoon eased, only to be replaced by steadily rising anxiety about the events to come. They say there are no atheists in foxholes. I don't know about that, but I know that I prayed hard that afternoon that all of us would make it through.

The house was silent. The only life I could see was young Jacob, prone behind his sandbag emplacement at the other corner of the porch. Every time I looked at him he was in motion, changing his position, adjusting his clothing, scratching something, rearranging his ammunition, checking his 30-30 Winchester. But he was doing it quietly, and staying well hidden, so I gave him a thumbs-up salute and stopped looking at him.

I knew that Brian was at the north upstairs window, behind sandbags that came up to the sill, watching the ridge along the stream bed that was the raiders' most likely approach unless they decided that was too obvious, and came in from another direction. Red Mahoney was at the south window upstairs, similarly protected by sandbags, watching the lane from the main road and the ridge to his left. The corresponding windows on the first level were shuttered on the outside, cargo-netted and blackout-curtained on the inside. Patsy and Jacob were stationed at the two east-facing downstairs windows covering the the slim back yard and the slope of the ridge leading down to it. They were watching, and would shoot, from behind the cargo nets and blackout curtains. Juanita Ramirez, with little Carla at her side, was in reserve upstairs; when the action started she would be in a closet whose walls were hardened with steel plate, from which she could deliver ammunition, backup weapons, or first aid to the upstairs shooters. Sarah McInerny had a similar function downstairs.

The house bristled with guns and hummed with nervous energy, but outside there was no sign. It looked empty, abandoned.

As the light faded and the heat eased, as the first fireflies began to wink in the trees and a mocking bird tuned up for another singing binge, boredom began to suffocate the fear. The far-off thunderstorm was still muttering, but from the southeast now, it had gone past us, well to the south. Four twitchy hours passed, and a fifth. The last light of the sun was leaching from the sky when we heard from our radios a double click, and a muttered "coming in."

A bush that looked a lot like George trotted onto the porch and strode into the great room. The radios clicked again; "Join me. Except if you're on external post, stand fast."

When we are all there, and George had stripped off the ghillie suit and mopped the streaming sweat and oily cammo paint off his face, he started to talk.

"The good news is that they are not trained military people. Just a bunch of outlaws with old deer guns. They don't seem to be local, but they know the woods and the animals. They've been doing a pretty good job of keeping themselves alive, they're in pretty good condition. They don't know this place is here, all they know is four of their guys came down here to check things out and haven't come back."

"Four?" said Brian. I was wondering about the count, too.

"Yeah, they sent two after the two we met."

"And?"

"Same result. The other good news is that they are not rushing to get down here. They're worried and they're going to want the light, so I'd look for them at sunup tomorrow."

We all groaned. Not that we were spoiling for a fight. It's just that we wanted it to be over.

"The other good news? They're drinking on the problem, getting shit-faced as a matter of fact, so they are not going to be geniuses in the morning. Oh, and the other bad news. There are 20 of them. Six women and four adolescents."

"Did you see my Momma?" Billy had been huddled in a chair in the corner of the great room since he got here, and we had pretty much forgot he was there.

"Yes, I did, Billy. She's still lying on the porch. When this is over we'll go get her and bury her proper."

"Thank you. Can I have a gun?"

"Can you shoot a gun?"

"If I shoot at it, I hit it."

"Ever shot a person?"

"No. I never thought I'd want to."

"But you want to now."

"Yes, sir."

"I will get you a gun."

"Thank you, sir."

George regarded Billy for a moment, respect growing in his face like a slow sunrise. Then he turned to the rest of us. "We'd better rest in place, just in case, so get pillows, a blanket, whatever you need at your post. Charge your radios, fully, before you settle in. Eat something. Stay hydrated. Try and sleep. Gonna be a busy morning. Gimme a charged radio before I go."

"Where you going?" Brian wanted to know.

"Out and about. Make sure they find us okay." He clipped a fresh radio on his belt. "Work the plan, folks, it's a thing of beauty."

And then he was gone.

The stars began to bleed out at about five in the morning. I had been dreaming I was sleeping, or just wishing it, but when I saw the signs of oncoming light I gave it up. I forced down some water, although it was hard to get the tension to let go of my throat muscles so I could swallow. I chided myself for being afraid. Hell, it was as good a day to go see Dottie as any, and better I should go than any of the others. I hoped dying wouldn't take too long. I hoped I would acquit myself as I should.

It had been light enough to see for a half hour – the sun would be erupting over the eastern horizon any minute, although we would not see it here behind the ridge for hours yet – before we heard from George. First the double click, then his voice pitched low, barely above a whisper.

"This is a rummy bunch, boys and girls, but rise and shine, here we come. They're still staggering around in circles but will be heading your way in a few minutes. It'll take em an hour and a half to get there. I'll follow em in, watch for any sneaky moves. Talk to

196

you when we're closer."

Some of us stood up, stretched. walked around our positions. Wed checked our weapons, rearranged our extra ammo, chatted a little bit, then went back to watching and waiting. In 45 minutes the clicks came again.

"These guys are bums. They're coming down the mountain like a mob, no flankers out, no scouts, nobody watching their ass. They have old repeating weapons, lever and bolt action, and big old pistols. They will be right on top of you before they see the house, and they don't seem to have a plan.

"Who's on OP, Daniel? Yeah, come on in to your secondary, we don't need to worry about the road now. Everybody in place? Ready?"

We all rogered him. Showtime in 30 minutes, he said, and reminded us to be sure of our targets, as he was coming in hot on their trail. Then he signed off. Jacob and I gathered up our mats, ammunition and weapons and went inside, shutting but not netting the front door and taking up posts on either side of it. We took turns keeping watch through the view port.

George might not have thought much of their tactics, but the men were hunters. They made no noise coming down the side of the ridge along the stream, and by the time they approached the clearing where the house was they had fanned out into a line abreast. They stopped in the shadows of the tree line 50 yards north of the house. Inside, we wouldn't have known, but somebody – I think it was CJ – keyed his mike and whispered, "They're here."

The intruders stared at the silent house. They thought things over, and consulted with each other in whispers. They didn't know if this house had anything to do with their missing men. They didn't know if it was even occupied. But it was a house in good repair, and might have provisions in it, and that had to be checked out.

After what seemed like hours but probably was about five minutes, they tried their first gambit. A woman limped into the clearing, hobbling along with a stick supporting one leg. She was a wizened walnut of a woman, sunburned and wrinkled and weathered to the point that she looked mummified.

"Hello, the house!" she shrieked. "Help! I'm hurt!" She stopped 10 yards from the trees, looked around apprehensively, tried again. "Can you help me please? I'm hurt!" She accentuated the limp even more to demonstrate how hurt she was, and struggled to about halfway between the tree line and the house. She yelled a few more times.

Getting no response, she turned, looked back at the trees and raised both her hands as if to say, "What do I do now?"

In response to some signal, she huffed a theatrical sigh, and came the rest of the way to the front porch, almost forgetting to limp at all now. She stomped up to the front door and banged on it with her stick. "Can you help me here? I'm hurt, I need help!" Then, to herself, barely audible to me through the door, "Assholes."

She tried the door. She went to both windows, picked at the thick wooden shutters bolted in place, tried to move them, tried to peek around them. Went around to the back, tried that door, peered at those shutters. Then threw her stick away and strode back to her people.

They talked. We waited. After a while a few of them broke cover, emerging from the trees with their weapons at the ready, peering around nervously. When nothing happened, more of them stepped out, until they were all standing around in a group, arguing about what to do next.

At their center was an elder, a stick-figure of a man in bib overalls that hung loosely on him, the bones of a sweat-stained straw hat clinging to his bald head, who moved as if his joints had rusted. His eyes darted around the house and yard like those of a hawk looking for a mouse. At length he gestured to two of his people, pointed back at the trees, and yelled something at them. They trotted over to some packs they had left leaning against the trees, extracted something from one of them, and started walking toward the house. Each of them had a two- or three-feet-long stick he appeared to be unwrapping. Halfway to the house, each of them grappled something out of his pocket, held it under his stick, clicked at and whump! They had torches.

"Oh, shit!" Justin said. He and I were watching through a tiny crack in the shutters of the north facing great-room window.

"They're gonna burn us!"

Two clicks from the radio. "Steady, all," George murmured. "They're not gonna burn food. They're bluffing."

Each of the men took a porch, one front, one back. They held the smoking torches down against the wall out of our sight. Black smoke billowed up across the windows. It was a really bad moment.

One click on the radio. "Daniel here. I have eyes on the one in back. He is not – repeat not-- setting anything on fire."

After a few minutes of making smoke, the two ran back to their pack. "Your house is on fire!" somebody yelled. "You better come out now with your hands in the air!"

They tried that a few more times, and then gave that up, too. They were drifting closer to the house. The old man sent some of them to the barn. They returned after a few minutes with a half dozen axes and picks. With its vanguard thus equipped, the whole group moved on the house, energized now with a sense of purpose.

Two clicks. "Ready folks. On my call."

The mob was 30 yards from the house. 25. 20.

"Open fire."

Behind the mob's left flank, CJ flung the top off a spider hole he'd been in since last night and leaped up into an L-shaped space behind two large limestone boulders. He flung his AR-15 across the top of one of them and began firing. So did Daniel, from behind another boulder up the ridge to the mob's left front, the secondary position he had taken when he left the OP. To the mob's right, a little trap door popped open on the side of the barn and Patsy blasted away with her shotgun from a position armored in front with steel plate on the walls and hidden from the barn's interior by hay bales. Justin and I tore through the door and both took up positions behind by sandbag position on the porch and started looking for targets. Meanwhile the roar of firing from the upstairs window – two or three guns simultaneously – was constant.

I do not think it was more than sixty seconds later that all the people who had come to kill us were dead. Except for one.

25. LIFE IN DEATH

Her name was Shirley. She was 12 or 13 years old. We found her when we were picking up the bodies. We had fired up the tractor with the backhoe attachment, we figured a little more noise was not going to bring us to the attention of anyone who missed the colossal eruption of gunfire. With the backhoe, we dug a trench in the far corner of an open meadow beyond the goat pasture. Then we picked up bodies and stacked them, three at a time, on the tractor's front bucket and took them out for burial. The copper smell of human blood was thick in the humid air. The grass was slick with it, the ground was saturated with it, it ran in turgid rivulets down the slope of our yard. When CJ and Red grabbed Shirley's hands and feet to throw her on the bucket, she moaned and opened her eyes.

She had been shot twice, high in the left shoulder and low in the right thigh. Her skin was peppered with buckshot. Her shapeless dress was soaked with blood, although there was no way of knowing whether it was all hers. Her wounds did not appear to be bleeding badly. She looked wildly, uncomprehendingly, around. She was deeply in shock.

Without a moment's hesitation George unshipped his sidearm and stepped toward the dazed girl. Just as quickly, Sarah Mulaney heaved her pregnant bulk in front of him. Her work that day had left her hands and feet and dress streaked and saturated with blood. "No, George. By God, no you will not."

George's left hand came up to sweep her aside, but Red leaped to her side. "Not that either, George. Let it go."

George glowered at them. "You will be very sorry. I have been here and done this. You don't know."

Sarah stepped even closer to him. "I know that we are not that kind of people. And if we ever become that kind of people, if we ever do that kind of thing, I will go out and hang myself from the nearest tree. Or something."

George holstered his weapon and stepped back. Sarah gestured to CJ for help. He went, reluctantly, to get a litter and a kit, and when he returned he and Sarah went to work on the girl. After a while they carried her into the house.

By late afternoon we had finished our grisly work, and we all craved to be washed clean of its vestiges. I left it to the others to overtax the house water system, and went to my spot in the creek to see if it was up to the challenge of cleaning my soul.

It wasn't. But it helped. We dragged in to supper in the grip of debilitating weariness – all of us, that is, except for Brian, who seemed normal, and George, who was on the high of a golfer who just recorded a hole in one. He recognized that we were not in the same place, and he lived with it for a while. We were sitting around the table, trying to choke down cold chicken sandwiches and salad, when he reached the limits of his restraint.

"So." he said to the room at large. "I thought that went pretty well."

"Jesus, George," said Sarah, who seemed on the way to becoming his nemesis. "That is what you call a good day? A massacre?"

"Yes, Sarah, it is." George sort of swelled up with irritation. "Do you know why? Because all of the people who were trying to kill us are dead. And we are all alive. That is the very definition of a good day."

"Christ." was all Sarah said, to her plate.

George regarded her for a moment, then looked at all of us. "Look, I know you folks aren't military, haven't seen or done what Brian and I have had to do. Back in the day we were the guys who went out and did the wars, and you were the people who stayed home and watched television – no offense, Pops, I'm talking about most people – and clucked your tongues in moral outrage when the people we killed were too young, or too old, or too innocent, or just too many.

"You all don't have that luxury now. We are all in the war, and in war you are either the windshield or the bug. So suck it up, people. Tough shit that you had to do and see today what you used to hire soldiers to go out and do and see for you. The point is, you did it, and you won, and they are in the ground and we are here eating sandwiches. End of story. "

"Really?" Tears of frustration threatened to escape Sarah's eyes. "The end of the story? We've gone through all of this so we can be the best savages, and kill the most people?"

"No, Sarah," Brian cut in, "we went through all this so we could survive. Sarah, for God's sake, those people attacked us. Were going to kill us. What are you talking about?"

"Ooohhh." She gave in to the tears now. "I don't know. I mean, I know we had to defend ourselves. But it's nothing to be proud about. And to kill that little girl...."

"It isn't about being proud, Sarah." George was speaking quietly in a way that made it seem he was shouting. "It's about perspective. Those were savages. They were evil. When you see evil you either give it a wide berth or you kill it. You don't take it into your house and feed it."

Sarah started to reply, hotly, but George cut her off.

"Listen to me, Sarah. In Iraq they used to send sweet little girls, hardly more than toddlers, out to ask us for candy. They'd be dragging their favorite Teddy bear, packed with explosives on a cell-phone activator. We lost a lot of nice guys before we figured it out. That was evil coming toward us, and we had two choices."

"But we can't. We just can't." Sarah was through with logic.

"We do what we have to do," said Brian. "I had to go get Kathryn. You had to take care of this girl."

"Yes, and you both put all of us in danger," George shot back. "You got away with it. Doesn't mean she will."

"George, she's a little girl!" Sarah wailed.

"Are y'all talkin' about me?"

She had come down the stairs while we were snapping at each other. Limping badly, one arm in a sling, pale as snow blowing in a freezing wind, her thin little frame almost lost in the billows of a borrowed cotton night dress. Her eyes glittered as she looked at us. They were not the eyes of a child, there was no expression in them. Just glitter. "Are y'all tryin to decide whether to shoot me or not?"

"Oh, sweetie, no!" Sarah rushed to her, knelt beside her, tried to hug her. The child ignored her, and stiffened herself. Sarah might as well try to hug a wire coat hanger.

"Y'all go ahead. Shoot me. You shot my whole family, din't ya."

"Shirley, honey, we are so sorry!" Sarah had stopped trying to hold the girl, and was kneeling at her side, trying to make eye contact, and failing. "We didn't mean to hurt you. We're going to help you get better, and then we'll be your new family."

The girl ignored her. She was looking directly at George, who stared back at her impassively. The rest of us tried to find somewhere else to look.

At length the girl said, so quietly we could barely hear her, "Yeah. That'll work." And then she allowed Sarah to lead her back up to bed.

We sat for a long time in silence. And then we went to bed, too.

It took a long time to emerge from the shock of the battle. We all wanted to go back to our routines, and let familiar drudgery heal us, but the old routines weren't exactly there. Now there was Billy, who refused to go back to live in the house where his mother had been murdered, and insisted on sleeping on our porch at night, and who followed me around by day. And Shirley, who became Sarah's shadow, and peered warily at the rest of us from the lee of Sarah's skirts with those glittering avian eyes.

September came, and brought the gifts it had always offered; a less oppressive heat in the day, and nights that sometimes were so cool they were like a long drink of creek water from a tin dipper. Leaves received their mysterious cue, and joyously abandoned the drab green of their summer life to put on the gaudy gold and crimson vestments of their approaching death. The air lost the mildewy closeness of late summer and began to move again, carrying the smells of hay and loam and pine needles.

As Brian had predicted years ago, climate change was not

affecting the West Virginia mountains as much as it had affected most other parts of the country. Summers were hotter, but not unbearably so; winters were more jagged, with warm spells interspersed with vicious cold snaps and howling blizzards. The most noticeable thing was that the weather systems moved more slowly, and instead of the weather changing every three to five days as it always had, dry spells and wet spells and cold snaps and warm ups often lasted for many weeks at a time. It was different, but we did not have to contend with the rising sea that was inundating Miami and Norfolk and New York, or the drought that had been depopulating Arizona, New Mexico and Nevada, or the tornado swarms that lashed the Midwest.

Not that things were serene at the Farm that November, far from it. Harvest had started in August – actually, the intervention of the attack on us had caused us to lose many pounds of tomatoes and squash. We were all in a frenzy now to can and freeze enough produce, and to secure enough root crops in the cold room, to see us through the winter. We knew we would make it through this winter, thanks to the stores laid in in advance, yet we were keenly aware of how depleted the reserves already were, and knew that we had better learn the lessons well this year because next year there would be little margin for error.

During the day we dug potatoes, picked tomatoes, squash, cabbages, beans and peas, and delivered the produce to Sarah's crew in the kitchen (the potatoes went into barrels in the cold room). There they sliced and diced, preparing the material for either canning or freezing. Both required hot water, and thus could not be done in daylight or on clear moonlit nights, because the smoke from the wood stove would be a beacon to the nearby world. So Patsy and her crew worked from dark until dawn, scalding and cooking and sterilizing until the light returned.

We became accustomed to Shirley's presence in the kitchen, chopping vegetables and stoking the stove and darting about on errands always assigned by Sarah. Sarah was enormous now, only weeks away from delivering her first child, and while she threw her bulk around the kitchen with remarkable agility, she used Shirley to extend her reach and take a lot of steps for her. Shirley paid no attention to anyone else, and regarded the rest of us with her impassive face and ravens' eyes, never smiling, rarely speaking, always withdrawn. We got used to Billy, who was almost as quiet as Shirley, but who labored without reserve in the gardens and wherever else we asked him to go, doing more than his share.

The healing grass obscured the signs of our terrible conflict, weeks of hard work eased the residual tension from our muscles, and the passage of each week allowed our minds to bury the jagged sights and sounds of that day, so that although they were still there they did not command our attention all the time.

So we were all in a mellow mood on the mellow October morning that Red Mulaney stumbled sleepily in from the overnight shift at the OP, went upstairs to go to bed, opened his bedroom door and began screaming at the sight of Sarah's lifeless body lying in a massive pool of blood from her severed neck. Shirley was long gone.

We had not thought about where to put our dead. Now it was Red's choice. When he had reclaimed his mind, while the women were cleaning Sarah's body and the room, he disappeared in the woods for four hours. It was about noon when he came back in, got a drink of water, and nodded to us without saying anything. We picked up Sarah's body, wrapped in a poncho and slung in a hammock so six of us could get a grip, and we all followed him in grim procession to a small, level clearing he had found low on the ridge north, or upstream, from the house. From it we could look over our little hollow and a slice of the greater valley beyond. He had already dug the grave. It was only four feet deep, that was as far as anyone could get down into the thin and rocky soil, but with an overlay of thick limestone slabs, it would do.

The whistling shriek of a red-tailed hawk, wheeling high in the clear sky against the fierce sun, greeted us as we lay our burden down beside the grave. Crows barked insolently in the distance. Somewhere high up on the ridge a drummer grouse fired off a machine-gun percussion solo that felt as though it was your own heart hammering in your chest. Daubs of dusty color, where the leaves were turning, smeared the flanks of the ridges, the mighty fossil waves of stone that rolled away to the horizon. The slight wind, gentle as it was, had an edgy aftertaste that spoke of fall, and winter, to come. Everyone gathered around, and looked at me.

I knew they were going to do that. I knew they wanted someone to make sense of this. I didn't feel qualified, but I had to try.

"She hated evil," I said. "She stood up against it, spoke out against it. She lived her life as a rebuke to evil. And yet evil took her, and her unborn child." Red sagged against Brian, who threw an arm around him and held him up.

"How could God let this happen? That's the question we're asking today. It's the wrong question.

"Do you see this day? Do you see the grace of God falling like rain upon us, drizzling the world with beauty and light? Maybe not. Maybe the grief is too hard right now. But I can promise you this: tomorrow will not be quite as bad, nor will the day after, and one day soon you will feel the grace again. You will smile again.

"But how do we reconcile with a God who allowed evil to do what it did to Sarah, and yet gives us a day like today? To start, we have to recognize something about God, or the Creator or the Universe or whatever you want to call the supreme being, that is not like us. God does not hate death like we do. If you believe he made the world, you must realize that he made it so that everything dies; every one of us, every animal and fish and bug, every society, continent, planet, moon and star. Look at the reality; God must love death. A writer named Richard Bach, once said: 'What the caterpillar calls the end of the world, the master calls a butterfly.'

"As for evil, look at reality again. There is no way to know what light is if we have not been in the dark, nor to recognize pleasure if we have not suffered pain, nor sweet without sour nor good without evil. These things are not at war with each other, any more than two ends of a stick fight each other – they are necessary parts of the stick, no stick has just one end. Death is. And evil is. And they have both come to us today. Yet listen."

Another musical shriek came whirling down from the red tailed hawk.

"Sounds like a welcome for two new butterflies. Sounds like the grace of God."

It wasn't much, but it was all I had. While Brian and George closed the grave, and Red leaned against a tree and watched, the rest of us straggled down the ridge, in the fading, smoky twilight of the October afternoon, feeling the cold coming, trudging toward our beds, hoping for some rest so that we could rise refreshed and take up our lives again.

26. A LINE IN THE SNOW

We were not troubled by any more intrusions until winter, which arrived in mid-October with a howling, six-day blizzard that dumped three feet of snow in below-zero temperatures, drove the snow like nails with 60-mile-per-hour winds and encased the world in white. Then a two-week warm spell with temperatures well above freezing melted almost all the snow. Weeks of blustery weather followed, with frequent snow squalls that coated the ground once again.

We did not mind the snow storms. The first big one did make getting to the barn and back difficult. Nothing is quite as exhausting as struggling through thigh-deep powder. But that was about all we had to do outside (we did not man the OP in such weather) and inside, life was better during the storms. Because of the wind and cloud we could stoke the wood fire all day without worrying about our security. Not only was the house warmer than the solar heaters could keep it during the day, but we could all keep a regular schedule, active during the day and sleeping at night.

Not that we were very active. Taking care of the animals consisted of making sure they had unfrozen water, feed and dry bedding. (We did not clean the stalls in winter, just added enough fresh straw to freshen the surface. The fermentation that started deep in the material actually warmed the bedding slightly.) All that took at most a couple of hours a day. The rest of the time we repaired tools, mended clothing, helped Red Mulaney distill alcohol, which, on special occasions, we diverted cautiously from its purpose as fuel to its secondary function as an inebriant.

The day after Sarah died, Kathryn followed me out to the barn when I went to do my chores. She gestured to the goats' milking stand. "Show me," she said. She apparently had decided she was going to take over Sarah's duties. I showed her how to get the nannies up on the stand, how to squeeze the teats. It was hard for her at first, but she would not let me take over, nor would she quit until all the goats that needed milking were tended to. At one point she stopped and rested, working a cramp put of her left hand. Not looking at me, she said, "Is it hard for you?"

"What?"

"Being here. Knowing you didn't help build it. I mean, I know you weren't against it like I was, but still. You weren't part of it, either. I just wondered if it bothered you."

"It did at first. But Brian and the others made it clear that I had knowledge and skills that they needed, that I wasn't dead weight. The more work I did, the less I thought about it."

"Yeah." She sounded wistful. "I wonder if they'll ever stop thinking of me as dead weight."

"I don't know where you got that, Kathryn. Do you understand how much it means to us, that you're here? It means we have Brian, whole again, firing on all his cylinders for the first time in a long time. It means Daniel and Julie aren't crippled by grief. And you've been pulling your weight, even without this." I gestured at the nannie on her milking stand.

She looked at me then, her eyes glistening. "You don't think I'm dead weight?"

"Nobody thinks that, Kathryn. Nobody."

In the weeks after Sarah's funeral we were a somber lot. It was so quiet in the house we could hear Red's wretched weeping from his room, where he stayed for about a month. But even the worst wounds heal eventually, if they do not kill, and before long we were playing card games, and encouraging Brian and CJ to break out their guitars, and planning next year's garden.

January brought a spell of cold, clear weather. We could not run the wood stove during the day, so we reverted to mostly nocturnal life. Which is why most of us were asleep, or trying to sleep, on the day around noon when the alarm sounded through the house. "AWK! AWK! AWK! AWK! AWK!"

Brian was first to the house radio. CJ was on OP duty. "What have you got, CJ?"

"Guy walking down the road. From the north, toward us. Better go on defense."

George came up to Brian's side. He gestured, and Brian gave him the mike. "One guy, CJ?"

"Yep."

"How long you have him in sight?"

"Couple minutes."

"Nobody else near him?"

"Naw. I can see 20 yards behind him now, there's nobody."

"Is he armed?"

"He's carrying a stick. Got a shotgun slung on his back."

Brian and George looked at each other, their expressions saying, "What the fuck?"

George spoke as if he could not believe what he was saying. "What is he doing with the stick?"

"He's dragging it. Down the middle of the road."

Brian took the mike back. "CJ, you've got glasses on him, right? What kind of shape is he in?"

"Good. He's walking strong, got good clothes, boots. Looks healthy."

"How does he seem? Nervous?"

"Naw, he looks like he's going for a walk in the park."

"Awright, let's hold off on defense right now. Tell us what he does when he gets to the lane."

"Roger."

George looked around. "Daniel, could you man the rear OP for a while? Just in case this is the lamest attempt at distraction anybody ever tried, and this guy's got friends trying to crawl up our backside?"

Daniel groaned. "You know how much snow is on top of that trap door?" But he was shrugging into his snow gear as he grumbled. He was hardly out the door when CJ came on the radio again. "You wanted to know what he did when he got to the lane? Nothing. Didn't so much as glance this way. Kept on walking."

"Huh." George was staring into middle distance. "Man walking a strange road, doesn't look to see what's down a side road? That make any sense? Where did this fucker come from, and what is he doing?"

"Well, he's gone now. Can't see him any more."

George started to pace up and down the great room. "Walking in plain sight. Leaving tracks like billboards. Could somebody that dumb have survived this long?"

Brian was similarly agitated, but didn't pace. "Well, obviously he has. So he's not dumb. He had a reason for doing that. He's probably not alone, either."

"I'm gonna track him."

"Hold on, George, don't you think that's kind of obvious? Like, what he'd expect? Hell of a way to find out where his friends are."

"I'm not going to walk into an ambush. I'm gonna find out where that sucker lives."

"And leave tracks like billboards leading right back here?"

"Brian. Please." George shrugged into his outdoor gear and some snow-camo overalls, grabbed an AR-15 from the rack and was at the door when the radio squawked.

"He's coming back!"

We all stood there looking at each other as CJ reported that the lone walker returned, unhurried, whence he had come. George slipped out the door. The rest of us chewed on what had happened. Who was he? Where had he come from? Was he alone or part of a group? What were his intentions? Of course without more evidence we had no way of answering any of these questions, and of course we could not stop ourselves from asking them of each other, over and over again. I thought I had a clue about a few of the answers, but held my peace.

When George returned a couple of hours later, in the very last of the day's cold light, he had little to add. The man's tracks had emerged from a stream bed, where it went under the road through a culvert, and had returned to the stream bed at the same place. George had gone nearly a mile up the stream but had not been able to see where the man had accessed the stream. "He's either very good at this shit," as George put it, "or he's a ghost."

The animated conversation continued, as pointless and circular as a hamster's wheel, while we ramped up the night's activities, stoking the stoves and starting the cooking. It was quite a while before Brian noticed I had not been participating. "Pops? You got something?"

Everybody got quiet. "Maybe. Just a guess, really. A series of guesses. I think he represents another group. I think they know about us, probably have for some time."

This offended George. "How? There hasn't been anybody anywhere near us, especially since it's been snowing. We check all the time."

"Thas' right." Billy spoke up from the corner. He was our ranger, especially since winter had set in. He disappeared most days early in the morning and sometimes did not come in until after dark. We had no idea where he went.

"No offense, guys, but I think they know. And I think the line in the snow is a proposed boundary between us and them."

"Bull shit!" George erupted. "They think they can waltz in here and tell us we can't cross the road?"

"C'mon, George," Brian cut in, "just listen for a minute, will you? In all the time we have been coming here we have never, ever crossed that road."

George muttered as I continued my guesswork. "I think he's trying to open negotiations without putting us on the defensive. That business of not looking at us, as if he were saying, 'Go ahead and keep pretending you're invisible, if you want, I'll play along.' I think he'll be back tomorrow, to see how we respond."

Brian was intrigued. "And how should we respond?"

That's what I'd been mulling over when he had started asking me questions. "I think at first light we should draw a line in the snow, just this side of his line. Leave our footprints there, opposite his."

"Beautiful," Brian grinned, "ball returned to his court, in bounds. Let's do it."

George regarded me balefully. "Then can I shoot him?"

Brian went over and slapped him on the shoulder. "George, go to your room and play with your guns. The grownups are going to handle this one." Laughing, they went out back for wood to stoke the stoves.

At noon the next day our new friend appeared, now using his branch as a walking stick, not a marker, and with something else strapped to his back in addition to the shotgun. When he saw the long line we had drawn in the snow parallel to his, he nodded. He stopped, nearly opposite the entrance to the lane, and unslung the tubular package from his back. He unwrapped it, unfolded it, and plopped it down in the snow, on the line, facing us. A camp chair. Then he left.

So our discussion, long into the night, was whether to do the meeting, and whom to send. Nobody really argued against the obvious conclusions: of course we would meet, and of course it would be me, the most expendable among us, who would appear. George, of course, tried to insist that he and Brian set up on the ridge opposite ours to guard against an ambush or attack. I was vehement in my opposition. "We just agreed, symbolically, to accept a boundary between us. So the first thing we do is break that agreement? Great way to begin, guys."

George yielded. He and Brian would watch over me from the OP. From then on, the discussion was all about what might be said, and how we might answer, and what his answer might be, and on and on. Pretty pointless, I thought, and I went to bed.

The morning came up clear and cold and calm. The snow cover was not thick, but it was everywhere, diamond-hard in the cold and diamond-bright in the sunlight that came roaring down from an empty sky. I walked out the lane toward noon, wearing sunglasses to ward off snow blindness and a parka against the cold, my footsteps crunching loudly in the still glare that made the woods look like an overexposed, black-and-white photograph. I went to a spot opposite his camp chair, shook out my own, and plopped down to wait.

It wasn't long before I heard him coming. I stood and faced him, so he could see my hands were empty. Like him, of course, I carried a shotgun, slung. We still occasionally saw packs of feral dogs, and every once in a while of feral pigs, that were very hungry and seemed not to have much fear of humans.

He came on without pausing, on his side of the line, until he was directly opposite me. Then he faced me, whipped off high right glove, and stuck out his hand. "Jared MacGyver. Congratulations on making it through."

The man was a greyhound, about my height, six feet, but lean. His grip was pure iron, without being aggressive. Pale blue eyes regarded me from a face bristling with salt-and-pepper beard that had been hacked short. I realized I still had my sunglasses on, and whipped them off to respond to his greeting.

He stepped back involuntarily, as if hit by an electric shock. "My God!!" he said. I looked around to see what on earth the matter was. "William Trent! Mr. President, sir! Good Lord, is this a government installation?"

I had lived so long, and come so far, since I had last thought of myself as the President that I was momentarily discombobulated. "No, no," I said, waving my hands as if to ward off bees, "No, I'm not ... I was out of government long before ... all this ... happened. No, this is family."

"Well. You gave me quite a start, Mr. President. The last thing I expected. Well. Let's see if I can get my mind back on business. Will you sit, Mr. President?"

"Sure." And we did. "But Mr. MacGyver, please don't bother with the Mr. President stuff. I used to endure it because it showed respect for the office. But the office is gone. And the country is gone. And it's William Trent, just William, please."

MacGyver slouched in his camp chair, looking like a drawn bow, and regarded me for a moment. "Begging your pardon, sir, but I wasn't using the title to show respect for the office, I was doing it to show respect for you. You gave us a chance to avoid all this, you threw your career, your office, your good name into a fight you knew you could not win. If you do not want to be addressed as a former president, that's your right, sir, but you will never be just William. Not to me. Sir."

"Well." Something was making me tear up a little, I guess the strong light was getting to me. I wanted to put my sunglasses back on, but knew it would be impolite. "Thank you. As you wish."

He sat for another minute, composing himself. "Now." He began briskly. "We are a group from over there," he gestured over his left shoulder, toward the northwest. "You are a group from over here." He pointed over my left shoulder. to the southeast. "We have agreed on this informal boundary between our areas. Right so far?"

"Right. How many of you are there?"

"We'll not get into that just yet. If you don't mind. Sir."

"Okay. Try this, then. How did you know we were here?"

He thought carefully. "Let's just say that we command a view of this mountain, and all of its hollows. Your smoke security has been good, but not perfect. And that firefight you had back in the fall was a pretty good clue."

"So you waited a long time before reaching out to us. Why?"

"We wanted to be sure about you. And, really, about us. We've had a lot to do, as I'm sure you have. And having got this far, we think we're going to make it, and we imagine you do, too."

"So what do you want from us?"

"What makes you think we want anything?"

"You initiated this meeting."

"Not because we need anything from you. Because we both need to take the next step."

"Which is?"

MacGyver sighed. "Mr. Pres – Mr. Trent, I understand your caution, but I am hoping you will join me in this conversation pretty soon. Look. You know as well as I, better in fact, that what we have managed to do – survive the end of the world as we knew it – was the easy part. Now, if what we have been through is to have any meaning, we have to put the world back together."

It was my turn to sigh. "Yes, I know. We have to get it right, don't we?"

"Yes. We do." He looked off into the distance for a moment. "You are the leader here?"

"Naw, I'm the guy they send out into the open alone to see if there's any danger." He didn't seem to think that was especially funny. "Really, we don't have an anointed leader. We have a guy who takes charge when there's fighting to be done. The guy who saw this coming first, and led us here, is influential, of course. But we try to insist that any major decision is unanimous."

"Hm. We elected officers, the old way. But we have renounced the ownership of private property. Of anything beyond personal effects – clothes, tools, that sort of thing. We are determined not to feed the greed. We think that's what brought the old world down, basically, letting the greed run. We don't want anything to do with the hoarding of personal wealth."

"Huh. Well, we haven't explicitly dealt with that idea, but actually, now that I think of it, we live that way. As if the place belonged to all of us. You know, I've been thinking a lot lately about the native people who were here when the white man came. I've been thinking that what they were doing was successful for ten thousand years, while it took us only 500 years to blow it all up. Maybe we should have talked to them, before we wiped them out."

"And what would we have learned?" MacGyver looked skeptical.

"Well, the unanimous decision thing, and the shared leadership. It drove the British completely nuts, not being able to deal with a single person, and having to wait forever for a decision."

"I think it might drive me nuts, too, trying to get unanimous agreement on everything."

"Well, you have to have the context. You have to have a group that is not divided, by race or gender or class or possessions, so that people will not have any need to work at cross purposes."

"You think we could live like that?"

"I think we should learn from that. It's one thing to live in our – what? Villages? Tribes? – and work things out with our family and friends. But could we extend it, say, to a country? Well, the Iroquois Confederacy did it, over about a third of North America. Are there any more of us, do you think? In North America?"

"We're in touch with 10 groups now."

The answer startled me. "Really? How? Where are they?"

"Ham radio. One of our members was a hobbyist, insisted on setting up a solar-powered rig. At one time there were nearly 20 communities in touch, but half of them have signed off. They won't say where they are, could be anywhere."

"Why won't they say where they are?"

"Some of them think the government is still out there, listening, planning to take things over again. Some of them think the United Nations, or the Chinese Army, or somebody, is trying to map them. They're like us, they don't know what's going on ten miles away from them."

"Have you seen any signs of other people in this area?"

"We've seen wisps of smoke to the north, and to the east. Maybe people, maybe not. Too far away to matter, right now."

"But we matter."

"Yes."

"Why is that?"

MacGyver sighed. "Now we are playing dumb again. You know very well."

"Children, you mean."

"Of course. We didn't come through all this just to die off slower than everybody else. Which is what we'll do if we just huddle in our compounds. We have to reach out, get organized, start having intercourse again."

"You mean social intercourse."

"Hell, no. I mean sex!"

We laughed for a minute, as friends do. But we were getting cold, sitting there, and I felt it was time to sum up. "So you came here to see if we were interested in, um, social intercourse, in starting to put things back together."

"Exactly."

"I will take it to my people. But I'm pretty confident we're ready."

"Excellent."

"When do we meet again?"

"Five miles north of here, on the main road, there's an old gas station and restaurant. Room for a good sized group to sit around and talk. Bring two or three of your people, a week from today, about dark. We'll fire up the stove and talk."

27. INDIAN WINTER

The idea that had been tweaking at the edges of my mind for months, that had emerged into my discussion with MacGyver, now took over my waking thoughts. It seemed to me we had before us a map for refashioning our lives and our society, for keeping them out of the ruts that had led the world to disaster. Okay, that's not quite right. I didn't have a map, but I thought I knew how to begin drawing one. I laid out the whole idea for the first time at our gas-station meeting with MacGyver's group.

It was a bitter winter day in late January, the whole world shades of stainless steel behind charcoal-sketched trees. Swollen clouds billowed low overhead like squadrons of airships off to snow-bomb a distant enemy, while the northwest wind lashed everything with barbed whips of frozen air.

Patsy, Brian and I went. We had debated long and hard over who should attend, deciding in the end that I had to go because I had started the conversation, Brian was our founder and chief strategist, and that there should be a female among us, none better than Patsy with her practical, no-nonsense approach to everything. MacGyver's people must have had similar thoughts, because he brought his wife – as thin and tightly coiled a whippet as he was, a woman whose eyes darted constantly around as if she were deeply afraid of everything – along with a man he identified as the vice president of their group, John Stockman. Stockman was, well, stocky, a blunt block of a man who, alongside the MacGyvers, was a dour bulldog between tense greyhounds.

"If John is vice president," I said to MacGyver, "I suppose, then, to be correct, I should address you as Mr. President."

He laughed and his wife tittered uncertainly, as if someone might find it inappropriate. "We voted for you, Mr. Trent," she said, "It's such a pleasure to meet you." Stockman smiled like it hurt him, and glared at me as if he thought I might be faking my own identity.

We chatted for awhile about our situations. Brian gave them a brief history of the Farm and how we came to be there. Stockman wanted to know about the attack, where it came from and how we had fended it off, and Brian told the story in an abbreviated and general way.

They told us that they occupied an old farm about five or six miles as the crow flies to the northwest, fifty or so acres of cleared fields far back into a hollow, reached by a single road that was easily closed and defended. The property included an old fire tower on a high ridge that gave them a superb observation platform. They had not been attacked, they said, but had been ready, and had been apprehensive that the gunfire they heard from our location meant marauders were coming their way. I got the impression, although everyone was still being careful not to give too much away, that there were more people in the MacGyver group than in ours.

We talked in general terms about what we expected of each other, and it soon became obvious that we were of the same mind. We intended to continue our lives as we had laid them out, had no desire to interfere with each other, and indeed did not see much reason to have much to do with each other except in a social way. We talked about our informal boundary, and the fact that as we did not need to defend it from each other, we could concentrate on looking outward, them to the north and west, us to the south and east, to watch for aggression or activity. We talked about the possibility of sending out scouting expeditions to search for more settlements.

It was then, when we were talking about what we might say to a new contact somewhere out there, that I laid out the vision I was developing about how we might shed the destructive baggage of the old world and nurture a new and sustainable way of living. We couldn't just forbid greed and exploitation and hoarding and all the things that had brought the old world down, we had to live in such a way that such things would be unthinkable. If our world was going to be renewed, it had to be new from the ground up, and I told them, briefly, how I thought we might do it.

There was a long silence when I had finished. Even Brian and Patsy were a little taken aback, because although we had often talked about the subject, I had never presented them with my argument, because I hadn't really formulated it until, well, that moment. So no one had really reacted to it, until John Stockman did.

"Jesus Christ on a crutch! You want us to live like a bunch of savages? Why don't we just crawl back into caves and forget we invented fire?"

I had expected the back draft to start this way. "John, when we got into the habit of calling them savages, it was because they did not dress like us, they did not have the weapons we had and they didn't pursue wealth like we did. We were wrong then, and it's wrong now."

"God Damn! They scalped us! They butchered women and children! What the fuck are you talking about?"

I kept my voice low and even. "Tell me how it's possible, John, to be as angry as you are right now over things that happened centuries ago?" He was red-faced, seemed to be having difficulty breathing. "You know why? Because our people kept the rage stoked, all this time. Reviling them was the only way we could forgive ourselves for what we did to them. It was genocide, John and we did it to them. Not the other way around.

"But look. That doesn't matter now. I'm not talking about reliving what happened back then, I'm talking about how we live now. How do we keep from doing everything all over again? Are we going to run out now and start the cars up and figure out how to make gas and keep on burning up the world? Are we going to go out and find the money lying around and put it back in circulation and start hoarding it? Divide ourselves up into rich people and poor people? Or are we going to try something different? We have to decide! Now, at the beginning!"

"Well, shit!" John had come down off his rage a little, but was still sputtering. "Sounds like you want us to run out and make arrows and war paint."

"No. That's not what I want. But it's for another time." I stood, grinning, to show that although I wanted to pause the discussion, I didn't think it was over and I certainly didn't feel beaten. We shook hands all around and I drifted toward the pile of coats on a table next to the door.

MacGyver quickly maneuvered to my side, so that we were a little way off from the others and facing away from them. "I understand," he said quietly, "that you have a doctor among you?"

"A medic. CJ is his name. Well. What we call him."

"John's wife," he said even more quietly, "is very sick. Bedridden for the last three weeks. Is it possible do you think, that your man could take a look at her?"

"I'll ask him."

"I think it's urgent. Could I come and get your answer tomorrow, at dark? And if he agrees, take him to her?"

I thought about that for a minute. "That's a lot of traveling."

"Yes," was all he said.

I thought about it some more. "I don't imagine there will be any objection, but we'll have to discuss it. And – no disrespect – I don't think he should go alone."

"Of course. I'll come about an hour after dark, tomorrow. To find out what you've decided."

As he started to turn away, something else struck me. "Wait a minute. I notice it's not John asking. Is he going to be all right with this?"

"Sure. He's scared to death. They've been together a long time. He's a good, solid man, but he never has been very good at handling emotions."

We headed out then, everyone amicable except for John, who I suspected was seldom amicable, and we agreed to gather again in a few weeks, this time with each of us bringing six people.

To be out of the room, I soon found, was not to be out of the cross hairs. The wind that had fought us at every step on the way here, filming our eyes with tears, trying to turn our coats into sails, now shoved and poked and slapped our backs, trying to make us run.

It did not deter Brian from coming alongside and opening fire.

"Hey, Dad! Quite a departure from the unanimous-consent rule in there."

"How so?"

"I don't recall us deciding we were going to be missionaries. I thought we were going to have a general conversation, see what's what, and leave it at that."

"Well, I didn't plan to get into that. But it was only my opinion."

"Your opinion! You were representing all of us in there! And I'm not sure we're ready to start living like Indians!"

"What do you mean?"

"I mean all that First People stuff you're talking about. I'm not at all sure we want to do that, let alone persuade anybody else to do it."

"Brian, we're already living exactly like that. I'm not talking about changing anything we're doing. Think about it. We don't have managers, or police, or officers, or money. What we have, we have together, what we do, we do because it's what we need to do. I don't want to change anything. I want to articulate it, affirm it, so the old ways never come back. Brian, if we don't make this effort, we'll turn into the same people we were before, grasping and competitive and money-hungry. We have to help each other not do that. That's what I'm trying to figure out here."

"Huh." Brian was quiet after that, until we got home and put supper on the table, and then we wrangled it all over again until dawn came and I could flop into bed, exhausted. There was something about comparing the way we were living to the way the Native Americans lived that offended a lot of people, and I knew I was going to have to find a way to get around that if I was going to make any headway.

"Look," I tried as we gathered for breakfast the next evening, "we don't have to worry about going back to the Stone Age, we're already there. This stuff of ours, the hydro generator, the solar panels, even the tools, they're all going to wear out, and we don't have any way of making new ones. I mean, technology is gone, and we're curling our lips at the idea of learning something from people who lived this life successfully? What's up with that?"

Patsy had been subdued throughout the discussions of the previous night, apparently working something out for herself. Now she spoke up. "I think it's the whole idea of going back. I mean, we've been conditioned to think that everything is always being reinvented. Including ourselves. 'Progress is our most important product.' 'We can make a smarter planet,' remember that one? For our whole lives it's been Up! and Onward! and More! and Newer! We're just not wired to consider a step down, or backward, as a good thing. Never mind suggesting that we – we! – have something to learn from primitive people."

I realized she'd been working hard on this. "So how do we do it, Patsy? How do we get people to think that way?"

"Some people never will. You'll just have to wait until they die. Others are going to get it after a while. But they're really going to have to kill off a big part of who they were."

"Has it been so hard, living the way we do here?"

"No, but in the back of your mind it's always, like, one day the lights are going to come back on. Or somebody's going to drive in the lane and say come on out, the party's back on. You know? It really hasn't sunk in yet, that the world's gone. Part of what's going on is, you're asking us to face it. And we don't want to."

I got her point. It was a good one. "But you know what's going to happen if we don't face it, and deal with it? Something like this: We're going to have some kind of social event with the MacGyver group. And Red will take along some shots of his potato vodka, which they probably don't have. And some of the fellows over there will ask him to make them some, and offer him things in trade. And pretty soon he'll be wanting to run his still instead of doing the work we need done. And he'll need a safe place for the stuff he's getting in trade. And in a year or so he'll want a patch of ground of his own to grow potatoes for his business. He'll be accumulating wealth, an entrepreneur,"

"Sounds good to me," said Red, with a grin. "What's the downside?" He said it like he was kidding. But he wasn't.

"The downside is, it starts the whole vicious circle all over again. Your interests become different from the interests of the people you're living with. You start to accumulate stuff. You set yourself and your possessions apart. You're depriving us of some of your attention and caring and work. Does that harm us? You don't care because you're accumulating lots of stuff. And how about the people you're selling to – were some of them recovering alcoholics back in the world, and did you just help them go back to a place they never needed to see again? You don't care, you've got your stuff. And away we go."

"Oh." Red had stopped grinning. "Other than that, though, it would be okay?"

"What would be okay is, we all talk about what we're going to take to the social. We talk about whether it would be a good idea to introduce alcohol, and I would think we'd want to know them pretty well before we took the risk. And if they did like it, and wanted more, then we would all decide how much, and when, and we would all benefit from whatever was given in trade."

Brian was squirming. "Dad, you know, that first scenario, it's so ingrained in us to go into business, to better ourselves. I mean, you were describing it and I'm thinking, yeah, some of us will become blacksmiths, and we'll need millers, and of course they should be paid for what they do. How do you even get to a place where that doesn't seem right?"

George was at the table, scowling down at his hands clenched in front of him. "You become a Communist."

"Communist!" I looked at him, incredulous. "Is that what we've been, these past few months, what you all have been for years, working on this place? Communists?"

"Sounds like it, the way you describe it."

"George, for God's sake. We worked out a way to live together and survive. I could also describe it so it sounds exactly like the early Christians. Or Uigher Chinese Muslim communities in Xinjiang. What does it matter what it sounds like?"

"It matters. I spent a good part of my life in the military, fighting for my country. Now it sounds to me like you want to betray everything we stood for."

"George, with all due respect, horse shit. I speak as a former commander in chief of the military you served. And I am here to tell you that when you were in Iraq, as admirable as your service was in terms of courage and loyalty, you were not defending your country of fighting for it. You were a mercenary in service to American oil companies."

George came halfway out of his chair. "Ex president or not, I think I'm going to whip your ass."

Wearily, I motioned him back down. "No, you're not, George. Listen. The military you served is gone. The country we served is gone. It's just us now. Patriotism for a dead country isn't going to help us now. Hatred for Communists or terrorists or Jews or black people – it's all pointless. It needs to be in the grave with all that other crap. We have to get on with it."

Brian had got a far off look that told me he was chasing a big idea. He paid no more attention to George's threat than I had. "You know," he said tentatively after a while, "Patsy said something about waiting for the people who cling to the old ideas to die. But what if we could kill off the ideas? Maybe we should have some kind of ceremony, a funeral for all the old ways of thinking."

"Huh." I was intrigued. "Ritual."

"Yeah!" Brian was getting animated now. "You know, one of the things that was just gone from our lives, back in the world, was ritual that had any meaning. Because nobody believed in anything. Even the people who went to church just snored through it, there was no real connection with their lives. And weddings. Don't get me started. White dresses for purity? Rice for fertility? Veils for modesty? Eternal vows of faithfulness and then six months later, hey, I didn't sign up for this? Give me a break.

"But what if we had real rituals, that signified something important, that helped us focus on beliefs that all of us shared. That might be intense."

"I think," I said mildly, "that was what they were supposed to be. Originally."

"A funeral for the old ways." He was designing it, in his head.

"What about real religion?" CJ wanted to know. I knew that he and Juanita were devout Catholics. "You going to throw that out too?"

"CJ, please. I'm not trying to give orders here, or to make decisions for everybody. I'm trying to feel out a way we can live together in a new way. I don't want to trash religion, I want anyone who has one to bring it forward, into his life, share it with everybody. I just don't want him telling me that I have to worship like he does or I'll go to hell. And I hope he won't go off one day a week, to a special house set aside from everyone else, to worship. We can be with each other and with our God, each in our own way, at the same time. I remember reading that a Jesuit missionary asked an elder of one of the Iroquois Confederacy tribes what his religion was. The old man asked for a lot of clarification about what a "religion" was, and finally said, 'I don't have a religion. I have a life.'"

"Huh. Well. What about this medical call we're gonna make? You want me to get some rattles and drums? Do a little dance?"

"What I'd like is for you to find a real sense of humor somewhere, and transplant it." Then a thought hit me, and I stared at him, turning it over.

Made him nervous. "What?"

"Well, there is one thing along those lines I think you should consider."

"Aw, Pops, I ain't gonna wear no feathers."

"No, better. A white coat. You have a white coat? Tell me you have a white coat."

CJ was bewildered. "A white coat? Well, yeah, maybe I got one in the back of the closet from when I worked at the hospital. Was gonna use it for rags."

"Get it."

"What the hell, Pops? What difference a white coat gonna make?"

"All the difference. You made me think of it when you mentioned the stuff a medicine man used, the drums and rattle and paint. You know why he did that? Because they were symbols of his power, symbols the people used in all their relations with the spirit world. They were familiar with them , and they believed in them, believed in the man who wielded them. Now, obviously, we don't have any such belief system, except for those who believe in miracles, and I'm not saying there's anything wrong with that, CJ, I'm just saying there aren't very many.

"But what symbolizes the power of the doctor to heal us? The white coat. And to the extent we believe in our doctor, we are helped by him. Or her. Now, we don't have an operating room, or a stocked pharmacy. And you're not a surgeon, or an internist. You're a medic, and if it turns out you can help John's wife that's great. But what I think is that you'll be more effective – you'll help her more – if she believes in you. And chances are that when she sees your white coat, and you have one of those thingies, what do you call them? Stethoscopes? hanging around your neck, she is going to believe!"

"AWK! AWK! AWK! AWK! AWK!"

Even though we were expecting it, the klaxon alarm released unbelievable amounts of adrenaline, standing all our hair on end. Jacob was on OP duty, and he knew he didn't have to do it. He needed a sense-of-humor transplant, too.

"Jacob, goddammit," George yelled into the radio when he got to it. "Why'd you do that?"

"Got a man coming up the lane, Dad."

"I figured that. We're expecting MacGyver."

"I know. Thought you'd like to know he's on a horse, and he's leading two others."

George and Brian and I exchanged glances. "They got horses?" Brian said quietly. "Wonder what else they're keeping to themselves?

CJ looked a little ill. "Horses?" he said weakly.

George was more emphatic. "I didn't sign up for any fuckin horses."

"Don't worry, George," Brian grinned. "Just explain to the horse that if he does anything you don't like, you'll shoot him."

CJ looked even more ill as he stood up and headed for the stairs. "I gotta go find my white coat and my face paint," he moaned.

They were quite a sight as they departed the yard, MacGyver leading at a brisk trot. CJ reminded me of a monkey I had seen in some circus clinging desperately to the back of a greyhound. George, on the other hand, was a grim-faced pile driver, rising up and falling on the horse with sledgehammer blows. MacGyver glanced back, saw what he was dealing with, and slowed to a walk. He looked a little discomfited. The trip was going to take longer than he thought.

More than twice as long. It was four miles north to Mathias, then four miles west. Since he could go no faster than a walk, it took two and a half hours to reach the jumble of downed trees across the road, ten feet high, that required them to enter a narrow passage, single file, double back sharply, then turn again to exit the other side – all under the view of manned platforms in the trees a short distance away.

Then it was another mile before they came to a large building on the left – the administration building of the old Lost River State Park. "Really?" said George, "You guys took this over? Cool!" They could see cabins salted away in the woods along the continuation of the road they were on, George thought there must be a couple dozen of them, and in the distance a huge horse barn with a paddock alongside. Well-used snow trails indicated that most of the cabins were in use. George thought there must be 50 people here, at least, but they were staying out of sight.

In the main room of the Admin building, in front of a huge stone fireplace with a fire made with dry oak and kept so hot it made no smoke, John Stockman waited for them. His wife, he said, was in a bed they had put in one of the offices behind him. CJ, groaning with every step he took on his battered legs, made himself ready and went in.

CJ told us later that Mrs. Stockman was riddled with some kind of cancer and was definitely terminal. But on the other hand, she brightened visibly when he entered the room, wearing his white coat. "Oh, thank God," she said, tears welling from her eyes, "a doctor at last."

CJ felt a little embarrassed, but played the part as he took her vitals and looked her over. "Am I going to die, Doctor?" she asked weakly.

"Not any time soon, my dear. I'm going to give you some medicine that's going to make you feel better." And he did – a small jar of an infusion, based on Red's potato vodka, of ginger, cayenne and white willow bark to ease her pain and nausea. Murmuring reassuringly, CJ limped out of the room.

"Is she gonna die, doc?" Once again it was MacGyver asking the questions. John Stockman sat glumly near the fireplace, seemingly unable to speak.

"Yeah. Pretty soon." As a battlefield and accident-scene medic, CJ had had little practice dealing with the next of kin. His bluntness sucked all the oxygen from the room for a minute. "Sorry I couldn't do anything."

Nevertheless, as we would learn, his attendance on Mrs. Stockman buoyed her considerably, and for most of her remaining days she was alert, in reasonably good spirits (nipping frequently at her little jar, which we replaced twice) and in only moderate pain. When she died, she died well, at peace and in the company of her people. There were no beeping machines, no brusque strangers sweeping in and out of the sterile, foreign room, and no lifelong debt for the survivors. Just a passing, made a little easier by a white coat.

28. VISION QUEST

"I'm going to go on a vision quest."

"What did you say, Pops?" Brian was helping Patsy make breakfast, scrambling eggs at the wood stove, and I was seated at the big table. It was morning. We had said to hell with the upside-down living, sleeping in the daytime and working at night, the chances that there was anybody to see our smoke were too small, and the disruptions of nocturnal life were too big.

"Okay, not a vision quest. I just want to go out in the woods for a while. Get the peace of the woods, think this thing through."

"Pops, it's still February. You'll freeze your ass off. What thing?"

"The way of life thing. The Indian thing. I know what I think about it but I'm not getting it across. I'm not doing it the right way, and I need to. So I'll do what they did when they needed to get it right."

"Wouldn't you be more comfortable thinking in your room? We'll leave you alone."

I drew breath for an irritated reply, but I saw he was grinning. We had hunted together, after all. He knew the peace of the woods, knew exactly what I was looking for.

"Tell you what," he continued. "Before you go, let's try that ceremony I've been working on."

"That born-again thing?"

"I wish you would not call it that. It's a funeral for the old ways, a christening of the new person. I'm thinking of it as a Waking ceremony. I'd be interested to see how it goes over."

"Who's gonna be your first guinea pig?"

"You."

"Oh."

"Best case, it'll set you up for your quest. And there is no worst case."

So we did it that evening after supper. Everyone gathered in the great room, seated in a big circle around the table, a few feet back from it. There was a lot of giggling and self-consciousness, especially on my part when Brian made me climb up on the table and stretch out on my back. I was to close my eyes and look as if I was in my coffin. "You know," I said to him, "when you reach a certain age this sort of thing loses its appeal."

"Yeah, yeah." He waited for everybody to get over the silliness, finish with the wisecracks. He doused most of the lights except for some candles on the table near my head. "Look," he said then, "this is a meditation for all of us, focused right now on Dad. It's an exercise to put our minds on what we've lost, and what we've gained, and how we're going to go on from here. So shut up, pay attention, and try to get something out of this."

By this time Julie and Juanita had a hopeless case of the giggles, and Brian just waited, looking disgusted, until they snuffled into silence. Then he nodded to CJ. CJ began to strum his guitar, a single, minor chord, over and over, at the rhythm of a heartbeat. That's when something came into the room.

Brian waited for a minute, then another. I went to another place, not sleep, far from it, but a place where there was nothing but my strumming heartbeat and that visitor, listening. Finally, Brian spoke. His voice was sonorous and powerful, and he weaved it around the cadences of the guitar.

"William Trent died with the world.

He was president of the United States, commander of vast and far flung forces, but his power died;

He was a citizen of the United States, and believed his country would do no wrong, but his country did wrong, and died because of it;

He was a wealthy man, who paid a heavy price for the cash that he could put away from others, but his money died;

232

He was a proud man, proud of his achievements, but his pride did not survive.

Who lives now?
A man lives, who hears the song of the red-tailed hawk and feels his soul lift and fly with it;
A man lives, who begins and ends each day with his family and needs no other people;
A man lives, who learns something new about the ground he walks every day, and needs no other place;
A man lives, who knows he is in the world not on it, a part of it not in charge of it, with many brethren of all kinds, and has no right to take more than he needs.

William Trent is dead.
William Red Hawk is alive in a new world."

As he concluded he walked over to the table, took my hands and helped me sit up, then swing my legs over the side and stand. I came back to the room as if from a far place, where I had heard the piping of the red-tailed hawk in the warm company of the friendly presence who had come into our room but had now withdrawn. Everyone else in the room, like me, shook themselves back into the present as if from a deep sleep. Nobody knew what to say. Except CJ.

"You think we could throw in a few more chords next time, man? That is one boring gig."

We laughed the nervous laughter of people who did not quite know what to make of what we had just experienced. None of us expected the power with which it had touched us. It was just Brian, after all, fooling around. So we had thought, until something else came into the room.

"That was peaceful," Patsy offered at last, "Will you do me next, Brian?"

"Sure, Patsy. Another time."

The next day I made my preparations. Not much food, just some deer jerky and dried berries, fasting was part of the deal. Plenty of tinder and fatwood – making a fire in the snow is a bitch. Water, my mountain sleeping bag (I know, sleep deprivation is supposed t be part of the deal, too, but not at my age), a one-man tent, some "possibles," as mountain men used to call their miscellaneous gear. I told Brian where I was going to be and for about how long – I thought no more than four days. I wasn't a teenager hanging out in a summer dream, and if I wasn't back in four days I bloody well wanted someone to come and get me.

I slung my pack and a 30-30 carbine and headed up the stream bed at midday, with plenty of time to reach the spot I had in mind and make camp before dark. It was cold, but not dangerously so if you took care. About 10 degrees Fahrenheit. There were two or three feet of snow on the ground, on average, but it had been blown around so that there were deep drifts in some places and bare ground in others. In the open, especially near the stream, the surface had been beaten by the wind, then slightly melted and refrozen, until there was a gilding of ice on the drifts and rocks alike. A broken ankle begging to happen.

Among the trees the snow was deeper but loose, and while it was a labor pushing snow up to the knees, it was tolerable. I paused often, not because I needed to rest – certainly not! – but because I was cleverly avoiding sweating too much. Wet underclothes would be a bear to deal with later.

A couple of hours of this brought me to the top of the ridge, a couple of miles northeast of where the house was nestled against its western flank. I crossed over the crest and dropped down below it, for protection from the northwest wind, to where I knew there was a small flat with a special feature. Twin blue spruces towered over a level, rough circle no more than 30 feet in diameter. As I had expected, the downward-then-outward sweeping branches formed a large if somewhat leaky double-topped tipi, under which there was little snow and a thick mat of shed needles.

I shed my pack, sat down with my back against one of the massive trunks, drank some water and waited for my legs to stop trembling and my core to cool down a little. It was a delicious rest, but I could not wait long. Thick, cottony clouds had tumbleweeded in from the west, sapping the weak winter light and hinting of heavy weather to come. I strung a line between the two trunks and hung a poncho over it, lean-to fashion, to shelter my pack and possibles. I laid out the tent parallel to it and maybe eight feet away, rolled out my sleeping bag in it, laid the 30-30 alongside and then between the tent and the lean-to dug a little fire pit, found some rocks to put around it, and struck up a small blaze with my flint and steel. For the rest of the time I had before full dark, I gathered in firewood.

I boiled a small kettle of water, poured some into an old military canteen cup and threw in a pinch of dried dandelion root from Patsy's stores. Then I resumed my seat, leaned back on the spruce, held my hot tea to my face, and let the woods take me.

Silence and darkness, inextricably mingled, thickened around me. Time melted. The ancient tree and I watched, waiting, in our different time zones. A gentle snow started, coming straight down in the windless air. Far off in the hollow below, a snowy owl complained that he could not hunt. I sat in my yellow flickering globe of firelight under the spruce, a starship now, cast loose from the body of earth, bobbing on the tides that move the planets.

My body became light, and my eyelids heavy. After a few minutes, or a few hours, I crawled into the tent, wrestled off my boots and parka, and squirmed into the mountain bag. My eyes closed and my breathing slowed, but my journey continued.

When I opened my eyes again I did not know if a few minutes had passed, or a few hours. I poked my head out of the tent flap. I could see, but the light was diffuse, I didn't know if it was the moon or the sun behind the thick clouds. A sifting of new snow dusted my things and the fire pit; beyond the spruce branches it looked like new drifts had formed.

I heard a sound. A faint snuffling, coming closer. What in the world? Then I saw a gaunt form flicking through the trees, nose to ground, tail high. Wolf! Jesus! I leapt from the tent, standing in snow in my sock feet, gaping around to see if there were more. Just the one apparently. He kept circling, ten yards or so out from the spruce. I realized I had left the 30-30 in the tent, but the wolf did not seem aggressive. He seemed to be looking for something. He circled closer.

And then, in a little clearing where I could see him perfectly, he stopped dead, turned, and looked straight at me. That was no wolf. It was my dog.

"Beauty!" I yelled. An eruption of joy welled up in me and forced a fountain of tears from my eyes. I floundered toward her through the snow. She bowed low over her extended front legs, saying. "Oh, good, let's play," and bounded away. "No, Beauty, come!" But she was away, among dark trees, where I could barely see her, so I followed as best I could.

She was the only dog I ever had. For years she had been my best friend, playmate, protector, shadow. She was never disappointed in me. Just being with me made her deliriously happy, and she never wanted anything else. Then, when I was 12, she died.

I had never hurt so bad in my life, and never did again until Dottie died. Whenever I had thought of getting another dog, I had remembered that hurt, and could not do it. And now she was here!

But she wouldn't stop. I called her, and ran after her, until my throat was sore and my feet were so cold I couldn't feel them, and I couldn't see Beauty any more. I turned back. I had been crying for joy, but now deep sobs of despair wracked me. Why wouldn't she come? She had found me after all this time, why wouldn't she come? Hardly able to see, I somehow got a fire going, put on dry socks, got my boots on, slumped against the spruce tree.

Minutes passed, or hours, and then I heard something, and looked up, and there she came, bounding through the snow, leaping into my arms, frantically licking my face, her tail wagging so fast it looked like a propeller.

And I woke up. I guess that's what I did. It didn't occur to me until later, but I didn't wake up in my sleeping bag, but seated against the spruce tree, my boots on my cold feet, tears leaking from my eyes. A fire burning.

Anyway, there I was. I made a cup of dandelion tea, chewed a stick of jerky, and thought about my dream for a few hours, or a few days. And then I went home.

Brian was at the table in the great room, working intently on something that had a lot of small parts, I think it was off the hydro generator. He glanced my way as I came in. "Back already?"

"Yes," I said, "I am."

236

"That was fast. Did you have a vision?"

"Yes," I said. "I did."

He glanced at me again, curious about my flat tone. "You want to talk about it?"

"No," I said, "I don't."

"I thought that was part of the deal. You have a vision, then you come back and share it with everybody."

"That's when you're a teenager and you need guidance to interpret what you saw. I'm not, and I don't."

"Huh. Well, it didn't improve your mood any."

"That's not what it was for." I went to my room.

I wasn't in a bad mood, really, it was just that the explosions of emotions that I usually held closely in check had left me exhausted. I wanted to sleep, and reflect, and when I had done so I began to understand what I had seen. That I had....that...that I ..

29. THE NEXT CHAPTER

This is Julie, of the Red Hawk Clan. I have no maternal clan, because none of my mother's family survived the end of the Old World. Although I live with my husband and children now in Old Park (where Mr. MacGyver's people settled), I have been coming home to Mint Creek almost every day this year to record the history of the People as my grandfather William lived it. I decided to leave my transcript of his account as it is, to show how suddenly he left us. He was telling me about his night in the woods when he sort of hesitated, looked off a long way over my shoulder, whispered, "I see beauty," and was gone. Or maybe it was his dog Beauty that he saw. Anyway, he did not seem reluctant to go.

He was almost 90. He lived more than 20 years after the contact with MacGyver's people, and thought of those years as the most important of his life. I am sorry he was not with us long enough to tell the rest of the story. I will do my best to finish it.

After his retreat and vision, he became for a time quiet and withdrawn. He never again mentioned the ways of the Native Americans, unless someone asked him a direct question about them. This was confusing to my father, and Patsy and some of the others who had become almost convinced he was right about our returning to the way they had lived. And it was a while before he explained.

"What I saw out there," he finally said after supper one night (remember, we never knew what he had seen, until he told the story for this record) "taught me this: whatever it is you desire, do not chase it, but be still, and wait, and if it is right it will come to you.

"I realized that it is not right to imitate the ways of another people. For one thing, we really don't know that much about them, only scraps, mostly related by people who didn't understand what they were seeing. But more than that, people have to find their own way to react to the world they live in, they can learn from others, but their ways have to be authentic, born of their need, and not mimicked."

And so he no longer argued or advocated, he waited. After a while Patsy asked if she could have a Waking ceremony, and grandfather arranged it with my father. Once again, although no one took it particularly seriously at first, it was curiously moving, and left us all with the sense, as grandfather put it, of something in the room with us, something powerful and friendly.

After another while, CJ said he'd like to do it, and by spring we all had gone through it, had felt its odd power, and had taken the names of our spirit friends. For a long time before mine I had been seeing a fawn frequently in the woods. It seemed to me that I saw her whenever I was upset, or especially happy, and sometimes she seemed to peer at me as if trying to impart something. So I took Small Deer as my Waking Name. And it really was an awakening, for me anyway, to all the spirit friends around us, to all the many subtle connections we had with the great, friendly spirit that enfolded us all.

We began to see the people of Old Park more often, and the Waking Ceremony came up in conversation, and before too long one of them, I don't remember who it was, asked if they could have one, and then another, and so on. When Mr. MacGyver heard about it he called it "a bunch of superstitious nonsense" and forbade his people to have anything to do with our "pagan rituals," but lots of them did anyway.

The first great controversy between the towns was over a proposal, in the early summer of the year we met the people from Old Park, that we conduct a scouting and scavenging expedition to the Old World towns of Broadway and Timberville, some 20 miles to eastward, to gather things that might be useful to us and to see if any people were alive. It was Mr. MacGyver's idea, and he brought it to my grandfather one day early in June.

By that time, visits back and forth had become normal and frequent. On this day he and his son Johnny sort of wandered around the yard until they found grandfather and me trimming goats' feet. I was leading them up onto the stand and locking the stanchion while he checked and trimmed their hooves. I remember this visit mainly because it was the first time I noticed that Johnny, who was about my age, was looking at me a lot. And it was the first time I noticed how weird that made me feel.

"I've decided to take an expedition out east," Mr. MacGyver said in his bluff, no-nonsense way. "Thought you folks might want to take part."

Grandfather finished the foot he was working on, signaled to me to take the goat away to the pen, and sat down on the stand, wiping sweat from his eyes and flexing the hand that had been working the trimmer. "What kind of expedition?"

MacGyver explained what they wanted to do, take a pack-horse train east to see if anyone was around, and to gather such supplies and equipment as they might find. "Could use a couple of your guns along, especially that George fellow. 'Course we'll split what we find."

"Well," grandfather said slowly, "we'll council on it. Let you know."

"Council on it? Why don't you just decide?"

"Not the way we do things, Jared. We'll need to talk about it."

"What the hell?" Mr. MacGyver was more puzzled than angry. "Are you in charge here, or not?"

"I'm not. I've told you, we decide together."

"How in the world do you get anything done? Look, we're leaving in two days, if you can't make your mind up about it we'll just go without you." Mr. MacGyver turned as if to go.

"Well, that will be all right," said grandfather. "But we could council tonight. Why don't you stay for it?"

"Yes!" I thought to myself. "Yes! Stay!" I didn't care about any expedition, but I liked the idea of Johnny being around a while longer.

"What? Listen to a bunch of people hash over a simple yes-or-no question for hours on end? I've got better things to do."

"Maybe so. But if this expedition goes wrong for any reason, folks won't look back on it as a simple yes-or-no decision. That George fellow, as you call him, has quite a lot of experience moving around in hostile territory. So does Brian. Sit in, Jared. You might even like it."

Without losing his appearance of annoyance at the unnecessary dithering, Mr. MacGyver allowed himself to be persuaded. After supper (before which, Johnny and I managed to get in a long walk along the stream, an ordinary walk and talk that was thrilling to me in a way I had never known before) everyone gathered in the great room.

"Mr. MacGyver proposes," my grandfather began, "that we join him in a patrol to the east to check for survivors and to glean supplies and material."

For a long time no one spoke at all. We were comfortable with taking our time, but Mr. MacGyver got the squirms real bad. He acted like we were wasting his valuable time.

"Could be fun," Charles said at long last. "How many people?"

"We're sending five men with five pack horses." Mr. MacGyver was brusque like this was a done deal and time was being wasted.

"Deployed how?"

"What – two men riding unencumbered, the other three leading the pack horses."

"All together?"

"Of course."

"Not good. You have to have someone on point, 500 yards out, and two people on the flanks."

Mr. MacGyver was not used to being contradicted. He was getting red in the face, and his voice was getting more and more clipped. "We don't expect any trouble. We've been watching, and we don't think there's anybody out there."

"That's exactly what gets people killed."

Mr. MacGyver turned to my grandfather and sort of snarled, "Is he making this decision?"

"No," my grandfather answered amiably, "We are. Have you

read our military history, Jared? If you have, you know it's a long procession of people who weren't expecting trouble. General Braddock at Fort Duquesne, Custer at the Little Big Horn, Colonel Rall and his Hessians at Trenton in 1776. You know what they say about people who don't know their history." There was another quiet interlude, during which Mr. MacGyver's discomfort grew. "Billy, you look like you're chewing on something."

Billy, as always, was seated in the farthest corner of the room, scrunched down and inconspicuous, but as he had grown more comfortable with us, he had revealed a depth of knowledge about his natural surroundings, and a native common sense about things, that made him valuable to us in all our discussions. We just had to overcome his crippling shyness to get him to tell us what he thought, and with a stranger in the room he was even more reticent. "Well," he began reluctantly, "I'se just thinkin, lots of folks around here have – well, had – root cellars or store rooms with a year, two year's food in 'em. Could be folks like us in lots of places."

"Exactly." Brian joined in. "Except you know what, Billy, they're not like us. They likely won't have expected the breakdown, they won't have prepared for it. So they have until the food runs out and that's it. Now if they're good people, eating their own food, that's one thing. But if they're marauders, the lower the food gets, the antsier they'll get, looking for another stash. You don't want to walk into their world. Not yet. It's too soon."

Mr. MacGyver was simmering. On top of being contradicted, he was being contradicted by a simple man – we had told him Billy's story. Now it got worse, when a mere lad, Jacob, spoke up. "What I wonder about," he said, with no deference at all, "is what we have to gain? I mean, what do we need? That makes it worth risking a fight?"

"Yeah," said Patsy, standing as usual at the sink, her back propped against the counter, hurling her comment into the middle of the room like a mortar round, "and who's gonna keep up with the work around here with all you geniuses off looking for buried treasure? We got a garden going, guys, needs weeding and watering and bugs picked off."

"Oh, for Heaven's sake!" Mr. MacGyver exploded. "I heard a

child crying upstairs earlier. Should we see what it thinks, too?"

"Hey," Patsy shot back, "King Arthur. You want these guys traipsing all over the country, they're gonna need supplies, and you don't want to try getting into my pantries without my consent."

Grandfather was watching Mr. MacGyver's discomfiture with growing amusement, which he did little to conceal. "Jared." he said with a smile, "It doesn't look like you have the votes. Especially when we require unanimous consent."

"Good Lord! I don't understand how you people have survived this long." He stood up, then drew himself up farther, then seemed to swell. "I'm sorry I have wasted your time. And mine. Good evening to you."

He stamped out of the house and across the yard to where he had tethered his horse. Johnny followed, more slowly, looking embarrassed, and thoughtful. He managed to shoot me a long, despairing look before his father snapped, "John! Mount up!" Then they rode away into the night.

The story of his frustration, we learned later, spread through Old Park like a rash, mainly because of Johnny. When, two days later, Mr. MacGyver tried to order the expedition out, he faced something of an uprising, and he had to back down. Except that he ordered a patrol of his two top scouts to reconnoiter the towns and report back on what might be found there.

They never returned.

Mr. MacGyver was devastated by their loss. His confidence deserted him, his leadership faltered. "You see what happens," grandfather said, "when you make one man do all your thinking for you. It will disappoint you, and break him."

When his restive people demanded an election of new leaders, Mr. MacGyver did not resist, nor did he compete. There was much discussion of the way things were done in Mint Creek, and one of the candidates advocated involving everyone in decision-making. In the end, however, they elected Mr. Stockman, Mr. MacGyver's close friend and fellow authoritarian. But he realized that he presided over a people who were nearly equally divided between those who had won the election, and those who had lost it, and in order to heal the divide he began to invite more people into the decision making, to take more time and engage in more discussions before a decision was reached.

My grandfather was gratified by these events. "You see the way of Beauty," he said, rather enigmatically, "you see how the People assert themselves, calmly, until they are one. It is necessary only to wait."

Our daily life flowed steadily now, and our memory of the great dying receded until it seemed like a legend, a fantastical account of how the People came to be. With every month that passed it got harder to imagine the way we had been, and thought. Had we really accepted that people were supposed to leave home to "make a living," rather than staying home and making a life? That children were supposed to leave home to be educated by an industrial machine, for use in the industrial machine, rather than staying home and learning what they needed to know, when they needed to know it?

A young man from Old Park came to our house one day and asked my grandfather to teach him to be a leader. "No." was grandfather's immediate answer. "Only your people can make you a leader. It's not something you do for them, it's something they do for you. But we can talk, you and I, about what we think we know."

In the second winter of our new life, we found a new enclave of survivors. They were in a hollow 15 miles to the southeast, nestled in the mountains behind the little crossroads of Criders. They were people who had lived in the area, who had not prepared for the crash, but had reacted to it. They had not stockpiled, or set up energy systems, or prepared a garden large enough for their needs. They had had a very hard time of it, especially the first winter when five of their number died. But they were so far away from any large settlements that they had not been intruded upon, and had been able to prepare reasonably well for their second winter. Watchers from the fire tower at Old Park picked up their smoke several times that fall and early winter, and when the fall work was done an expedition went out to see who they were.

This time it was my grandfather who walked in front of their sentinels, drew the line in the snow and then waited. These folks were not as quick on the uptake as we had been, and it was three days before anyone took the challenge and came out to talk. My grandfather charmed them, organized help for them, asked their questions, and in the year to come knitted them into our little society.

By now my Dad and Pops – that's actually what we still called him – had devised a Sleeping Ceremony for funerals, a Harvest Song as a kind of thanksgiving, and a morning chant for beginning the day. They fashioned large hand drums, thin hoops two or three feet in circumference covered with tanned goat skin, whose sonorous, gong-like beat replaced the guitars (because there were only two guitars). Such ceremonies became a frequent, comforting accompaniment to our lives, and always made me feel secure and loved.

Another contact that winter didn't go so well. This group was holed up east of us, across two mountain ranges, near Orkney Springs. When grandfather set his camp chair on the line and sank into it, a rough voice called out from the woods, "Have you been born again, and do you accept Jesus Christ as your personal lord and Savior?"

When Pops hesitated, trying to think how to answer, the man screamed, "You are from the devil, sir, Satan himself!" And they opened fire. Pops left the camp chair behind. After a few more tries over the following weeks, with the same result (George said either they were just firing warning shots, or were terrible marksmen), we gave up, and left them alone. Within a year they had all gone to be with Jesus.

The years began to flow together. We adapted to the hotter summers and the stronger storms; we wore less, and built stronger (mostly bermed buildings now, showing only a hump of earth to the north and west). Some summers were very dry, and some winters brought little snow, but we did not suffer an extended drought and we worked hard on our water husbandry. We had to watch out for new things such as Africanized bees and fire ants, as well as for the now familiar threats from feral dogs and pigs.

No one had a career. People specialized, of course, George taught people military tactics and weapons use, CJ shared his medical knowledge, Kathryn held seminars on all the things you can get from a goat, people from Old Park taught horsemanship.

But no one profited from his or her knowledge, we all profited. We had no loners, no disaffected and sullen children, no drunks or psychotics or criminals. For that matter, we had no police, no judges, no managers. We were just people.

We began to speak differently. Our language gradually shed its technological references, its psycho-babble and money-speak, its Facebook glitziness and Twitter airiness. It became leaner, more direct and simple.

And every year there were more of us. Babies began to be born, mine and Johnny's among them. And we found new groups of survivors. My grandfather waited for each new contact like a spider waits in his web, patient and still, but keenly attuned to any flutter in his farflung strands.

The day came, a few years before his death, when there were seven towns in communication, at various stages of melding into the same kind of people. The idea spread to have a congress, to celebrate our union and talk about our future. It was held in the fall, at Old Park (because they had a great meeting hall) and nearly a hundred people came. The first thing they heard was my grandfather's speech of welcome, which has become sacred among us as the Oration of Red Hawk at the First Congress of the People.

When he died, there were two hundred people at his Sleeping Ceremony, and my father read his words again. With them I will close this account of how we came through the great tribulation and became the People.

The Oration of Red Hawk
at
The First Congress of the People

My friends: I have been an old man in two worlds. In the old world, I lived among people who had more luxury than any people in the history of the world. Like them, I did not know that after a while we would have to pay dearly for that luxury. In that world, I held in my hands more power than anybody ever did before. Yet I could not save my people, or my country, from paying the terrible price.

That is a burden that I have grown tired of carrying, and that

I will be pleased to lay down one day soon. I have lived enough.

But here I am, an old man in a new world, carrying my burden of memory, yet able to see to the east a great light growing. Able to see the people, at one with each other, at one with the earth, springing up like grass in spring. And if these old eyes do not deceive me, I see a way before the people, leading to a shining place, where they can stay. I am here with one foot in the old world, one in the new, and maybe only from this place can the path be seen. If that is so, I must tell you what I see. Then you can decide what to do.

I see that we have resolved to occupy ourselves with our families, in the places where we live, to nurture them and raise them and grow old with them and never leave them. And our families have resolved to stay with us, to ease us through sickness and old age and into death. And I see that whatever burden weighs a family down, is raised up by the hands of all the other families nearby. No one is alone. No family is alone. This is the way of the People.

I see that when we decide something for our family, it is with all the family. If it is for our town, then all the people of the town decide together. If several towns, then the representatives of the towns must all agree. We make no effort to decide things more quickly, or more efficiently, because we know decisions have to ripen like apples, and should not be used before their time.

I see that we are doing our best to leave greed behind us, in the old world, dead with all its works. We do not pretend that each of us owns a piece of the earth by ourselves, to make us rich and deny its benefits to others, any more than we hoard water, or air, to ourselves. We do not measure each other by what we have in our pockets or our granaries, but by what we give to the people. This is the way of the people.

I see that we have left off the worshiping of gods and prophets put before us by others, and have found our own spirits in the world, friends who guide us toward the place where everything is just one thing. We understand now that the mystery is too great for us, that no one alive knows it or can stand between it and the people. We know now that the only right response to the mystery is to live in awe of it, and in harmony with it. So we have *left off having a religion and we live our whole lives in the mystery.*

In all of this, I see we have closed a great circle. Five hundred years ago our European ancestors came here and began the destruction of the people they found here. They did it for wealth. They did it with guns. And they did it with contempt, never bothering to learn even the right names of the people they killed.

And then we, the greed-crazed descendants of those marauders, destroyed ourselves. Now we who still live reach back to the First People, to say we are sorry for our grandfathers, and to ask for help to clear their sickness from our minds, to come out from the darkness of greed and evil, to be the People again and live in sunlight. Thus the circle is closed. We honor them by asking their help. We ask with humility that they accept the honor, and forgive us, and help us. This is a great thing to ask, but they were a great people.

We will make mistakes. Weeds will grow among us. When trouble comes we must not clamor, but sit quietly in our councils, talk calmly with our families, and be patient until the smoke blows away, and the clouds scatter, and our minds clear, and the sun shines once again on the way of the People.

I cannot go much farther with you. But I can bless you, and maybe from where I am, I can light your path a little. Walk in sunlight. Be the People.

THE END

Thomas A. Lewis is a veteran journalist and broadcaster who has written six non-fiction books, two of which received favorable critical attention nationwide. He became alarmed about the state of the environment while working as the executive editor of the Time-Life Books 18-volume series on the earth sciences, "Planet Earth," and later when, as roving editor for *National Wildlife* Magazine, he traveled from Alaska to Costa Rica to chronicle the distress of animals and their ecosystems.

It was while writing "EQ Index," an annual assessment of the state of the US environment for *National Wildlife* and *The World Almanac,* that he began to suspect that pollution and exploitation of natural resources had reached a point of no return. That conviction led to his latest non-fiction work, *Brace for Impact: Surviving the Crash of the Industrial Age* -- and to the present work of fiction, which imagines how that crash might happen, and how an American family might deal with it.

Lewis lives on what he calls a "sustainable-ready" farm in West Virginia where he has learned, he says, that "if my life depended on my sustainable-living skills I'd be dead now." He chronicles the ongoing crash of the industrial age on *The Daily Impact*, found at www.dailyimpact.net